Chasing the Red
The Dominion Falls Series 8

Sarah Cass

Historical Romance
Romantic Suspense
Historical Western Romance

A Divine Roses Ink Book
Historical Romance
Romantic Suspense
Historical Western Romance

Copyright © 2023 Sarah Cass
First publication: February 2024

Cover design by Sarah Cass
Edited by Annie Farrell
Proofread by Mary Terrani
All cover art and logo copyright © 2013 by Sarah Cass

PUBLISHER
Divine Roses Ink
http://www.divinerosesink.com

Other Books in
The Dominion Falls Series

Independent Brake
Changing Tracks
Derailed
Dark Territory
Green Eye
Runaway Train
Home Signal
Red Zone
Dust Raiser

Coming Soon in
The Dominion Falls Series

Blizzard Lights
Dead Man's Switch
Bird Cage
A Highball Arrangement
Douse the Glim
Blood
Grave Digger
Bad Order

Books by Sarah Cass

The Tribe Series
The Tribe
The Wolf
The Chief
The Raven
The Lake Point Series
Santa, Maybe
Deep-Fried Sweethearts
Stalled Independence
Witch Way
A Thorough Thanksgiving
Eve's New Year
Heartstrings & Hockey Pucks
Luck of the Cowgirl
Stars, Stripes & Motorbikes
Free Falling
Love for Hire
Haunted Hearts
Stand Alone Novels
Masked Hearts
Leap

Dedication

To all the girls who tried to blend in,
That thought they had to.
To all the girls stepping into their power.

Shine.

Content Warning

Pregnancy loss, miscarriage.

Protect your mental health.
Protect your peace.

                                          Sarah Cass

Table of Contents

Work and play are words used to describe the same thing under differing conditions.
—Mark Twain

Cole pushed, then pulled, then pushed again. His muscles trembled with every run of the saw through the large tree. Tom mirrored his motions on the other side of the tree. He grit his teeth with determination. The tree would be down by lunch come hell or high water.

This day was set by Jane. Her grand idea to gather the whole family to clean up the new claims so they might accommodate paying guests.

All Jane's idea. Yet, it seemed as though he and Tom were the only ones doing any work. Jane, Willow, and Sally had disappeared on the guise of cleaning up rocks to form a trail. He'd seen neither hide nor tail of them for an hour. While he hadn't seen them, he'd heard plenty of laughter carrying through the trees.

Jesse and Jay gave up all pretense of helping near an hour ago. They'd decided climbing trees to be a more productive use of their time. Alma sat on a large rock nearby. A small stream trickled down the hill beside her while she read. The only ones currently not on the claims were the twins, who were with Millie and Lee; and Cindy and Lizzie, who'd already planned to do something with Kat's friend Patrick.

Tom held up a hand to halt the progress. He took a few deep breaths. With a swipe to his brow he shook his head. He caught the canteen Cole tossed his way. "I think we're getting played."

"I was thinking the same thing." Cole caught the return of the canteen, taking a deep swig of the ginger-laced water. "I'm pretty sure we're the only ones actually working."

"No, Ma." Sally's voice carried down through the trees. "Like this."

A few moments of quiet passed.

"Yes. Exactly." Sally's voice tittered with laughter. "Your arm up like that, but your hand swings upward."

Tom grimaced. "I think she's teaching Jane to fight."

"About damn time that woman learned about more than slapping and shooting." After all Jane had been through since he'd known her, Cole wasn't about to complain if she learned how to defend herself better.

Leaves rustled above. Several dead leaves drifted down on top of them.

Cole lifted his gaze toward the sky. He frowned at what he found. "Jesse. Your ma will kill you if she finds you that high in a tree."

"Aww, but I can see the whole town from here." Jesse didn't move to climb back down. He tapped Jay's shoulder beside him, pointing east toward town.

"It's your neck." Cole shifted his attention to the boy in the branch beside Jesse. "You too, Jay. Jane'll have both your hides."

Tom chuckled, wiping the sweat on his brow again. "Can't contain those two anymore. They're going to be plenty trouble. They're even worse when Isaac's around."

"Or Stephen," Cole confirmed. Stephen was the brother of Matthew Coleman, the rancher that had won the purse at the race during Statehood ceremonies. When the four of them got together, it was utter chaos. Though Isaac was enthusiastic, Stephen teetered on the edge of actual troublemaker.

"I think the whole town knows it. They remind me of the group of troublemakers Nick and his pals were, though one short." For a brief second Tom's jovial grin faded. He replaced it as quick. "At least they aren't constant companions."

"Don't I know it. I think the only thing that saves us is Jesse doesn't live at our place full time." Cole grabbed his end the saw. "Let's finish this up before lunch arrives."

They got back to it, sawing back and forth until a great crack rent the air. The tree fell in slow motion. Small pops and cracks carrying through the trees. Even Alma lifted her gaze from her book to watch the trees descent.

The tree landed with a soft fwoomp, the landing cushioned by leaves and branches. Alma returned to her reading soon as it landed. Silence returned to the claim for a few moments. Cole took another swig of water. "That's the worst of it. The rest are smaller. Jane wanted most of the big trees kept in place, this one was on the clearest path to the site, though."

A small rock bounced past them. Several more rocks and pebbles tumbled down the hill toward them. Cole turned in time to spot Jane skidding down the hill behind it.

Laughing the whole way, she held her arms out for balance. It did her no good, several feet away she slipped right onto her ass. "Oh. Ow. We need to make some form of steps, or at least something for people to hold onto to."

Cole laughed when she dropped on her back, only to repeat her *ow* at the action. "You go and forget your injuries again?"

"Shut your—Jesse Michael Schaffer!"

Cole blinked at the change in subject. He glanced toward the trees. "Don't say I didn't warn you."

"What are you doing all the way up in that tree?" She pushed onto her hands. Her features narrowed in a glare. She pointed at the boys. "And Jaybird? Both of you get down here, now."

Cole smirked as the boys grumbled their way to the ground. He nudged Jane gently. "What were you lot doing up the hill? It wasn't moving rocks."

"We moved some rocks." She strode to the tree soon as the boys hit ground. Rather than yell, she tugged them both into a hug. "Don't you scare me like that. This is almost pure rock face down here. If you'd fallen, you could have died."

Jesse wrinkled his features at the kiss she pressed to his temple. "Aw, Ma. Stop."

Jay grunted, ducking away from the same treatment.

"Are we at a good stopping point? Leanne should be along soon with our lunch." Jane brushed dirt from her skirts. "I, myself, am starving."

"From doing what?" Tom scoffed. "We're the ones that've been working. All you've been doing up there is playing."

"I wasn't playing," Jane objected. "Don't you worry none about what we're doing. So long as these claims get cleaned out and ready for use. The sooner we can use them, the sooner we can make money off them."

Tom clicked his heels together and offered Jane a sharp salute. "Ma'am. Yes, Ma'am."

Jane stuck her tongue out at her brother.

"I see Leanne," Cole offered by way of interruption to their burgeoning argument. He turned to holler up the hill. "Girls, come on down from there. Food's here."

Once again small stones trickled down the hill before the girls skidded toward them. They both laughed the whole way down to the level of the others. Sally fell much in the same place Jane had, while Willow made it down to the stream before falling as well.

Cole chuckled at their falls. His grin faded when he caught a glimpse of Jane. Her eyes had taken on a faraway look he was all too familiar with. "Jane."

"Hm?" She cast her gaze up the hill, retracing the sliding trail of the girls.

"What are you scheming?" Cole didn't trust that look one bit. It had always proven to be expensive. "Better yet, how much is it going to cost me?"

"Not a thing." Jane's grin broadened. "Oh, I do have to speak to Michael soon."

"That'll be difficult." Tommy helped her down toward the stream bed. "He's been real grumpy of late."

"Has he? I don't believe I've seen him in weeks. Not since the statehood celebration." Jane's brows pursed as she stared down her brother. "I've only seen Lee or Reuben at the train station to greet guests. What about you two?"

"That's all I've seen there." Cole shrugged. He didn't see what that mattered. Lee Schaffer and Reuben Miller were the managers at Mike's hotel, after all. "I didn't think it was strange or nothing. Figured he was staying back working like we do. Tom and Chauncey go for us sometimes, and Chauncey isn't even a manager."

"He should be floor manager. He's been handling the tables long enough." Jane pursed her lips. "It isn't like Michael not to be around. I should have paid more attention. Things have been off kilter with him for a while."

Cole thought of the questions Jane had asked him about Daisy. "Is it—"

"Well, don't you three look a miserable for such a beautiful afternoon?" Leanne approached, the basket she'd been carrying no longer in her hands. A quick glance told Cole the children had absconded with it.

"I should go talk to him now, and quickly." Jane tore down the hill before Cole could grab her to talk some sense into her.

Tom blinked a few times as she approached the horses. "What put a bee in her bonnet?"

"Not sure, to be honest. I got ideas, but not sure they're right." Cole narrowed his eyes when Jane made to leap onto Faro. "Wait a minute, Jane. You're not supposed to—"

Damn her. She'd taken off on Faro at a breakneck speed. They'd ridden on him together to get to the claim, since

Andrew had suggested using care after the abuse so early in her pregnancy.

Leanne's brow furrowed. "Would someone tell me what in heavens is going on? I thought she wasn't supposed to be riding."

"She's allowed to ride nice and easy, not that damn fool speed she just took off at." Cole glared off in the direction Jane had gone. "She mentioned having to talk to Mike, but when Tom said he'd been grumpy, she decided it was urgent, I guess."

"It's not the first time Mike's been grumpy." Leanne slung her arm through both Cole's and Tom's. "No need to race off."

"She already had a mind to see him." Tom shrugged. "When she realized she hadn't really seen him since the first, she got nonplussed."

"Hm. Do you think he knows what Jane suspects?" When both men turned toward her, she quirked a brow. "You know, that she thinks Daisy might be a whore again."

Tom blustered at those words, but Cole narrowed his eyes at his half-sister. "How'd you know? She just told me a few days ago."

"And her and I are extremely close, like sisters, you could say." Leanne winked. "We talked over dinner last night. I'm certain you missed it in the chaos."

"Guess so." Cole settled on the blanket among the kids so they could eat. "Either way, I don't care none why she went. Don't even care that she's running faster than the doc wants. I just care that she took my damn horse."

Tom laughed outright. He tugged Leanne close against him. "Guess you're walking, then."

"The hell I am. You and Leanne can ride together. I'm taking Brag."

"We'll see if you can beat me to the horses."

"It's a bet."

"Loser walks home."

As a cure for worrying,
work is better than whiskey.
-Thomas A. Edison

Jane slowed Faro in front of Mike's hotel, The Sage Brush Resort and Health Spa. Faro stomped once beneath her before he fell still. She let her gaze rise above the hotel to the foothills beyond. She wondered who might own the lands, and if it would be difficult for Michael to purchase the acreage needed to pursue her idea.

That was, if he was even interested. Only way to find out would be to go in and tell him about it. She alit from the saddle to head inside.

A murmur of voices came from the clinic room on her right. Likely Daisy had a patient inside. Jane nodded to the man behind the counter across from the door. "Good afternoon, Mr. Billock. Is my brother in?"

"Jane." Joe Billock nodded in return. "I'm afraid he's not. Reuben's in today. No sign of Daisy, either. Figured she and Mr. Young took the day together."

"She's not?" Jane glanced toward the room where she'd heard voices. Before she could inquire further, the office door opened.

Rueben Miller, one of Mike's managers, emerged. A small man with beady eyes, a round face, yet a thin body. Jane had never really cared for him, but he was polite enough. He looked up from the papers in his hand. Spotting Jane, he stopped short. "Miss Spencer. I wasn't expecting you today."

"I stopped by to see my brother. Mr. Billock just informed me he's not here today. I thought you were off on Wednesday's."

"I usually am. Mike said he wanted the day off, and I offered to work." Reuben adjusted his glasses. "We were without a doctor today as well."

Jane noted an oddly bitter bite to his words at this. "I've just heard. Daisy isn't here either?"

"I imagine they're off together." Reuben turned his attention back to the papers in his hand. "If you'll excuse me."

"Of course." She stepped aside to let him pass. Once he had moved off toward the dining room, she turned her attention back to the desk. "If Michael happens to come through, would you let him know I'm looking for him?"

"Sure thing." Joe bent over to write down the information.

"Thank you." Jane turned to leave, pausing when the clinic door opened. A tall gentlemen exited the office. He passed right by Jane without acknowledgment, not that she expected any. The man was a stranger. The one who exited behind him was not, however. "Dr. Cross. What a pleasant surprise."

"Jane." Andrew smiled brightly, extending his hand. "I could say the same."

"I came to visit my brother, but apparently he's gone astray. I heard Daisy had as well."

"Yes. When I arrived at the clinic, Dr. Young was making preparations to come out to take care of Dr. Pearson's appointments. Seeing as he had more appointments than I did today, I offered to come in his stead."

"Kind of you." Jane headed toward the door with him. "I hope it wasn't too tedious for you."

Andrew glanced around the empty lobby, then again along the porch when they stepped outside. He lowered his voice. "It is quite tedious. I don't know how Dr. Pearson does it every day. They all hope for a quick fix using tinctures. I tried to offer as few of those as I could."

She sighed heavily. "I've tried to dissuade my brother from offering the snake oil. He insists he's only offering what his clientele wants. Plus I've heard word he adds in the allure of Indian herbs being added."

"Those are actually surprisingly effective. I spent a couple of hours with Black Moon going over the various offerings he's added to the shelves in the clinic. Have them all written down here." He lifted a notebook half out of his bag. "I'm intrigued by their properties. I've asked him to come to the clinic so I might get more information."

"You would use Indian medicine?"

"If it works, why not? Yarrow is well known among cowboys as a stop-gap for wounds. It's an old Indian remedy, of course it was also used by the ancient Greeks. Besides, in the winter sometimes the trains can't get through and Dr.

Young says supplies can get scarce. We might as well use all at our disposal."

She couldn't deny the logic of the sentiment.

"You're using Indian medicine, you know."

She stopped at Faro's side, turning to face Andrew. "I'm sorry?"

"The salve, for your wounds on your back. It's made with herbs and it has yarrow."

"Intriguing. I wouldn't mind learning more myself. If I'm going to raise two children with Indian roots, I must do all I can to encourage their heritage. I imagine Sally will be quite intrigued by the information as well."

"I've no doubt. Sally has quite the curious mind. She soaks up knowledge eagerly."

Jane lifted a brow, studying the young man before her. "You speak of her quite highly. Is there something I should know about?"

"Hm? What? Oh, no." Andrew's features flushed. "No, ma'am."

"If you're certain."

"Sally is a wonderful girl, make no mistake. We're no more than friends."

"I'm glad you feel that way. You're a fine young man. I'd hate to see her break your heart as well. She's still figuring out her way."

"And it's a joy to watch her find herself." He set his hat on his head. "I'll leave you to your day. I must go see about getting the carriage to get back to town."

"Carriage? You still aren't riding, Andrew? You must learn. A carriage won't help you in all endeavors here."

"I know how, mostly. I prefer a carriage."

Jane did her best to hide her grin as Andrew made his way around the hotel. She'd eat her hat if he ever learned to ride as he should.

She got back on Faro. Before she went home, she'd swing by Michael's homestead to see if he was there. She turned Faro south to ride the few miles to Michael's.

The closer she got, the more she doubted her resolve to go see him before going home. His home appeared empty. Curtains drawn, quiet all around. She slowed near the door, glancing around the property. Through the barn door she saw his horse.

"Odd." Jane drew closer to the house. "Michael?"

No response came. She hopped down and tied Faro's lead loosely around a post. "Michael? Where are you?"

She froze with her hand at the door. Perhaps Daisy was over and they wanted privacy. Well, if they wanted privacy, they would ignore her knock. She rapped a few times on the door.

At first, she heard nothing. Right as she was about to return to Faro, she heard something inside. She hesitated. "Probably imagined it."

The click of the lock made her stop untying Faro. Mike pulled open the door. "Jane?"

She stared at him for several minutes. His normally pristine features unshaven, dark circles under his eyes. He squinted out into the sunlight. Jane frowned at the change in her brother. "Michael? Are you ill?"

"No. No. Just tired." He sighed heavily. "What are you doing here?"

"I had an idea I wanted to share with you. If you have a minute."

"Sure. I guess."

Jane followed him inside. The room was dark with all the curtains drawn. The faint musty scent of dust lingered in the air. She was used to Mike's home being warm and cheerful. They'd lived together once, in the homestead that now belonged to David. He'd been more successful than herself at making it seem a home. "Michael."

"I've had a headache. A megrim, by Charlie's way of thinking. The light bothers me."

"You poor thing. How long?"

"Days." He slumped onto the sofa.

"Days? Why did Charles tell you? Why didn't Daisy?" When he didn't immediately respond, she made her way across the darkened living room. She turned up the lamp just enough that she could see to make some tea. "Let me make you some tea."

"Tea would be nice, thank you."

"Did Charles give you anything to treat the megrim with? I can add it to your tea." She poured some hot water into the teapot to warm it before returning the tea to boil.

"There's a tincture on the table." Mike pinched the bridge of his nose. "What did you come to pester me about? Or was it just about Daisy again?"

"Actually, Daisy was only on my mind because I stopped by the hotel before here thinking you were working. Neither you nor Daisy was there. Dr. Cook ran the clinic this morning. I simply assumed the pair of you were together. I apologize."

"No need. Don't know where she is."

She didn't react to the comment, not wishing to upset him further. For a newly engaged couple, such time apart seemed odd, but what did she know? She'd married days after her proposal. Not that many souls knew such a thing.

"No lecture?"

"I didn't come to lecture, and I certainly won't finding you in this state." She slipped into the cellar to grab the milk. Unable to stop herself from pondering what Daisy's absence meant. If she'd been by the clinic in town at any point in the past couple of days she'd know Michael was ill. Why wouldn't she check on him?

In the bright, sunlit pantry she gathered the tea tin from the shelf to buy another moments contemplation. Perhaps she should tell Mike her suspicions, but then again what right did she have? There was no proof. Perhaps the melancholy from the losses during the epidemic lingered enough. Jane certainly understood melancholy.

With some reluctance she left the warmth and light of the pantry to return to the darkened room. After she'd dumped the water from the teapot, she spooned in some tea leaves to pour the boiling water on top.

Michael remained quiet while she got the tray together. Even when she sat beside him preparing his cup for him, dropping some of the tincture into his tea. Once she'd set the warm cup in his hand, she began on her own cup.

"Would you like the distraction of my idea? Or would you prefer to suffer in silence for a time? I'm happy to do either."

"You can't be silent. You're wholly incapable."

Her lips twitched against her better judgment. "You aren't so poorly you can't be a beast of a brother to me, I see."

The first stirrings of a smile tickled light into his ragged features. "You'd be far more worried if I weren't."

"Quite true."

"Tell me your idea. I'll sip my tea and listen."

"We were out at our new claims today, cleaning them for use."

"Who was cleaning?"

"We all were. Thomas and Cole were cutting trees, while Sally and I worked on clearing rocks along what seemed a good trail." Jane sipped her own tea. "When I was coming down for lunch, I slid right down the hill. The gravel carried me until I fell. Willow and Sally did the same. I have to say it was great fun before we fell on our rears."

His cup had lowered and he studied her through his half-close lids. "Where, may I ask, are you going with this?"

"The slide down the hill reminded me of an article I read a few years back. A new sort of resort opened out in New Hampshire."

"Sliding down a hill brought to mind an article several years old? Your mind is a mysterious thing, Jane."

"Don't I know it?" She tapped his knee in an effort to chide without jarring him too harshly. "Now, listen. It was what they called a ski club. I thought since you already own the land back behind the hill that snows up so well every winter, perhaps you could offer something similar."

"I don't own that much. I'd need more land for such a thing."

"I'm certain between Norman and Nicholas you can find out who owns the land to make an offer. I imagine if there isn't much gold in that stretch, you'd be fine."

"A ski club?" He sat a little straighter. "Might be an even better draw than the health resort, especially seeing as we aren't the ones with the hot springs."

"But you have the fresh mountain air, best for consumption." Try though she might, she wasn't able to keep all of the sarcasm from her tone. "Along with your tonics and tinctures."

"Be nice."

"That was nice."

He hummed, taking another long sip of tea. "I bought the land up the foothill for privacy, but to use it for such a thing might not be a bad idea. I'll have to look into it further, to see how successful the resort in New Hamphshire is."

"I'm glad to hear you'll think about it."

"I am intrigued."

"Good. Soon as you're better, you'll start."

"I'll think about it."

No man is exempt from saying silly things;
the mischief is to say them deliberately.
-Michel de Montaigne

Sally moved down the line of bottles Andrew had laid out on his table while he cleaned the clinic's laboratory. Truthfully, he'd taken over most of the room seeing as he also used it for autopsies when they were necessary.

She was fascinated by the different chemicals and what they could reveal about so many things; poisons, ailments, water contamination. He'd told her plenty of stories of the different uses he'd put many of these to while working with the coroner in Buffalo.

Most recently he'd begun to add in herbs from the Indian medicine. Some of them seemed familiar, as she believed Charlie used a few of those himself. Both he and Andrew had told stories of how the land around Buffalo had once been rich with natives. Between their passed-on knowledge, plus the old folk remedies from their family histories had rounded their stores.

While Andrew had his back turned, she grabbed the vial of vinegar, and a smaller vial of iron shavings to add to her collection she was testing on his recommendation. She pulled a rack of tubes in front of her. Her notebook sat beside her, writing down notes from his commentary as she remembered. "Ma ordered me the book you recommended."

"I could have let you borrow it, you know." He lifted a capped beaker, studying the contents before making a jot in his inventory.

"I know, but it seems to be a comfort book for you."

"A—what?" He lowered the beaker. When he turned, his brow puckered.

"Comfort book. Like Leaves of Grass for Ma. She always has several copies even though she has every word up here." Sally tapped her temple. "Pa said that his room became their room the day she left that book in there."

Andrew smiled warmly. "You light up when you talk about them."

"They give me hope that I'll find love like that sometime." She sighed, tilting some water into the first tube. She carefully administered one drop of phenolphthalein into the tube. With a small set of tweezers, she pulled a small piece of potassium from another tube. After a quick check to double-check her notes, she dropped the metal into the tube. The water began to turn purple before her eyes. "Fascinating."

"I'm aware." Andrew chuckled, though he'd returned to his work. "So you think my chemistry book is my comfort book."

"You touch it when you pass the desk." Sally jotted down her observations on the reaction.

"I do not."

"Do too."

"You're lying."

"Am not."

"Are."

"Andrew! I'm not. You might not realize it, but you touch it every time you pass the desk. Haven't you noticed you never need to retrieve it from the shelf because it's always on your desk?" Before he could answer, the tube she'd added potassium to sparked. She jumped, letting out a small squeak. "You distracted me. I missed it."

"Sounds like you didn't."

She narrowed her eyes at his back. Her plan for a prank had been meant for later, after she'd had a chance to test more reactions. His attitude made sooner seem like a better option. Perhaps she could make a quick escape and come back another day to experiment.

Surreptitiously she poured some filings into a test tube.

"I never noticed that," Andrew said quietly. His back still to her, he continued making marks on his inventory.

Distracted from her task, she stared at his back. "What?"

"The book. How did you notice? You've known me only a short time."

"Most of our interactions have been here in this office. It's difficult to miss."

"You have a keen eye."

The compliment soothed her temper. If she'd been the sort, she would have preened at the kindness. "Tommy says as much sometimes."

"I see why he's encouraged you on this path, though you have the brains to do even more."

"I don't see what's less about wanting to be a detective."

"I didn't say it was less. You have the sort of constitution that could handle many careers, I think. You could even be a doctor."

Sally snorted out her surprise, the vinegar in her hand splashed into several test tubes, including the iron filings. "Oh, damn."

"What?" Andrew turned at her curse. His gaze drifted from her down to the test tube.

She flung her arm across her nose as the smell of rotten eggs wafted quickly from the tube. "Oh, I meant to hold off doing that."

"You meant to do it?" He pulled the handkerchief from his pocket to cover his own nose.

"It was supposed to be a prank. Oh, dear." Sally rose to open a window, but the door to the laboratory opened first.

Charlie stepped in, "And this is our laboratory."

A very attractive young woman followed him in. Deep auburn hair, mismatched eyes of pale blue and green, and a pleasant smile that faded pretty quickly. Her nose wrinkled.

"Sorry." Sally scattered to the window, throwing it open before moving to the next.

"Sally Ann, what is that smell?" Charlie's nose wrinkled. "What did you do?"

"Sorry, really sorry. The timing was accidental." Fortunately, a light breeze fluttered through the room to help disperse the odor.

Oddly, Andrew hadn't moved or spoken. His gaze fixed on the doorway where the young woman stood. For several long moments he stood staring. Then his eyes flickered toward Sally and red flooded his cheeks as he realized she'd caught him staring.

Sally cleared her throat, turning her attention to the pair still standing in the doorway. "Uncle Charlie, that wasn't meant for you. It was repayment to Andrew for being wicked."

Charlie's brow rose, but he said nothing more on the matter. "Andrew, I was just giving our new nurse and midwife a tour of the clinic. This is Bonnie Coleman, Matthew's sister. She's finally mostly completed her care of her patients in Denver and is ready to join our clinic."

Andrew cleared his throat. His mouth opened to speak, but no sound emerged.

Biting her cheeks against her laughter, Sally stepped forward to rescue her friend. She extended her hand to the young woman. "Hello. It's nice to meet you. I'm Sally."

"Sally? It's nice to meet you." Bonnie shook her hand. "I thought the other nurse was Lydia."

"Oh, I'm not a nurse."

"This is my niece," Charlie supplied before Sally could. "She's been learning some about chemistry from Dr. Cross, apparently."

"And about autopsies." Sally grinned at Bonnie. "Sorry about that, truly. Andrew made me laugh and the experiment got away from me."

"It's fine." Bonnie glanced toward Andrew.

"This is Dr. Cross. He joined the clinic a few months ago and has been a valuable asset. A talented surgeon with experience as a coroner." Charlie gestured to Andrew.

"It's good to meet you, Dr. Cross." Bonnie smiled almost shyly.

Andrew finally seemed to get his wits about him to step forward. "Yes. It's good to meet you, too."

Sally smirked at her uncle while the two exchanged almost shy greetings. She cleared her throat when the pairs brief conversation stuttered to a stop. "Well, Bonnie. Are you glad to be back in Dominion Falls?"

"I am. Although I'm not as attached as my brothers. I went to Denver pretty soon after Ma and Pa Edwards brought us here. The ranch is home, though." Bonnie's gaze fell back on Sally. After her brief greeting with Andrew, a pleasing pink flush lit her cheeks. "Of course, it isn't the same without the Edwards."

"I am sorry for your loss. I didn't know them well, but they were always kind when I saw them in town." Sally tugged off the apron she'd donned for the experiments. "If you'll excuse me, I'll let you get back to your tour. I should probably check in with Ma."

"Leaving me with your mess?" Andrew scoffed. "Thank you so much."

"You were cleaning anyway." Sally darted from the room before he could protest further. She was still on the porch, tucking her notebook in her reticule when she heard someone call her name. When she lifted her gaze, she found Tommy waving at her.

"There you are. I've been looking all over for you."

Sally quirked a brow. "You have? Should I be learning detective work from you if you couldn't find little old me?"

"Har, har." He jovially punched her arm. "I saw Kilmurry a little bit ago. He said your order is ready. I thought you'd want to head over sooner rather than later."

"Oh, really? That's wonderful!" She laced her arm with his to head toward Second Street. "I hope they were able to successfully do as I asked."

"They made your ma the holster for her gun, and they hadn't done that before. I'm certain they've succeeded to your specifications."

"Oh, without a doubt they're talented. I'm worried about the quick release, though. How could they manage it?" Sally had requested wrist holsters for her knives. They had to fit her perfectly and release the knives into her palms quickly.

"It seems they do like a challenge." Tommy held open the door to the leathersmith. "Just ask your ma. She likes to challenge them."

"Ah, Miss Spencer." Luca Kilmurry smiled in greeting. "When Tom stopped by, I thought I might be seein' ya today."

"Tommy told me you had my order ready." Sally couldn't stop the bounce in her step as she drew close to the counter. "Is it true?"

"Aye, lass. Nessa, Sally's here." Kilmurry turned toward the back. "She wants those pieces she ordered."

Nessa swept from the back room carrying a paper wrapped bundle. "No need to shout, I heard them come in, Luca. Here you go, Miss Sally."

Sally barely thanked her before she tore open the package. Four wide leather cuffs sat inside. Two were longer, made for her calves, the other pair for her wrists. Tucked into fitted pockets of each sat one of her knives. Though she hadn't asked for it, flowers danced along the leather in elegant swirls. "Oh, my."

"Those were my idea, lass. Just because you plan to hide them, doesn't mean they don't need to have some life." Nessa pulled one of the wrist cuffs from the paper. "It was tricky, making it so the knives would release quick enough and still have them fit snug on these wrist pieces. I don't mind telling ya, Luca struggled with the right design for near a fortnight."

"I like a challenge. Your uncle here and your ma are usually the ones to do it." Luca chuckled softly. "Go on, try them on."

Sally took the cuff from Nessa with a bit of reverence. She shook off the awe to undo the buttons on her sleeve. After it had been rolled back, she set the cuff on her wrist so the knife handle settled toward her palm. Once she was certain she'd picked the one that would present the blade outward when the handle dropped in her palm, she began to tie the piece on.

Tommy leaned forward to examine the rest of the pieces while she worked on tying them one handed. "Fine work again, Kilmurry. I wondered if you'd be able to do something crazy like this woman thought of. You are a master."

Sally barely heard Luca's answer in her excitement over the straps that made it easy for her to tighten on the cuff even with her weaker left hand. A few tugs and a tuck through some metal rings and they seemed plenty tight. Eagerly, she slipped on the next cuff while the rest continued their conversation.

With both cuffs on, she studied the release. Using the dual metal rings, made so small the leather thong barely fit through them, she thought she saw how she could release them with some rapidity. She curled down the fingers of her right hand toward the strip of leather.

"You might need to use your other hand." Kilmurry leaned forward to point at the point where the strap and rings met. "If I'd made the strap longer, it would have been obvious, and you wanted them discreet."

"A piece of lace could solve that," she muttered absently to herself. Luca's words rang true as she couldn't quite reach what she needed to loosen the piece holding in the knife. "I'd like to not have to unless necessary."

Tommy chuckled along with Nessa. "Your perfect design and she's already making adjustments, Luca."

"I think we expected more, to be honest." Nessa leaned on the counter. "I can make the adjustment for ya, dearie. If you'd like."

"No." Sally dropped her arm. With a quick movement, she tugged the slender strap. The heft of the knife dropped down into her expectant fingers. She let her fingers curl around the hilt, then snapped the blade outward. "Lovely. You left enough of a slit in the leather for my blade to clear. Just as I asked."

"Aye. It helped with having it loose enough for the knife to come out." Kilmurry stood with a smile. "I'm pleased you like the final product."

"They're perfect. How much do I owe you?" Sally slipped the knife back in place, then tugged the leather taut.

"Nothing." Nessa's voice danced with laughter.

"What?" Sally stared wide-eyed at the pair. "Of course I owe you."

"They've been paid for." Nessa pushed the paper toward her. "Enjoy."

"What? Who?" Sally turned her gaze on Tommy. "You didn't."

"I didn't. I swear." Tommy met her gaze evenly. The man was good at lying, but was he?

"Then who?"

"Who do you think?"

Sally stared at him, wracking her brain. The only other people, would be Jane or Cole. "Ma?"

"And your Pa. They thought maybe they weren't supportive at the start, and maybe they should show more."

"But…this is too much."

"Tell them that. See how far it gets you."

*It's a poor sort of memory that only
works backwards.
-Lewis Carroll*

Jane slowed her pace toward the clinic when she spotted the two men approaching from the opposite direction. "Reverend Greene. Reverend Lyons. It's good to see you both."

"Hello, Jane." Reverend Greene shook her hand. "Eli and I thought it would be nice to take a walk. Rather than being cooped up in the clinic all day."

"I hadn't realized you were still staying at the clinic." Jane turned to Eli. She accepted his extended hand. "When will my pesky brother agree to release you, Reverend?"

"A few more weeks." Eli smiled warmly. "The good doctor says I'm mostly healed. It's my adjustment to a sightless life that delays my release, as well as a place to live."

"I can only imagine what it must be like for you. I hardly had the patience to live a soundless one when my tonsils were removed from the scarlet fever. I was quite contrary by all reports." Jane grinned at the Reverends' mutual laughter. "I'm relieved to hear you've healed so well otherwise, though."

"Physically, I am well-healed. Spiritually, I have been blessed with a wonderful mentor to help me through these difficult times." The young Reverend's head turned in his mentor's direction. "I must admit that I haven't been without my struggles."

"As anyone would." Jane winked at Reverend Greene. "I imagine you're a far sight less difficult to deal with than I was for the good Reverend in my worst times."

"I believe just about anyone is less difficult than you can be, Jane." Mark teased right back. "We are making do. I've been seeking somewhere for us to live now that the house is gone."

"You and about twenty families. I'll keep an ear out if anything appropriate comes available. Where are you staying in the meantime, Reverend?"

"At the church for now. If I were to seek a blessing in all of this, it's that I don't need to return to our old home without Mabel. It would be strange to not have her there with me." Mark returned the squeeze she offered to his hand. "For now, I'm quite content where I am until such time as Eli and I can find appropriate lodging."

"I'll pray that it's soon so that Reverend Lyons can truly adjust to his new situation." Jane shook both their hands, making apologies for the brief conversation. She headed for the clinic to make her appointment on time. Outside, she found Charlie smoking. "Charles. How is Millie getting along?"

"Impatient. Both of us are, I believe." He returned her hug warmly. "You're early for your appointment for a change."

"Sally is learning to discharge a weapon today, and I'd like to be present for the occasion. I figured the sooner I arrived, the sooner you'd be done with me." She leaned on the railing beside him. "I'm hoping it will be easier on my nerves if I see how she handles the first lesson."

"Nothing will be easier on your nerves. I do admire your attempts to support her rather than lock her in her room until she's done with this fool notion."

"It hadn't crossed my mind."

"I thought you didn't lie."

She huffed her annoyance. "Fine, it did. It's only my fears that let such intrusive thoughts rise into my brain."

"Thomas said you paid for her new accessories."

"Cole did, but I didn't stop him. Besides, Tommy has done nothing but expound over how well she's been doing." She didn't like to imagine what life would be like when Sally left home. In some ways it was hard to believe the girl had only been with them three years. A deep sigh rushed from her lungs with her thoughts. "I think she'll leave Dominion Falls when the time comes. Whether she becomes a Pinkerton or something else, I believe she'll leave."

"That means you did well, you know. That's what Ma always said. She knew she did her job well when we all left. Although, some of us went much farther than others."

"At least Sally said she's happy to know she'll always have a home here."

"That is good. You did right by that girl."

"I tried."

"You're becoming melancholy."

"Then change the subject."

"Did I tell you I'm looking to add another doctor to the clinic?" Charlie grinned at her surprise. "I've got a baby on the way any day. I'd like to know my clinic is in good hands when I can no longer spend so much time here."

"I'm truly surprised Millie has been so accommodating before now. You have been known to practically live here at times." Jane knew Charles had bought the clinic from Michael two years previous. It had been Michael's idea, seeing as Charles had experience running a clinic, and Michael had none. While Daisy had been offered a portion of ownership, she'd rejected the offer claiming she hadn't the funds to do such a thing.

"We haven't been without some rough patches due to my dedication to my work. Of course, that isn't saying Millie doesn't understand when things like the epidemic happen and there is no choice. However, the days I'd spend here without such an excuse tend to rile her."

"Can't say as I blame her. Now, you're looking to hire another doctor?"

"Andrew is proving to be a stellar physician. He fits in well despite his upbringing."

Jane attempted to turn her scoff into a cough.

"I meant with the people, not the horses." Charles chuckled softly. "With the exception of his horse-riding skills, he's done well getting himself established."

She let her laughter free. "I do remember our first meeting. The boy flopped right out of his saddle to the ground. Cole said Thomas had to push him into the saddle in the first place."

"Andrew is not a horseman by any means, to be certain. His sister is quite skilled by all accounts. Andrew prefers books to beasts.

"Ah yes, his sister. He mentioned they are twins?"

"Yes. They were the only children in his family, unlike us. Ma couldn't make a twin pregnancy stick, but she had seven of us. Four of us she lost a twin."

The reminder twisted her heart, but she pushed forward a grin. "Then she gained one with myself and Clara."

"And you weren't even a twin to start." He nudged her. "We're digressing. I'm looking for another woman doctor. I figure two men and two women, along with our nurses and midwife will complete the clinic for now. I believe most of the women are more comfortable going to Daisy. Not all, but many."

"Another woman doctor. How progressive of you."

"They have a difficult enough time finding positions to continue practicing. Daisy is rather skilled, and proves that being a woman doesn't make you less of a doctor."

"Ah, yes. I think it sounds wonderful. I imagine the men might grouse seeing as there's already one woman doctor, along with the two nurses."

"The men can grouse all they like. I'll hire whom I see fit." Charlie tossed aside his cigarette and gestured toward the door. "Shall we?"

"Does the fact you are looking for another doctor mean you're looking at building a larger hospital with more sincerity now?" She followed him inside while they continued their conversation.

"If the town continues to grow as it is, yes. They're already grading to add Fourth Street. There are so many families in the settlement now with the expansion of the mines, the clinic is beginning to feel cramped some days."

She hopped onto the exam table, immediately discarding her bodice for the exam. "Have you thought much about a location?"

He started her exam at her neck this time. "Between here and the settlement would be ideal, and of course we'd keep a clinic here in town for immediate injuries. We'd likely downsize from this building."

"I don't know about that. You should probably keep it. There's no telling when another cowboy, or visitor, is going to bring in another epidemic. The more rooms the better in such situations, I would think."

"True. Isn't there another drive coming through town next week?"

"Matthew Coleman said as much. He's got a few heads of cattle heading this way with the drive to replace those he lost. He used the purse he won in the race to buy them, and to pay for Bonnie's ticket home."

"I would have paid for Bonnie's ticket. I told him several times over. Pride wouldn't allow him. He said he'd take care of his own family. Your back now, please."

Jane unbuttoned the front of her chemise so the shoulder slid down to reveal the still-healing wounds from the whip. "Matthew does seem the proud sort. I think he considers himself his siblings guardian, even if they were adopted by the Edwards."

"Either way, it's good that she's arrived. I gave her a tour, and she's eager to begin, but I suggested she spend some time with her family first." He touched the skin around the wounds. "I think she has one more patient in Denver, and needs to pick up some items from her boarding house. After that trip she'll be here on a rotating schedule with Lydia."

She winced under his examination. "See? Better?"

"Better, yes. Healed? No." Charlie moved to the cabinet, pulling out the salve he'd been giving her. "I've ordered more. I think you'll be using it for some time."

"Joy." She didn't bother to keep the sarcasm from her tone.

He chuckled as he moved behind her. "Believe me, I'd rather not continually have to treat your injuries, my dear sister. You must stop putting yourself in danger."

"All I did was greet someone, they're the one that went insane."

"Fair point." He tugged her straps back up. "You're all set for now."

"Thank you." She slid her bodice back into place. "Next week again?"

"I'll be here with bells on."

She smirked at him. "No need to be a boor. Now, you'll tell us when Millie is having the baby? You two aren't the only ones eager."

"Of course. Soon as we can." He kissed her offered cheek.

"See you soon." Jane left the clinic with a bounce in her step. The blasted wounds were healing well. Hopefully things were looking up. She'd stop in to see Cole, then head out for Sally's first firearm lesson.

The casino floor was pleasingly busy for an early afternoon. She nodded her greetings to those she passed. Behind the bar, Cole stood wiping a glass absently. His gaze sat fixed at the roulette table. A purse to his brow made him look both annoyed and confused. If he was confused, she imagined that meant he was also annoyed.

She cast a glance the direction he was staring. A few familiar faces stood around the table, and several new ones as well. Among them was a young woman. A fairly pretty one, at that. Jane found it difficult to determine her age. She could have been close to Sally's age, or even near thirty. Jane knew it was by design, and imagined she knew why Cole was staring.

Even if she did, that didn't mean Jane couldn't have fun. She approached Cole, poking him hard in the side. "I know we agreed scandal wasn't a bad idea, but to so blatantly stare at another woman in my own business?"

"Huh?" Cole did a double take, then paused on her. "Nah, it ain't that. I swear I know that woman from somewhere."

"Hm. Likely story." She poked him again. "Stop."

He drew her close almost automatically. "I told you, it isn't that."

"I said stop." This time she kept her voice low, putting some force into the words. Her tone had the correct effect to draw his gaze more clearly on hers. "Don't draw attention."

His brows knit together again. "Eh?"

"I said to not draw attention."

"She's drawing enough on her own. What's it matter?"

"There are reasons."

"You know her?"

"Personally? No. Never met her, myself. Not while I was fully conscious, anyhow."

He stared hard at her for several long minutes.

To jog his memory, she leaned closer. "You're blue."

"I'm...."

A slow smile grew. She swore she could see the pieces clicking together.

"She was the—"

Jane clamped her hands over his lips before he could say 'chambermaid'. "Yes."

Cole peeled her hand away. His gaze slid back to the table for a moment before passing over the entire casino. She knew he'd finally put two and two together. The woman was a friend of Tommy's. In fact, she'd participated in the grand scheme to save Jane herself from the clutches of the madman Bingham.

In doing so, she'd saved Cole's neck when Alan had returned to the room he was holding Jane in before Cole had been able to tear himself from her drug-addled side. Tommy had pointed her out after she'd checked in the day before.

"Why?" Cole fixed his gaze back on her.

"I imagine my brother has his reasons."

"Those reasons got anything to do with Sally?"

"Don't they always these days?"

Mistake not.
These pleasures are not pleasures that
trouble the quiet tranquility of life.
—Jeremy Taylor

Cole called out the winner of the roulette spin. A tap hit his shoulder as he raked in the losing bets. Chauncey jerked his thumb over his shoulder. "Janey's back. I'll take over."

"Thanks, Chaunce." Cole grinned at the approaching woman. Though her dress certainly was appropriate for the casino, the holster slung over her shoulders and buckled under her bosom was not normal for the day. He greeted her with a warm kiss. "Welcome back."

"Did you make Horace keep an eye out for me or something?" Jane glanced at the new croupier. "You didn't have to take over. I could have waited. Especially since I know you've worked all day and are supposed to be heading home."

Chauncey shrugged while the ball spun. Though he responded to Jane, he kept a sharp eye on the ball, the table, and the players. He knew how to handle the crowd, it's why he'd been working for Cole long before they had proper gambling. "Olive went off to some idiotic prayer meeting, I got nowhere else to be."

Jane's brows flickered in confusion. "Prayer meeting?"

Chauncey finished calling the winning number and placed the dolly on the table. "Eckles is having a prayer meeting," he said in response to her question. "She got roped into that nonsense by Nell. Told her Greene's got the better church, but she's been praying like mad of late atoning for things she ain't gotta atone for no more."

Cole's brow furrowed. "Thought Eckles didn't care for former whores none."

"Apparently if they repent enough he don't mind." Chauncey spun the wheel again. "You two go on. Don't worry about me, Janey. Cole's been running this table past few hours. I've been tending bar."

"Well, thank you, Horace." Jane laced her arm through Cole's. They walked back toward the bar.

"Figured you'd take that off before you came to work. Don't usually wear it on the casino floor." Cole gestured to the weapon strapped to her side. He knew she usually kept her gun in the room, leaving her trust in the several they had hidden around the casino in case of trouble.

"I came in through the front instead of the apartment. I'll remove it soon enough."

He noticed she hadn't stopped smiling since they'd parted Chauncey's company. "Did you have a good time?"

"I certainly did. I do enjoy besting Thomas in something. My aim with a pistol is one of the few places I can do such a thing." She tilted her gaze to meet his, a broad grin on her features. "I even attempted using my right hand to shoot today."

"You did? Never seen you do that. How'd you do?"

"Surprisingly well." She lifted the hand in question. "My aim isn't as dead on as it is with my left, but I still hit the target far more than poor Sally."

"Oh no. Sally didn't do well?"

She poured them both a coffee. "Unfortunately not."

"She was really looking forward to it, too." He knew Sally'd been waiting for weeks for her first lesson with a gun. The girl had been talking about it non-stop for several weeks.

"She's in a sour mood due to the whole debacle, I'm afraid."

"Where'd she run to hide?"

"The library for now."

"It was her first lesson."

"I'm aware. Doesn't make her any less frustrated, and embarrassed. It made no matter that Thomas pointed out she did a fair sight better than Clara during her first lesson when she nearly shot her Pa."

"And later lessons when you did shoot Nick."

"Precisely." Her mug stopped right near her lips. The features bright with laughter a moment before softened into an almost dream-like way. Her gaze drifted off, the words she spoke next quiet in wonderment. "Right in the calf."

His heart twisted in an odd way. "Jane?"

"Clara shot him right in the calf. Huh."

It couldn't be what he feared in a way he couldn't describe. She'd referred to her past self by name. She was still Jane. Silent, she stared off into nothingness. "Jane."

A slight jerk of her shoulders seemed to bring her back. She blinked a few times before meeting his gaze solid as ever. "I believe I just had a memory of Clara."

"Doesn't happen too often." He tried to keep his tone casual. The thought she had a real memory from her years as Clara took him off-guard. Since she'd first arrived, true memories were few and far between. Occasional spurts of facts like remembering the middle names of her brothers popped up, but those were less memory, more detail.

On the extremely rare occasion she had a real memory, he couldn't contain that sliver of fear that pierced right through his heart. What if one day she remembered everything? What if she no longer wanted this life she'd forged as Jane.

He swallowed against the sudden lump in his throat.

Her brow puckered in concern. "What's wrong?"

"Can't remember the last time you had a memory is all." Though he wanted to keep a casual tone, even hear could hear the strain through his words.

"One memory now and then doesn't mean I will ever be her."

"You don't know that."

"I do. It's been years and though a memory surfaces now and then, even if I did remember, I'm quite happy where I am." She leaned closer. "I am yours, through and through. Besides, you're the one with memories you can remember. I think I'd have far more cause to worry than you ever would."

"Nah. You don't." He tugged her closer. There was no good way to explain that his past was that, the past. Even if he didn't have amnesia like her, he'd buried his past long ago. He offered her a wink. "I'm yours."

"Then it's settled. Maybe we should get married."

Beer sputtered all over both of them from the man across the bar. The guilty party, Hammy, choked apologies. He wiped at his scruffy face, his tanned features growing ruddy. The man beside Hammy sat wide-eyed, his own drink frozen halfway to his lips.

Jane stepped back to stare at her dress where the beer had sprayed. Before he could say a word, she busted a gut laughing at their guest's reaction to her bold statement. Sure, not a soul knew they were married, had been for a few years, so many of the townsfolk liked to speculate if and when it would ever happen.

Cole wiped his shirt and the counter. He stared down first Hammy, then Carl Denner. "There a problem, gentleman?"

"Nope." Denner downed his drink. "You gonna answer her?"

"Janey knows good and well how I feel about marriage." Cole pursed his lips in response to Jane's audible snort at his words. "I'm guessing she said that for Hammy's benefit."

She nodded, still unable to speak for her laughter.

Cole chuckled, leaning on the bar in front of Hammy. "He's the one that keeps calling her Mrs. Mitchell when he thinks I don't hear it."

Hammy stammered, his features growing ever darker in his embarrassment.

Jane managed to gather herself together for the most part. Soft chuckles still flittered free through her words, though. "Oh, Mr. Hamm. I'm sorry. It was worth it to see the look on your face."

Hammy cleared his throat. "Sorry, Cole. I don't mean nothing by it."

"Yes ya do. No worries. I don't care what ya say. She *is* mine."

"When you say it like that, you sound like you own me." Jane bumped his hip.

"No man could."

She hummed in response, tucking a delicate finger under his chin. "Get the bourbon. Charles appears unhappy."

Cole hadn't even noticed the man enter. He'd been too busy enjoying the show. At her order, he knelt to open the cage of good liquor behind the bar. Jane continued to placate Hammy behind him. Cole poured a glass for Charlie, nudging it across the bar. "How's things?"

"Dandy." Charlie drank down the liquor quick.

"Something wrong with the baby?" Cole noticed Jane's head turn at his words.

"Nah. Still not here. Millie's going stir crazy." Charlie accepted the fresh pour. "Get it in my head I'm going to hire another doctor. Hell, at this point I might as well look for two."

Cole stared at him in confusion. "You're looking for more doctors?"

"I wanted a full staff so I might be able to spend more time with Millie, and the baby when it arrives. I only needed one more, but I'm thinking I should look for two."

Jane drew closer, her laughter fading the closer she got. Without a word, she grabbed the bourbon from the counter. She gestured for them both to follow her to a table in the secluded corner of the casino. Soon as he sat, she poured

Charlie another drink. "Why do you look fit to be tied? You were perfectly pleasant when I left my appointment."

"Daisy never showed up today. She had three appointments I had to cover as well as my own. If she's not going to bother to show up to work, I'm going to have to hire someone else to replace her. I can't leave my clinic in incompetent hands." This time Charlie nursed his drink slower and more deliberate. "I'm going to have to have a talk with her."

"Do it with a cool head and mind your words." A flash of a smile lit Jane's features again. "No ultimatums, just talk. You don't want to lose her just because you pissed her off."

"She's not you, Jane."

"Nah, but she's a woman, ain't she?" Cole grinned. "A stubborn mule of one at that. When it comes to her doctoring, anyway. Always got under my nerves when she got to doctor. Bossed me around like she owned the place instead of me."

"And we all know how much you hate bossy women." Jane's teasing tone kept him from bristling too much.

"Hey, now." He nudged her gently, riling her laughter again.

Charlie shook his head at the pair of them. "The problem with talking to her is I need to actually see her. She's been absent more than present lately."

"You're not the only one that needs to talk to her. I've been trying to keep a respectable distance since she yelled at me the other week, but I'm worried about her. A woman that's…" Jane's words trailed off suspiciously. Then she sighed. "Well, neither her nor Michael should be in such rotten states as they have been of late."

Cole eyed her, wondering what she'd left unsaid.

"Well, whomever gets to talk to her first, I hope we make some headway." Charlie glanced at his pocket watch. "Thank you for the bourbon and conversation. I'd hoped to release my frustration before I met my wife. You've succeeded."

"Happy to help." She waved off her brother. Once Charlie'd gone, she propped her feet on Cole's legs. "Now, my darling scoundrel."

"Yes?" At the teasing tone she offered, he slipped his hand under her skirts. Inch by inch he teased his fingers along her calf. "Did you need something?"

"You."

"You've got that." He grinned slow and steady, offering a familiar smirk that made her eyes darken with heat every time. Her back sat to the crowd on the floor. The table she'd selected had them pressed deep in the corner of the pit. Their near-perfect seclusion meant she didn't offer a lick of argument when his fingers continued their teasing trail up her leg. "What else?"

"I thought it was implied with the *scoundrel*."

"I thought I got your meaning right." He tugged her chair closer with his free hand.

Her features flushed as he brushed his fingers along her folds.

"Or am I wrong?" He dipped one finger in her already moist heat. "Don't seem like it."

She swallowed once, shaking her head. "No. No. You got it."

He grinned at her small gasp when he gave one last tug to her chair, which buried his two ready fingers inside her. "Do I?"

She pinched her delectable lips between her teeth. One of her legs dropped to the floor as her hips rocked into his touch. Her voice emerged in a husky whisper. "Yes."

"You sure?" He circled his thumb on her clit. Every tiny shudder she couldn't contain pleased him. He leaned in to whisper. "I could stop."

"Don't you dare." Her eyes opened to meet his, dark with need. "You know how grumpy I can be if left unsatisfied."

"Is that an order?"

"You'd better believe it."

"Yes ma'am."

Skill to do comes of doing.
-Ralph Waldo Emerson

Sally made her way through the thin crowd on Third Street. A light freezing mist made the roads and portions of sidewalk uncovered by roofs slick. To that end, she kept a slow pace, taking care between buildings.

She'd promised Jane she'd stop by the Kilmurry's shop to pick up some scrap leather for Willow. It seemed odd Jane would ask her instead of making the trip herself. Jane enjoyed visiting with Nessa and Luca. For that matter, she liked visiting with anyone most days. Jane had claimed tiredness due to the baby, so Sally had acquiesced to the trip in her stead.

As she walked, she tapped her pencil on the small notebook she carried. Inside were puzzles Tommy had created for her, along with the notes she'd been compiling about all the odd deaths and activity of late.

For the time being she worked on the logic puzzle Tommy had left for her. She bit the end of her pencil as she wondered over how to solve the complicated run of clues.

"Morning, Miss Sally." Hammy offered a bow. "What brings ya out here today?"

"Ma asked me to pick something up at the Kilmurry's." Leanne peeked at the stack of wood in his wagon. "What are you working on today, Hammy?"

"New building up on Third where the bank used to be. Gonna be a confec—con—sweet shop." He grinned. "Kids'll love it."

"As will many adults, I imagine." Sally tipped her head when he bowed again. "Have a good afternoon, Hammy."

The man climbed into his wagon with a wave.

For some odd reason, the hair on the back of Sally's neck stood on end. Someone was watching her. On the pretense of checking for something in her reticule, Sally searched the street behind her for anything out of place.

Nothing stood out, but the feeling did not subside. Hammy's wagon departed in a series of rattles and the clatter of lumber. Sally sidestepped onto the boardwalk, no longer lost in her book, rather more engaged in her surroundings.

Last thing she wanted to do was tip off whomever it was that she knew she was being followed. She resorted to a casual stroll. With every passerby she exchanged a friendly greeting so she might be able to look behind her without the move being obvious.

It had to be Tommy. Didn't it? Truthfully, she hoped so. Then, at least, she'd know what to expect. He'd said she wouldn't know the next time he would test her skill again, after all.

Though she hadn't expected such a bold move in the midst of town, it made sense.

Unfortunately her theory quickly dissipated. She spotted Tommy yards away down the street with Nick. Not following her. The brothers leaned on the railing in front of the cigar shop, rather ensconced in conversation.

If not Tommy, then who? What was going on?

Sally paused to lean on the nearest railing, figuring she might as well let whomever it was come to her, if they dared. Within a few minutes someone did approach rather close, even paused at her side. Then they passed by, determinedly ignoring her.

She frowned when she realized who it was. "Arthur?"

He paused his pace, hands clenched at his sides. Her life had been busy enough that she'd hardly noticed, but with him in front of her she realized she'd hardly seen him since the disastrous proposal. Her name emerged from a taut jaw. "Sally."

"Have you been following me?"

"What? No." Arthur's body half turned toward her. He seemed to change his mind quick and turned away again. "You don't want to talk to me. Why would I follow you?"

"Who said I didn't want to talk to you?"

"You haven't. Not once since I left you there by the lake. I'm leaving in a couple of weeks anyway, so I guess it doesn't matter."

Sally lowered her gaze to the ground, unsure what to say. No matter her answer, it wouldn't satisfy him and would seem more an excuse. Then again, she wasn't the only one avoiding what had happened that night, before the attack at least. "Well neither have you."

"Didn't figure you'd forgiven me."

"Forgiven you? For what? I'm the one that said no to your proposal. I didn't figure you'd forgiven me."

"I left you out there all alone, and then…"

"You aren't the one that hurt me." Sally moved closer. "Oh, Arthur. I've not been angry at you, not even a little bit. I certainly don't blame you for something you had no way of knowing would happen. I thought you were angry at me for ending our courtship."

"I wasn't happy," he muttered.

"How much longer are you in town?"

"A couple of weeks. Leave mid-September."

"Good. Why don't we have lunch while you're still here? I'd like to hear about your plans for when you get to college."

"Really?" He finally turned to face her.

"Yes. If you can forgive me."

"I'm trying." He took her hand in his. "Tomorrow? We never did talk like you said we would that night. I'd like to try."

"That sounds wonderful." She squeezed his hand, turning her cheek to accept his chaste kiss. He was right. She'd said they could talk and such a thing had never happened. At the very least she owed him that much for the pain she'd caused.

After he'd gotten to Miner's Row and turned the corner, Sally became distinctly aware that the feeling of being watched remained. It hadn't been Arthur after all. She looked down the street to find Tommy and Nick still outside the shop, each of them now puffing on a large cigar. For a moment she could have sworn Tommy looked right at her.

From this distance she couldn't be sure she wasn't imagining things.

Sally resolved to once again wait out whomever continued to follow her. Several minutes passed in relative quiet. Impatience set in for the wait. Sally tapped her pencil rapidly on her palm to try to disperse some of the nervous energy building.

Maybe she'd been imagining things the whole time. No one was there. Tommy had told her to trust her instincts, but for the moment they were proving faulty. No one approached, no one seemed out of place.

After nearly ten minutes of listening to the footfalls crossing behind her on the boardwalk, one set stopped near her. The pencil stilled against her palm. She stood the pencil on her palm and slid her fingers down to get a good grasp.

Something solid pressed against her back. She offered little reaction to its presence. This time when she stole a glance toward Tommy, she had no doubt he was watching. "Friend of Tommy's, are you?"

A low chuckle was her only response. This made her believe the answer was yes, though she couldn't be one hundred percent certain. Sally took a small step backwards to press harder against the object against her back. No sharp point pierced her clothing. Not a knife. Best guess at an alternative was a gun. "All right, then."

"Move." The voice was unusual. Oddly neither masculine nor feminine, deep nor high. An accent she couldn't place due to the one syllable coated the 'o' in a thick tone. "To the alley."

"No. I don't think I will."

A soft click confirmed her guess at a gun. "Now."

"I still don't believe I will." Sally adjusted her grip on the pencil until it felt good and secure in her palm. Pointed end toward her right where the gun pressed to her side. In one quick motion, she swung her hand back toward the arm holding the weapon.

The stranger spun the second Sally moved so that the pencil hit something hard rather than the arm or hand of her attacker. A corset bone of all things.

Sally allowed a moment of surprise to take in the sight of the woman facing her. The momentary distraction was too long. The woman's leg moved before Sally caught the motion. A strong kick to her stomach had her flying back onto the slick cobblestone.

The hard landing jolted some sense back into her. Rather than fly to her feet, she allowed herself to fall back with a gasp as if the impact had knocked the breath out of her. As the stranger took several quick steps toward her on the right, Sally grabbed the woman's ankle.

A moment's pause in the stranger's step allowed Sally to swing her own legs around. Her body slid along the slippery cobblestone easily. Before the woman had turned to follow her progress, Sally kicked off the porch post to slide again straight at the woman's legs. She had just enough power to knock the woman's legs out from under her.

Sally rolled away toward the boardwalk where the slickness of the icy mist wasn't so strong. On the way to her feet, she grabbed her knife. Though she heard shouts in the periphery, she kept her focus on the woman now getting to her feet.

A smile graced her lovely face. She approached Sally slowly, her hands raised. Not fooled for second, Sally kept her knife tucked behind her. When the woman held out her left hand as if to shake, Sally ducked to the right to avoid the oncoming punch.

She grabbed the extended wrist and spun the stranger right back toward the slick street. While she stumbled to regain her footing Sally tore into the alley. One surefire advantage she had over the stranger was her knowledge of the area.

Sally didn't even glance over her shoulder even as she heard footsteps pounding behind her. At the corner of the grocery she ducked to the right and leaped over the short fence of the chicken coop she knew to be there. She tore through the scattering chickens to leap over the other side.

A loud curse behind her let her know the woman hadn't seen the coop in time, just as Sally had hoped. Sally ran through the barn at top speed, only to stop to the left of the door. She crouched low to the ground, listening for the sounds of footsteps to either side of her. The stranger could either come through the barn or around it.

She tucked her knife back into its holster and pulled the leather strap to lock it in place. With all her might she kept her breath quiet to listen for any noise. None came, but a glimmer to her left made her move. She launched upward with the heel of her hand targeted toward the weapon, which went flying. The woman parried with a punch to Sally's kidneys, but Sally didn't stop moving a second.

She spun to the right, bending low to swipe the woman's legs out from under her. With a dive to the ground, she grabbed the weapon that had landed feet away. A sharp kick to her ribs stunned her the briefest moment. The woman used it to her advantage and plowed her elbow into Sally's shoulder near her neck.

Sally grunted at the impact, but loosened the knife on her free hand by tugging on the lace she'd added to the straps. The knife slid down into her hand easily. With one swipe she strategically cut the woman's leather belt so she wouldn't be seriously harmed.

When the woman startled for the briefest of seconds at the impact, Sally leveled the gun at her. That's when she fully realized what it was. She furrowed her brow. "A Derringer? You were holding me at gunpoint with a lousy Derringer?"

"Zey can be quite effective eef you know how to use zem." The stranger bowed her head with a sly smile. Thick lashes covered her eyes as she studied Sally. The same odd affect to her voice left it neither masculine nor feminine. The accent had thickened. "Eet is not loaded."

"Are we good, or is there more?

"Ve are good. Isn't zat so, Thomas?"

"Drop the act, Molly." Thomas emerged from the barn. Surprisingly, Jane followed right behind him. "And yes, we are good. Nice thinking using the icy street, Sally."

Heat rose to Sally's cheeks at the compliment. "Thank you."

"I am impressed," Jane acknowledged. Her face was a little paler than normal, tension in her eyes expressed worry she didn't. A warm smile graced her lips nonetheless.

Sally lowered the weapon slow. She took a moment to tuck her knife back in its sheath. After she'd risen to her feet, she offered the stranger a nod. "Molly, is it?"

"It is." This time when she spoke, the woman's voice was soft, almost melodious. No hint of an accent carried on the words. "I'm an old friend of Tommy's."

"I gathered." Sally wasn't ready to offer the Derringer back to the woman quite yet.

"I reached out to Molly because she is the queen of disguise. In appearance, affect, and voice, the woman can become almost anyone." Tommy moved to the female Pinkerton's side. "She's a far better choice to teach you in such things than I. She tells me she's happy to take on the challenge."

Sally checked the Derringer to be sure it was truly empty, then handed it back to Molly. "What about Ma? She knows about a lot of that, too."

"I may have read plenty about how Clara disguised herself, but I'm not skilled at it in any way myself. I certainly wouldn't know accents or multiple languages." Jane approached, nodding to Molly. "Miss Malone will be staying at the hotel for a while."

"Wait." Sally narrowed her eyes at the woman. "Molly? Malone? You mean to tell me your name is Molly Malone? That's a song."

"Aye, lass. That it is." A thick brogue wove through the words. "You catch on fast."

"Ah, Molly." Tommy slung an arm over her shoulder. "In Dublin's fair city.."

At his nod, Sally finished the verse in full song. "Where girls are so pretty, I first set my eyes on sweet Molly Malone."

Molly's eyes widened, revealing them to be a light brown, nearly amber. "Oh, what a delightful extra talent to have. It will help with learning voices and accents. Tell me, my dear, can you move as well as you sing?"

"She can," Jane supplied when Sally flushed under the inquiry. "The leader of our burlesque continually tries to get her to join the troup."

"Oh, ma. You're overstating things." Sally cleared her throat. "Then you'll be teaching me accents and voice changes."

"Among other things." Molly tucked a finger under Sally's chin. "Many other things."

What is more agreeable than one's home?
-Marcus Tilius

Jane fought back a yawn. For the moment things were blissfully peaceful. She didn't want to ruin the moment by sleeping through it. She lowered the book in her hands a moment to take in the scene again.

Colton curled against her left side, half asleep with a book laid out on the sofa in front of him. Across the room Sally lounged on the settee pondering something in the notebook she carried with her everywhere. Clara sprawled across the young woman's lap, mouth hanging open in her deep slumber. She'd played hard that morning with Jaybird and the dogs.

Speaking of which, both hounds were curled up on either side of Alma. She herself leaned against Jane's legs with a book of her own in her hand. Alma's fingers danced along Whiskey's ears, toying with the soft fur in a self-soothing action.

Jay and Willow sat near the stove playing a game of checkers. Seemingly in deference to the relaxed air of the room, they cheered their wins almost silently.

The quiet comfort of the winter afternoon could have been made better only by the presence of Jesse, Cindy, and Lizzie. Then again, if those three were present, she doubted there would be anything peaceful.

Other than that, she only missed Cole's presence.

As if her wish had been heard, the door opened a few moments later to reveal the man himself. She held her finger to her lips to keep him quiet. If he dared wake Clara the subdued afternoon would dissipate in moments.

Cole obliged her request with a nod. After he'd toed off his boots, he crossed the room to lie on the couch, his head in her lap. She leaned down to give him a soft kiss. "How's the saloon?"

"Fine. Wil is objecting to getting another bartender. He says the amount you, me, and Tom cover is plenty." He shrugged. "It's up to him."

"Not really, it's our place. I'd like to have someone to cover in an emergency, seeing as we tend toward them." Jane raised an eyebrow at Sally's snort. "Hush, child."

Sally's eyes widened in mock innocence.

Cole poked Jane in the side. "Then you talk to him. I gave my best argument."

"Liar." She set her book in his stomach, then laced her fingers with his. "Any other news?"

"No. Saw Daisy."

"Oh? How is she?"

"Odd." His brow furrowed. "Every time I see her now I think about what you asked me, about pitying her. I think you got my brain too confused. I swear she's dressing different."

Jane pondered the idea. "You'd notice."

"What's that supposed to mean?"

"You've known her all her time in Dominion Falls. You've seen her as a proper woman, as a whore, and after."

"Never did go back to what she was. Didn't even go back to Caroline, kept Daisy all these years." His frown grew deeper. "She cleaned up some when Mikey opened the hotel, but there was always…"

"I know what you mean." Jane, too, had noticed that though she'd donned *proper* dresses, there was always something that lingered from her life as a whore. She kept her powders and rouge, and wore her hair loose. The dresses she chose were also more risqué. "What do you mean changed? More proper?"

"Less. No hoops, her bodice wasn't covering much. Not even her arms."

"That's it, I need to make a concerted effort to go see her." She glanced around the room. "Soon. I don't care to leave. Everything is quite lovely right now."

Cole's head turned toward the settee. A wicked smirk creased his features. "Won't be the second the wild one finishes her nap. Maybe we'd better make an escape."

She chuckled low and smacked his stomach. "Be nice to your daughter."

"Perfectly nice. She's still wild. Starting to see what your brothers mean when they talk about young Clara."

"You and me both."

A light tapping on the back door got the attention of the dots. Their heads lifted, the first rumblings of a howl working its way through Bourbon's throat.

"No, Bourbon." Jane tapped the dog's nose lightly with a finger.

Cole flew to his feet to answer before they knocked again. A minimal groaning noise emerged from the dog instead of a full-on howl.

Jane pointed her finger at the pup. "There's a time and place for such a racket. Now is not it."

Bourbon huffed out a blast of air, his gaze on the door. After a moment he grumbled again and lowered his head. Jane was relieved that though they'd only been there a couple of months, Cole hadn't disappointed with his training of them. They were still very much puppies and far too fond of howling, but they were settling well. More importantly, they listened when it mattered.

When Jane straightened, she was surprised to find that someone had entered the apartment with Cole. With her right ear still nearly deaf, and the fact that Bourbon had laid back down instead of rushing to greet anyone, she'd thought Cole had sent whomever it was away.

Instead, Nick approached the couch. He leaned down to kiss her cheek. "Millie is in labor."

"Oh, how wonderful. How is Charles handling it?"

"You'd be delighted to see him now. All those years of doctoring and he's a mess." Nick allowed a rare bright grin to break his stoic features before it disappeared. "Andrew and Bonnie are with them now."

"Andrew? I thought Daisy was caring for Millie." Cole perched on the low table in front of the sofa when Nick took the seat next to Jane. "Is she totally hiding from doctoring now?"

"Don't know, I just know we couldn't locate her." Nick scanned the room, then turned his attention back to Jane. "Kat went out to see if she could bring her by. I thought, seeing as your last encounter with her didn't go well, she'd be best."

"Yes. I do plan on going to see Daisy soon, though. Cole saw her today in town." Jane hadn't missed the fact that Sally was listening rather intently. "Yes, Sally?"

"What's going on?" Sally narrowed her eyes. "I thought you and Daisy were friends. What about what Cole was talking about? What have I missed?"

"Little pitchers have big ears," Jane noted.

"En Français?" Sally looked hopeful. Jane had been teaching her French for some time. Perhaps it could work, but what to tell her.

Straight forward and factual would be best. She'd tell her Daisy had been acting odd since the epidemic, and there was suspicion she'd been prostituting again. "Daisy n'est plus elle-même dupuis l'épidémie. On soupçonne qu'elle pourrait se prostituer à nouveau."

"Mais pourquoi?"

"I wish I knew, Sally." Jane sighed. "I should go check on Charles and Millie. Has anyone told Lee?"

"Cindy and Lizzie begged to take on that particular task." Though his expression remained neutral as ever, Nick's eyes twinkled with laughter. "I believe Lizzie merely wanted to visit with a certain young man."

"Jesse and Lizzie are proving rather inseparable." Jane sighed. "I almost wish they weren't. Young love can be rather fragile and they are still but children."

Cole chuckled low. "Can't tell them nothing, though."

"Definitely not. We must simply remain nearby should they break each other's hearts." Jane leaned closer to Nick. "Speaking of hearts."

"Do not tread down a path with snares, Jane." Nick cast a dark look her way. "I am content. Leave it at that."

"Are you, though? Truly?" Jane laced her hand with his. "The divorce was several years ago. That's a long time to be alone."

"Jane."

Cole cleared his throat, offering a small shake of his head to Jane. "Do you really want to push your luck?"

"I do." She squeezed Nick's hand again. "I only worry for your happiness, Nicholas."

A loud snort startled through their hushed conversation. Clara shot to sitting, rubbing her eyes with a huge yawn. When she lowered her hands a high squeal erupted before she tore across the room. She scrambled right over Cole's lap to launch into Nick's arms.

The dogs hopped on their hindquarters unleashing a long howl into the quiet after Clara's squeal.

Jane chuckled. "Let's not tell Thomas that Nicholas appears to be her favorite."

"It's only because she doesn't see me as often." Nick gruntled at the brutality of the hug from his niece. "My word, Clara."

The dogs by now were going loopy, Jay and Willow helped stir them up further. Even Alma was laughing and playing with the puppies.

"So much for my peaceful afternoon." Jane rose now that Alma no longer leaned against her. She glanced at Nick.

"Seeing as you're occupied with your niece, I'll talk to you later."

"No." Nick tried to argue, and even set aside Clara. The girl just climbed back into his lap chattering away fast as could be. "Jane, I—"

"No, no. Enjoy yourself. Sally is here if you have too much trouble." Jane grabbed Cole's hand to drag him from the apartment.

Cole chuckled under Nick's protests until Jane shut the door. "That wasn't nice. That girl's too much for us most days."

"Well, he needs to spend some time with them. Maybe one of these days I'll get him convinced to not remain a bachelor for the rest of his life. Why is it him, Thomas and Michael are all so difficult about it?"

"Tom and Nick had wives, remember?"

"Yes, and they are both good men. At least Thomas and Leanne are in a good, solid relationship. Michael should be happy and content, but things such as they are. Ah well, we'll see if we can't help him and Daisy out."

Cole tugged her to a stop before they got to the street. "You don't have to fix it."

"I care about them both. I have to at least try, don't I?"

"Always trying to fix everything."

"No. I'm simply trying to change this little world."

*As men, we are all equal in
the presence of death.
–Publilius Syrus*

Tommy loaded the last crate in the back of the wagon. On a whim, Jane had decided to change the glasses used in the casino. She'd also been talking lately of getting a fancy bartender in to make a wider variety of drinks. He had a feeling she'd get her wish at some point in time. Sooner, if she could. Later, if life continued to interrupt her trains of thought.

He counted over the boxes again to be sure he'd gotten them all. Callahan, the current owner of the mercantile, had been known to make mistakes from time to time. Ever since he'd decided to sell, it had gotten worse. Everything seemed in order, though.

A sharp whistle drew his gaze from the wagon. An elegant phaeton with white fringe approached from the hill. He recognized it instantly as Leanne's. As it drew near, he raised his hand in greeting. He rested his hand on the horse's nose when she pulled to a stop. "Afternoon."

"Afternoon." Leanne accepted his help to disembark. She met his kiss easily. "How is Millie? Has the baby arrived?"

"Just. Poor girl labored near a full day. She's exhausted, but they got a boy out of it. Charlie's named him George."

"After your brother?" Leanne smiled. "Wonderful."

"George and Charlie were always close, Charlie really looked up to him, even more than James." He smirked. "Or me."

"You were too close, you probably beat him up a bit, too."

"Me? I was a gentle soul."

She scoffed lightly. "Unlikely. You have your moments, for certain."

"You certainly know plenty of them."

A delectable flush lit her cheeks. "Hush."

"The madam is far from being embarrassed at suggestive talk."

"Fine, you should still hush." She nudged him gently. "How is Sally getting on with your friend Molly?"

"Thick as thieves awful quick, honestly. Molly's intrigued by Sally's skills."

"As you've been since you both started this fool notion."

"If it were a fool notion, I wouldn't be intrigued." He nodded down the street. "There they are, as a matter of fact. Molly's been asking what she knows. Finds it interesting she learned French in a matter of months from Jane."

"It's astonishing how quick she picked it up. Unfortunately, Jane and I can no longer have private conversations if she is around."

"What kind of private conversations are you and my sister having?"

Before Leanne could answer, a scream ripped through the town. Tommy spun to figure out where it had come from. Down Miner's Row he spotted a woman tearing through the street scantily clad, eyes wide in terror as she continued to scream. He recognized her as one of Tully's three whores.

Tom raced toward her, the impact of catching her nearly knocking her over. "Carrie!"

Carrie froze, staring at him hard.

"What happened?" When no response came, he gave her a small shake. "Carrie. What is it?"

"T-T-Tully…dead. He…"

He caught her as she fainted. He lifted his head, spotting Graham a few feet away. "Get her to the clinic."

Tom took off toward the small saloon near the end of Miner's Row soon as Graham grabbed the woman. He burst in to find the place dark and dingy as ever. Even with the gloom, he didn't have to look far to find Tully.

The man lay spread eagle on the floor. Bloody foam lingered on his lips, vomit on the floor beside him. Several empty whiskey bottles littered the floor and tables. Tom remained still where he was, taking in the scene.

Footsteps pounded to a stop behind him. Sally's voice broke the silence. "What the devil?"

"Looks like he drowned in his own sick," Molly offered quietly.

"Doesn't make sense," Sally said before Tom could.

"Why not? Look at him, and all those bottles? Man went on a bender." Molly took a few steps forward, but stopped when Tommy touched her arm. "What?"

"Tully didn't drink." Tom crouched down to take in the scene. Plenty of footprints marred the dust, but seeing as the man never cleaned the floor, they meant nothing.

"Not ever," Sally confirmed. "It's why Pa never tried to run the saloon out of town. He let the town think it was because it was small and only three whores that were nickel at best. It was because Pa respected him. He didn't drink and didn't cheat his customers. Didn't want to be bigger. Kind of like Hammy in that he was content with his little piece of the town."

More footfalls rattled the boards before skidding to a halt. "Oh, my."

"Hi, Andrew." Sally stepped around the scene in a broad circle. "I count four bottles. Molly's right on one thing, it looks almost like he drowned with the foam at his mouth."

"I'll be able to confirm or deny with an autopsy. I have Mr. Cooke bringing a stretcher to take the deceased to the clinic." Andrew drew up alongside Tommy. "May I inspect the body?"

Tom lifted his gaze to find the young woman who had stopped almost opposite him. "Sally? Are you ready?"

"Give me a minute, please." Sally drew closer to the body, still keeping her distance. She grabbed a lantern from a nearby table and lit it with a match. Back and forth she swept the lantern, then paused. "I know Tully never cleans, but this looks fresh."

"What?" Molly eyed the young woman. "How can you tell?"

"There's what looks like drag marks here. No footprints over it. They lead over here." Sally walked slowly along the floor, keeping the lantern low.

Molly glanced at Tommy. "She's good."

"I know." Tom watched Sally move slow and steady through the small room.

Molly nudged her chin toward Andrew, who was watching Sally as well. "What's he to her?"

"Friends only," Andrew spoke at the question. He turned his gaze on Molly. "It's rude to speak of someone as if they aren't right beside you. Dr. Andrew Cross, by the way."

"Molly Malone." Molly shook his hand.

Sally let out a strangled cry. "Oh, Lucy. You poor—oh! She's alive! Andrew, come quick."

Tom held out a hand to hold back the doctor. "Follow the path Sally took. Molly, go call for another litter."

Both did as they were told quickly. Tom circled around near Tully. He noted bruising on the man's arms, and the start of one on his cheek that looked suspiciously like a hand print.

Through the noise and yelling outside came David's calm voice. Lord save the town when David no longer wanted the sheriff job. Would be difficult to find another man like him. He kept a cool head under pressure and was good at calming a crowd. Qualities Tommy could admit he didn't possess in any strong measure.

David entered, took in the scene and frowned. "Another death?"

"This one doesn't look so innocent. What's one thing you know about Tully."

"Doesn't drink—oh." David stared at the bottles on the table and floor. "What else you got for me?"

"Not much. We just started, and I'll need to have the autopsy done. Cross is a little busy with the whore in the storeroom. Not sure what state she's in, but Sally thought her dead at first." Tom straightened back to his feet. "Whoever did this one didn't do as good a job of making it look like an accident. They're getting sloppy."

David's brow furrowed. "I thought we agreed Keller was an accident."

"Seems to be a lot of accidents happening, David. Keller, Ellis, and McKerney. If it had just been Keller I might agree with you. Instead it's three, not to mention what's been happening to women in this town. Sally, Jane, Emily, and now Lucy."

"It's been quite a few deaths in a short time, but you haven't had any clues for what happened to Sally, or Emily. Jane we know it was Mac. He never liked her."

Tom chose to keep his mouth shut rather than argue further. He sighed and shook his head. "Sally, Molly, and I are going to keep looking for answers for all of them. You don't have to worry about what we do, but let me know if you hear anything odd."

"Tommy." David rubbed his hand over his face.

"Trust me. My gut's rarely wrong. Remember, I'm the reason Jane's alive today. I know what I'm doing. Now I got Molly, too." Tom stopped when Graham, Molly, and several men entered with two litters.

He directed them to get the body, and the rest to circle around to the room where he assumed Andrew was working on saving Lucy. At a gesture from David, he moved off to the side with him. "What?"

"I know I can trust you, but this seems too much. I can't deny the whole thing comes out suspicious when you string it together like you did. What can I do?"

"What you're good at." Tom smiled at his friend and former brother-in-law. "Keeping order. You're best at handling the town's business, keeping calm and order. You weren't made for investigating. You're a great lawman, but you'd make a terrible detective. For one, you can't lie for nothing. You give yourself away every time."

"Now you sound like Jane."

"Won't deny it, either." Tom laughed with the sheriff. "We've got things under as much control as we can."

"Let's hope this is the end of it." David watched them carry out the body of Tully. "It's going to be harder to keep order if it keeps happening. Even worse, we've got cowboys coming in any day. Nearly impossible with that lot—and now Tully's is done for. One less saloon to keep them happy."

"One less saloon to make them drunk." Tom clapped him on the shoulder. "I'd best see what's going on with Lucy. Don't worry, I'll let you know if and when we figure anything out."

"Do you have any ideas right now?"

"Unfortunately, no. The women have a common theme, they're all whores, or at least they were. The men were all popular in town, and otherwise there's little similarities except they mostly seem like accidents." Tom glanced toward the door. He nodded to Cole when he peeked in. "Tully's dead."

"Damn." Cole slipped into the room toward them. "I hoped they were wrong out there all muttering about it. What happened?"

"Appears to have drank about four bottles of whiskey and choked on his own sick." Tom eyed Cole. "At least at first glance."

"Bullshit. Tully never drank. Didn't touch a whore, neither." Cole shook his head. "I'll let Jane know. She's not going to be happy to hear it."

"Tell her I'll talk to her soon. Fill her in on what we find out at the autopsy. I'm guessing Sally's going to want to be in on the autopsy herself." Tommy glanced toward the storeroom when there was movement. "Oh, and Lucy got hurt, too. Must be bad, Andrew's been in there working on her for a bit."

"What about Carrie? And Agnes?" Cole's frown deepened when the stretcher emerged from the room with Sally right behind.

"Carrie's how we knew it happened, came out to find Tully and got hysterical. Ran screaming down the street. No sign of Agnes, but we haven't finished searching the place." Tom nodded to Sally as she passed, noting she seemed a bit pale. Probably because Lucy didn't look much better than Sally herself had when she'd been attacked.

"I'm going to the clinic with them. See how she comes out, if it's looking good or not." David stepped forward. "I'll expect word from you as well, Tom. Keep me updated."

"Will do. If Lucy wakes up at all, try to get her to talk. She might know who did this." Tom blew out a heavy breath as silence fell on the saloon. "Damn."

"Tully was a good man. Didn't deserve whatever this was." Cole went to the bar, then crouched down behind it. There were several thumps, followed by a clatter. "Money's still here. Pretty much everyone knew where he kept it."

"We'll give some to the girls, send the rest to his family." Tom leaned on the back of a chair. "Help me close off the saloon. The girls and I will come back for a more thorough search after we're done checking on Lucy and Tully."

"Hold up. Let's check for Agnes first. If the girl's still here, she'll be right scared to find herself locked in." Cole paused, glancing toward the back, then at Tom. "Don't know which way you'd like me to move."

Tom chuckled. "Jane's been teaching you, I see."

"Complaining more like. Talks about how bored she gets listening to you and Sally talking about investigating all the time." A sly smirk creased his features. "I think she finds it more interesting than she'll admit, though."

"Of course she is. It's her worry for Sally that makes her grumpy. You can go that way." Tom gestured toward the path the rest had tread to bring Lucy out. "It's already messed up from everyone passing through."

Cole followed the path easily, checking the three rooms in the back. He called for Agnes several times, but came out with no sign of the girl. "Don't know where she's gone off to."

"Doesn't make her look good, but she wouldn't have had the strength to do that to Tully."

"No, she was a tiny slip of a thing." Cole approached. "I'd best go let Jane know, if she hasn't already heard through the grapevine. Let's get it closed up for you."

They worked together to close and lock the doors. They even blocked off the doorknob with some wood they grabbed off a scrap pile.

"Good luck," Cole called as he walked toward The Hangman's Inn.

"Yeah. I'm going to need it," Tom muttered.

I always like to know everything about
my new friends, and nothing about
my old ones.
-Oscar Wilde

Sally flipped through the pages of her notebook to the page where she'd drawn something similar to the knot Tommy had found tied around Bob Keller's leg. At least she'd drawn it based on his description. Beside it were brief notes describing how it might have been tied without his knowledge.

She drew a ribbon from her reticule. Still examining the directions, she pulled the other chair closer. "All right, around the leg."

Step by step she tied the knot. It was a complex version of a hitching knot. One Cole and Tommy both knew. They'd helped her write down the directions. She'd wanted to attempt it in private so she didn't embarrass herself. At the final step she pulled the line taught and it tightened around the chair easy as anything.

She pulled the free end and the knot untied just as easily. If Bob had one second awareness of the knot, he could have freed himself. Everything must have happened fast.

The bells on the door jingled, signaling a customer. Sally lifted her gaze to smile in greeting. "Good afternoon, Mrs. Johnson."

"Afternoon, Sally." A soft southern lilt carried on the woman's words. Though the Johnson's had been in town for several years now, Abby couldn't seem to shake the southern lilt. "I was wondering if Jane has a copy of *The Law and the Lady*."

"Oh a fascinating mystery. Yes, I know the library contains it, though I'm uncertain if anyone has checked it out. It's on the second floor, in the mysteries row, right there." Sally pointed to a point on the balcony. "Under Collins."

"Thank you kindly, Sally."

"Certainly. If it's been checked out, might I suggest something by Sheridan Le Fanu? I found *The Rose and the Key* an intriguing mystery."

"I'll look for it, thank you."

Sally nodded, then turned back to the desk. She rarely met another person interested in mysteries, she was pleased to be knowledgeable enough to assist as opposed to some other stories in the library.

She grabbed the ribbon to try again. This time the knot came much easier. She made some notes in her notebook about the knot to put in her own thoughts, not those of others. After that, she flipped the page to study the notes on Ellis.

The bells chimed again. This time when she lifted her gaze, Sally couldn't help but smile at the person who'd entered. "Molly. I wasn't expecting you."

"Tommy's off on some jaunt with that devilishly handsome Cole." Molly strode to the desk. "I thought we'd use this time to continue making our acquaintance."

"I certainly don't mind." Sally tried to deny the little flutter of enjoyment over Molly's continued interest. After all, it was a business matter for her. As a Pinkerton, she was used to playing whatever part suited her situation. According to Tommy, they all did. "However, I don't know what else we could go over."

"Well, we've only discussed the cases. I've yet to see your notes. Best way to get to know a soul is to see how they express their thoughts and ideas." Molly settled into the seat with the ribbon tied to it. She paused to study it. "That's not a normal hitch tie, this is meant to stay."

"It's how Tommy described the knot around Keller's leg. At least, I believe I got it correct."

"You did this based on a description alone?"

"I drew it out first." Sally flipped the pages of her notebook to return to the page. "Tommy described it. Pa was familiar with the knot and helped me further."

"Interesting. You actually drew the knot." Molly drew the notebook close, her fingers tracing over the knot in the direction of the arrows Sally had used to figure out the tie. "This could be in an instruction manual on knots. Quite good."

"It's a simple sketch is all."

"Modesty doesn't suit you. Have you learned nothing from your Ma?" Molly turned the page to the notes on Emily's attack. She flipped forward a page, then back. Rough outlines of the human form were drawn in miniature on the small pages, with marks for the wounds.

"I learned that from Andrew. It's how he keeps his notes on his autopsies."

"Using and adapting what you've learned." The words were quiet, perhaps Molly hadn't meant to speak them aloud. "Intriguing."

Footsteps on the stairs interrupted Sally's reply. She lifted her gaze to smile at the woman descending back to the lower level. "Did you find what you needed, Mrs. Johnson?"

"I did, and I selected the book you recommended as well." Abby set the books on the desk. While Sally entered them in the ledger, she nodded to Molly. "Sorry to interrupt."

"No worries." Molly waved her off. She barely lifted her gaze from Sally's notebook. "I'm just reading at the moment."

Sally fought the urge to roll her eyes, but handed the books to Abby with a smile. "Enjoy. Let me know what you think of *The Rose and the Key.*"

"I will. Thank you, again."

Molly sighed as the woman left. "I still can't get over you learning French in such a short time. It took me ages to learn my languages."

"How many do you know?"

"Two." Molly closed the notebook. "Working on number three. Latin, it's quite helpful in more ways than I expected."

"The other two?"

"Italian." Molly leaned on the desk, smiling warmly. "Also French, like you."

"Impressive."

"Not really. It took me years to master them. I acquire accents easily enough, the languages not so much. You, however, have mastered French in a short time. I think you could easily surpass me if you found enough able to help you learn their languages." Molly fluttered her lashes. "You're quite the linguist. A very talented tongue, I'd say."

Heat rose to Sally's cheeks so fast she shot to her feet to avoid it. "Would you like some tea?"

"If you're making it, I won't say no to a cup." Molly leaned back in her chair, her gaze returning to Sally's notebook. "One odd death is not suspicious. Three, however."

"Four now," Sally reminded her.

"Four is a pattern. Three that appear to be pure accident. A man caught by a rope, dragged by horses. A man with a penchant for moonshine falling in his own well. Another caught in his own trap."

"All well-liked men. Though that might be stretching it for McKellan. He tended to stay to himself. Preferred his traps and his small cabin to town life."

"How often did he come to town?"

"Twice a week. Wednesdays to trade, Sundays for church." Sally poured water over the tea. "Other than that he ran his traps and worked the furs. In off season we'd still see him occasionally on Wednesdays when he visited the casino or another saloon."

"A man of God."

"A decent man. All of them were. Ellis loved his wife and became more reclusive after. Still he'd come to town for church every week because it was his wife would have wanted. He sat on the Town Council a few years ago when it was first formed but left after his wife died."

"By all accounts Keller was more active in the town. He almost worked as a junior mayor to Archie, correct?"

"Yes." Sally found herself a little relieved that upon her return to the desk, Molly now sat ensconced in her own notes, writing as they spoke. She couldn't figure her reaction to Molly's teasing. It had been almost pleasurable, like when Patrick flirted with her. That wasn't right, though. It wasn't how it should be. Not according to the rules of propriety. She couldn't find a woman attractive. Not if she wanted to be accepted, could she? What would Jane think?

"Sally?"

"Hm?" Sally shook off her reverie to find Molly staring at her. "I'm sorry, what?"

"You didn't hear a word I said, did you?" Molly's musical laughter flittered right over the nerves jangled by Sally's train of thought.

"I'm afraid not. I was lost in my own thoughts."

"Must have been very interesting thoughts." Molly perched her chin on her hands. "What could be more distracting than murder and mayhem?"

"It was nothing. Tea?" Sally handed off the cup to Molly before taking her own. Rather than circle back to her chair sitting so close to Molly's, she took the one on the other side of the desk.

"Fine, I won't pry." After a sip of tea, Molly glanced at her notebook. "You and Tommy swear Tully didn't drink. So does the delicious specimen of a man that is your pa."

"Molly," Sally scolded as heat flooded her cheeks again. "Really."

"What? He is. Even the old biddies talk about him over their tea."

There was no way to deny the truth of Molly's words. Sally shrugged. "He's my pa. I became a whore at the Inn well after he stopped taking whores for his own pleasure. So, he's my pa and I can't…"

Molly laughed again. "Fair enough. As I was saying—according to you all this Tully didn't touch alcohol."

"He didn't. Plus, you know Andrew's autopsy showed signs of him being held down, forced to drink the whiskey."

"Bruises on his face, shoulders, even his thighs suggesting he was held down by several people. Too bad the whore isn't awake."

"It could be days before Lucy wakes, if she does. It was near a week before I woke after my beating. Worse, I don't remember much but a woman screaming *whore* at me." Sally pursed her lips. "If we could find Agnes, maybe she knows something."

"It's been a day. If she's hiding, she's barely had time to get hungry. She'll come around." Molly slurped her tea noisily. "This is quite good."

"It's Ma's favorite. I guess it's become mine as well." Sally tapped a fingernail on her cup.

"Heard your pa found a place for that whore. Also noticed it wasn't his place even though they've only got eleven and started with a clean dozen."

"One didn't make it past Ma. Besides, Tully's whores weren't up to standard for Pa. That's why they were at Tully's. He knows a guy in Manitou whose saloon Carrie will fit in well. If she gets over her fright, that is."

"Delicate females." Molly scoffed, closing her notebook. "People need to stop treating us as such. I've got more gumption than half the men in this town."

"Unfortunately, some women like Carrie fit into that pretty little picture of a weak female. Helps perpetuate such notions."

"Spoken like a true Spencer." Jane's voice cut through the conversation. Sally's Ma beamed at her from the door. "Good afternoon Sally, Molly. Sorry to interrupt."

"Not at all, Ma. What are you doing here? I thought you were spending the afternoon with Kat and the children."

"Well." Jane paused when a small boy peeked around her skirts. A few moments later two young ladies, and one young man traipsed into the library. "Everyone but Clara felt they needed new books."

Sally grinned at the three youths as they raced past her up the stairs. When she turned back, Colton toddled toward the shelves with books for the youngest readers. "Even Colton, I see."

"I'm beginning to think Cole is right. This child is reading already, even if he isn't doing so aloud." Jane stepped into the room with the stove. The space was equipped with a long table for her teas with the ladies of town, as well as a couple of comfortable chairs where she could read when the library was quiet. She reemerged with a cup of tea for herself.

"How old is that child?" Molly studied the boy who now sat on the floor with a book open on his lap.

"Two and a half, or thereabout," Sally supplied. "Been reading at Ma's knee since he was a babe. Clara has far less interest in books than he does."

Jane paused by the boy before drawing closer to the desk. Her gaze wandered toward the upper level when laughter sprinkled down. "Looks like he's grabbed *Nonsense Songs, Stories, Botany and Alphabets.*"

"If you're here, and most of the children, where is Kat?" Sally returned to her original chair so Jane might sit.

"Watching Clara, of course. Pa is working, and all of your uncles are occupied." Jane settled in with a sigh. Her hand rested where the first signs of weight gain could be spotted by a keen eye. "Now, why were we discussing weak women?"

"We were talking about that whore that discovered Tully." Molly had turned back to her notes. "Sally said she'd be moving to Manitou if she recovered from her fright."

Sally frowned slightly when Molly continued to refer to the woman as 'that whore'. "Her name is Carrie, and yes, she was quite frightened."

Molly lifted her gaze in surprise. "What does her name matter?"

"Because she's a person. All whores are. I'm a person." Sally lifted her chin.

"You're not a whore," Molly pointed out.

"I am. Or at least, I was." Sally couldn't help be offended by Molly's carelessness. "Ma never treats a whore as less than unless they act as such. Just because you spend your life pretending to be anyone but yourself doesn't mean we're all expendable."

For a moment Molly's features twisted into something akin to wounded, then straightened. "I do apologize for offending you. If you'll excuse me, I'm going to retire to my room."

Sally didn't try to stop the woman as she gathered her things. With great effort, she kept her gaze averted from Jane. Something told her that her ma was staring hard at her.

Soon as Molly left the building, Jane confirmed her impression. "What was that about?"

"It bothered me that she kept referring to Carrie like that. Lucy, too."

"Clearly. I understand your feelings on the matter, but you got quite upset. You snapped at that young woman like she'd wounded you personally."

"Well—it felt like she did."

"I see."

But how could she, when Sally herself wasn't entirely sure why she was so upset?

*True friendship multiplies the good in life
and divides its evils. Strive to have friends,
for life without friends is like
life on a desert island.
—Soren Kierkegaard*

Jane flipped through the guest book. With everything in order, she knew they had two suites left along with four standard rooms. Not too shabby for the time of year, what with winter predicted to hit within weeks.

"Jane." Patrick Warner approached, a bright smile on his handsome features. He extended his hand, kissing the back of hers when she offered it. "Fair Jane, I must throw myself at your feet and beg your assistance."

"My goodness, what in heaven could cause such desperation?"

"I have found myself in need of remaining in Dominion Falls for another few months."

"The horrors!" Jane clasped her hand to her chest for added effect. "You poor dear. No, worse, this poor town. Having to put up with your exceedingly pitiful countenance for several more months. What will the widows and young women do? They'll have sore knees from groveling at your feet for one dashing smile."

"It is a tragedy." Patrick's features fell in appropriate commiseration to her lament. "However, my darling CC has requested I remain for Christmas and beyond. I cannot deny that child when we were separated for so long before this visit."

"You spoil that child and she will desire for you to never leave." Jane flipped the book back open to the page with current guests. "Neither will her mother, or Leanne, or myself. Your company has been most enjoyable and welcomed."

"Unfortunately, I won't be able to remain much beyond the holiday. I do have business matters to attend to back home. Though I must say this quaint little town has charmed me in ways I had not expected."

"You will fall in love with this beautiful town if you remain much longer."

"Perhaps. This does not change the fact I must return to St. Louis at some point."

"Well Mr. Warner, you are in luck. Due to the rapidly approaching winter, we are not as busy as we were upon your arrival. You are welcome to your room for the next three months. Will you continue on in the Gold Room as well?"

"I would be delighted. The games have proved a challenge. You've gathered quite a group of skilled gamblers into your high-in rooms."

"We try to cultivate the best." Jane marked him down for both. Once he was set in their ledger, she circled the counter to lace her hand through his arm. "I'm delighted your earlier drive to leave has been eliminated. I must admit I doubted Katherine's stories could be quite as true as they've proven to be. You are a delight."

"Careful, Jane. You'll make me blush."

"I do find it rather fun to make the best scoundrels blush."

"I imagine you are quite adept at such a thing."

"I do try." She slowed as they approached the casino. "I'm quite serious. You're enjoyable company to have around."

"And you haven't even lain with me. Imagine if you had." He offered a sly wink. "Then again, it's probably for the best. I can only catch so many swooning maidens a day before my arms tire."

"It must be so tedious for you." Jane paused at the top of the pit with him. "What's your poison today, Patrick?"

His gaze wandered the room, only to pause on the roulette wheel where Sally currently covered for an ill Chauncey. "Roulette, I believe."

"I do not mind your interest, especially now that other matters are settled. I do implore you to remember your promise to be kind. The girl has only recently allowed excitement back into her life. She's new to such matters."

"Kind I can do." He kissed the back of her hand again before descending into the pit.

Jane released a sigh as he greeted Sally in such a way that the girl blushed down to her bosom. A hand settled at her waist. The familiar warmth drew her in until she happily leaned into Cole. "Hello there."

"Do I need to be worried?"

"Look at you, being all protective like her pa."

"She says I am."

"True enough. No, I wouldn't worry. Much like another rake I know, Patrick isn't all he seems. Sally longs to find excitement and stimulation. I can't fault her for that."

He tugged her close when she turned toward him. "You can't?"

"I certainly have plenty of both with you around."

"You saying you're just using me?"

"Most definitely. The best part being that you're using me right back. Often." She took his arm on their way through the restaurant. Along the way she paused at tables to greet friends and guests. When they emerged into the open air, she leaned on the railing with a contented sigh.

Cole opened his mouth to say something, but a deep rumbling like thunder distracted them both. Instead of fading, it grew in intensity. They both darted toward the railing on Main Street, gazes cast south. "Cowboy time."

"I'll go alert the floor, and Cora. Looks like Wil heard the noise as well." Across the way Wil stood on the saloon porch with what appeared to be every whore out on display.

"I'll go on over and check if he needs extra help for the rush." Cole leaned in to give her a kiss before hopping off the porch to cross the street.

Jane rushed inside to make appropriate warnings. Though the cowboys meant an uptick in business, it also lent a shadier aspect to the business dealings. There'd been plenty of men up to no good when they passed through town. David had even added an extra couple of deputies to cover the periods when a trail run came through.

After spreading the word, Jane grabbed her holster from the apartment and slung it over her shoulders. She stepped back onto the floor as she buckled it under her chest. Tommy nodded to her from behind the bar, patting the bar where a shotgun sat hooked beneath.

She stopped to check on Sally at the roulette wheel before she made it to the bar. Though the girl was still clearly flattered by Patrick's attentions, she was keeping a clear enough head to run a good game, so Jane didn't intervene.

"Cole at The Golden Touch?" Tommy asked as she stepped behind the bar with him.

"He said he'd check to see if Wil needed an extra hand to handle the crowd."

"And seeing as he's refused an extra bartender so far, that means Cole will be across the way for the rest of the night."

"Most likely." Though it would be several hours before the cattle were settled enough for the real crowd to begin, already a few of the cowboys trickled in.

For the next several hours Jane worked ceaselessly alongside her brother to take care of the stream of regulars and the mix of strangers that wandered in from the trail. Exhaustion hit early, but she worked through the debility. Seeing as Chauncey was ill, they needed as much help as they could manage.

At some point Tommy pulled a stool behind the bar for her to rest on as often as possible, which helped some. Near the end of the evening when she stood to greet another customer however, a strong pain hit her right side by her hip. "Oh. Ow. Hmmm."

"You all right, Janey?" Carl Denner eyed her with concern from across the bar.

"Yes. I think. It's just an ache." She rubbed the heel of her hand against the spot to try to relieve the pulling sensation. It wasn't like a contraction pain, or anywhere near the pain she'd had when she'd miscarried. All of that eased her initial panic into gentle concern.

"Should I get the doc?" Carl polished off his beer. "I don't mind."

"I believe I'm fine, but perhaps it wouldn't hurt to check. There's a free beer in it for you if you do me that favor. Two free beers if you get Dr. Cross instead of my brother." Granted Charlie was likely occupied with his newborn George, but if he caught wind of her trouble he might leave the clinic and his wife to help.

Carl winked and took off out of the casino.

Tom's brow furrowed as he approached. "What's wrong?"

"I have an ache, that's all. I believe I worked too much, or the baby is just reminding me he's there. Either way, I've already sent Mr. Denner for Andrew."

"Good girl." He edged her back onto the stool. "Take a rest. We've got a handle on things for a while. Kat showed up to lend a hand, so I'll put her to work."

"You mean you aren't going to run tattle on me to Cole?"

"Not until there's something worth tattling about. You handled things appropriately, didn't get stupid, and you're taking care of it. Therefore, there's nothing to report."

Jane patted his arm. "Thank you. Take it easy on Katherine, she's with child too."

"I know. The whole damn camp is."

"Except Millie and Lee. They've had their babies."

He chuckled. "Fair enough point."

"All right. I'm resting. Get back to work you lazy sod. We have a casino full of people. Cuddy's guarding the cage. See if you can't get a little more action at vingt-et-un. Edwards is looking a little lonely."

He clicked his heels together and performed a stiff salute. "Yes, ma'am."

Ten minutes of careful deliveries of drinks—each followed by rest—later Andrew arrived with Carl. Along with him was a lovely young woman with deep mahogany hair and startling eyes—both pale, but different colors. One was the celeste blue of the sky, the other the palest green that could only be called chartreuse. Jane extended her hand. "Hello, I'm Jane. You must be Bonnie. Your brother Matthew has spoken of you often."

"I am. It's good to meet you. I hope you don't mind that I tagged along with Andrew. I'm still gaining my footing, but seeing as this is about your baby, I thought I might help." Bonnie cast a smile at Andrew. "Andrew is very capable, but I do have more experience with pregnant women than he does."

"I'll not deny it either." Andrew's hand drifted toward Bonnie's waist before he pulled it back as if he'd only realized he was doing it.

"I don't mind at all. One moment." Jane poured a beer and set it in front of Carl. "You let Thomas or Katherine know that I said the next one is on the house as well."

Carl lifted his glass in thanks before setting about emptying it.

Jane led the doctor and midwife back to her apartment. "I apologize for disturbing you both. I'm already feeling better now that I've been resting, but given my history I tend to panic first rather than end up in dire straits."

"Andrew told me a little about your history when we were going over files. Why don't you tell us what happened tonight?" Bonnie took charge in a way Jane appreciated. At least Andrew wasn't too proud to allow it when it came to the baby.

Jane explained the course of her day and the location and nature of the pain that had struck. By the time she'd finished Bonnie had done a cursory exam, then deferred to Andrew to do the same. Jane sighed. "Please tell me I overreacted. I'd much rather hear that than any alternative."

"Given your history, I wouldn't call anything overreacting. However, I believe you're getting a pain rather common in pregnancy. It has to do with your body adjusting to the baby. Since you overdid it today, it would make sense you'd feel it. You said it happened when you stood up?" Bonnie perched on the side of the couch next to Jane. Her hand rested on the slight swell of Jane's abdomen.

"Yes. I'd been sitting on the stool. When someone walked up I moved to stand and it pulled right there." Jane rubbed the offended area again.

Andrew cleaned his hands and came to Jane's other side. He leaned on the back of the couch. "There's no sign of trouble that I can tell, and it seems Bonnie feels the same."

"Definitely. I would say you need to take it easy for the next couple of days." Bonnie's brow rose at Jane's undignified snort. "I understand there's a trail run in town which makes your businesses quite busy. However, I ask you rest whenever the opportunity arises, and remain off your feet when you can. As much as possible."

"Trust me, between my brother and Cole, once they hear my orders I will have no choice in the matter." Jane glanced pointedly at Andrew. "Am I wrong?"

"Not in the slightest. She's got a protective lot surrounding her at all times." Andrew squeezed her shoulder. "Back to your stool, and stay seated as much as possible the rest of the night. With the size of the crowd I know you'll never lie down."

"I really wish I could, but Chauncey is ill at home, and so we're short tonight. Sally was helping, but she's with Alma now." Jane got herself to sitting. "Well, it was lovely to finally meet you, Bonnie. I wish it had been on the street or in the restaurant rather than this way."

"Nonsense. This is how I meet most of my patients." Bonnie rose. "Shall we, Andrew?"

"Of course." Andrew extended his arm. "I hadn't finished your tour yet."

Jane eyed the pair as they left the apartment through the back. "Those two will be courting by Christmas or I'll eat my foot."

All truths are easy to understand once they are discovered; the point is to discover them.
—Galileo Galilei

Tommy sipped his coffee slow and steady. His gaze darted around the restaurant to go over every patron. He struggled to think of people capable of the evils befalling the town. He knew every person. Sure, there were ones that weren't the best people, but murderers? That would be stretching it.

Had he become too complacent? Never had he stuck around anywhere as long as he'd been in Dominion Falls. Not since his youth, anyway. Jane, Cole, and Leanne kept life interesting enough his eye had rarely wandered beyond their little valley.

Too long in one place must have dulled his skills, but it couldn't have made his instincts wrong, could it? Instinct told him most of the people in this group wouldn't hurt a fly, much less murder. Then again, he'd seen good people turn dark for the oddest reasons. So, if one of them had, what could be behind it?

"You look perfectly miserable," Jane said by way of greeting as she took her seat.

"Not miserable. Contemplating."

"You appear to be contemplating murder with that grumpy puss."

"I was."

"Thomas Eugene."

"Not committing it, the ones already committed." He shook off his reverie to face his sister. "What's wrong with you?"

"I'm missing a child."

"Easy to do, as many as you've got."

Her lips pursed against her next words, eyes narrowing.

"Not complaining, just stating facts."

"I suppose you do have a point." She released a long sigh as she settled back in her chair. "It's Sally. You haven't seen her, have you?"

"She's supposed to be in a lesson with Molly about now, isn't she?" He pulled his watch free of its pocket to check the time.

"I thought you were observant."

"I am."

She lifted a brow and gave him a sidelong glance.

"What? I am." He frowned at her continued stare. "The cowboys have been in town, I've been busy. What'd I miss, oh wise one?"

"She hasn't been taking lessons with Molly for several days. Not since their little tiff in the library. Of course, she's usually spending time with Andrew. I should check the clinic."

Before he could question her on the tiff she spoke of, she rose and departed the Inn. He scowled at her back. It was her intention to have him questioning this bit of information. She always liked to prove men were more gossipers than women. "Smartass."

Speaking of the devil, Molly strode into the room right then. Tommy flagged her down before she could make her leave. She flopped into the seat opposite him with a huff.

Rather than reveal his cards too early, he studied her. He turned his attention to the coffee in his hand. Cool and calculated, he took a sip. He thought it best to let her stew for a minute. When she huffed again, he set down the mug. "Thought you had a lesson with Sally today."

"Sally ain't interested in lessons right now." Her mouth twitched. "Or rather, lessons with me. Hanging out plenty with that Andrew fella."

"Reverting to the tongue of your former life? You're in a fit." He'd known her long enough to know she only reverted back to rough vernacular when she was too flustered to think straight.

"Am not."

"What happened?" Tommy leaned forward. "Last I knew, Sally was pretty damn excited for her lessons."

"Guess things changed."

"Care to elaborate?"

She huffed again. The approaching waitress got waved off. "Apparently I offended her."

"Did you now?"

"We were talking about that whore—"

"Carrie? Or Lucy?"

"Does it matter?"

That was enough to give Tom an idea what the tiff was about. "It does. And it does to Sally. She's got a good heart, and was once a whore herself."

"For a couple of years." She scoffed with cold derision. "I myself have played the part enough times."

"You played, she didn't. She, and her ma, see whores as people, not dispensable tools."

"I don't—"

"Mr. Young." Andrew panted his way to a halt at the table. "She's awake."

Tommy stared at the young doctor in confusion. "Who's awake?"

"Lucy. Sally is with her now." Andrew clutched a stitch at his side. "Oh, dear."

Tommy chuckled under his breath. Clearly the young man had to build up stamina as well as his horse-riding skills. Tom got to his feet with a nod to Molly. "Let's go."

He didn't wait to see if she'd follow, just walked quickly outside. The thoroughfare was busy enough he had to weave his way through people and greetings to get across the street to the clinic. By the time he got to the door, Molly was right on his heels.

They climbed the stairs without a bye or leave to Daisy, who sat at the front desk. However, when he got to the top of the stairs, he paused. He knew they'd put Lucy in a nearby room, and he could hear quiet words being exchanged behind the door.

He touched his finger to his lips before gesturing for Molly to follow. The door sat cracked, and he caught a glimpse of Sally perched on the edge of Lucy's bed. Sally held the whore's hand, whispering words of comfort to the crying girl.

"—am I going to do?" Lucy's shaky voice grew louder at the end of her question.

"Don't you worry about that," Sally soothed quietly. "You know Pa will find you somewhere to go. Somewhere far from here, away from whoever did this to you."

"Why? Where? How? I've got nothing."

"Ma and Pa will take care of you. If you want another place to work, they'll find it. If you want something else, they'll make sure that happens. You've got a little bit saved up, I'd bet."

"Not enough for…nothing."

Sally smiled at the young woman, then leaned in to whisper something in her ear.

Lucy broke down in sobs, wincing at every flinch of her body. "Why?"

"You know why. Just because you aren't part of their flock, doesn't mean they won't help. That's how they are. Helped Tully stay in business after Mac busted up the place last year, didn't they? It's who they are."

"I don't got a place to land like you."

"I got lucky, I won't deny that. Good part of that luck came from Ma and Pa. Ma will be by soon, I bet. She'll see what you want."

"I just want to be far from here. It's…I…"

Even from where he stood, Tommy could see the way Lucy's hand tightened on Sally's.

Sally folded Lucy into a hug, her words lost for a few minutes. When the embrace ended, Sally kept a hold of

Lucy's hand. "I felt that fear too. After what happened to me. Still do sometimes. I don't remember what happened even. Not after that woman screamed whore at me."

"Who?"

"I don't know," Sally admitted, a frustrated note in her voice. "It wasn't anyone familiar by the sound of their voice. It was dark, I couldn't have seen her clearly if I'd tried, then I got hit and I don't remember after that."

"It was dark, I couldn't see anything. Agnes's scream woke me."

"Agnes? Do you know what happened to her?"

"No. I-I-I think they got her. I heard her screams, and then Tully hollering."

Sally shifted in her seat, the only admission of her eagerness Tommy could note. He felt the same excitement that they might have a clue at last. Sally's free hand clasped over Lucy's so she held both hands in hers. "What about Carrie?"

"Sleeps like the dead." Lucy shuddered at her own simile. "Slept right through the tornado."

"I see. You said it was dark. You went out?"

"I don't know why, but yeah."

"Did you hear their voices?"

"I got hit." Lucy's hand fluttered to the back of her head. "It's all muddled. It was so dark. One of them dragged me away. He…"

Tommy held his breath, willing Sally to remain calm, to not push.

"Andrew told me what was done, you don't have to relive that." Sally brushed the girl's cheek as if to remove a tear. "Did he say anything?"

"He said…a lot. About hell and temptation." Lucy's voice trembled.

"You heard his voice. Lots of men pass through Tully's for a drink or entertainment. You've talked to most of them, I'd bet."

"It's part of the job."

Sally nodded quietly. "It's never all about sex. We learn how to keep them happy, drinking, talking, and spending money. We learn the men that come through, who to avoid, who is good, who brings in the money."

Lucy nodded quietly. Her eyes fluttered shut, pain flickering across her features.

"Try to focus on his voice over his words, over the blows. Just the man's voice."

A small gasp squeaked out of the whore, her eyes flying open. "It can't be."

"Can't be? Who?"

"Georgie."

Sally settled back, her face slack from shock. "Georgie Staub?"

"Yes. But, I have to be wrong. He was always good. Kind. Stopped coming by a few months ago, we were disappointed."

Tommy backed away from the door, unsurprised when Molly did the same. Though her gaze remained on the door, thoughtful. "Yes?"

"She's good."

"I know. She learned how to talk to people from her former life as a whore, and her ma. She's fair sight better at it than me."

"Well, you are a brute. So, who's this Georgie?"

"Just like Lucy said, always known him to be a decent man. Friendly-like, patron of Tully's, used to frequent The Hangman's Inn before the whores went away. Never would have thought this of him."

"She said he stopped going a few months ago. Wonder why."

"Good question." Tommy leaned sideways to check on Sally again. She sat with Lucy in a warm embrace, running her hands along her back.

Footsteps on the stairs caught his ear moments before his sister's voice. "Why are you spying?"

"Not spying. Letting your girl do what she does so well." Tommy turned to find Jane balancing a tray in her hands. "What's this?"

"I heard Lucy was awake and thought I'd bring her a hearty soup."

"You heard? Already?"

"Walked right past you, you big galoot. Entered behind Andrew. Anyhow, I doubt Lucy's mouth feels strong enough for a stew. Luckily Cora had a nice minestrone today." Jane glanced at Molly, who still stared toward the door. A quizzical gaze fell on Tommy.

He shrugged. Rather than address the curiosity of Jane, he nodded back toward the door. "Sally's already told the girl you'll help her find somewhere else."

"She's a smart girl."

"Brilliant," whispered Molly.

An amused twitch crossed Jane's lips before she returned to the conversation as though she'd not heard the woman. "Cole and I have already discussed options, depending on what she wishes to do moving forward. Does she know anything about Agnes?"

"Said she was in the middle of it, thinks whoever they were took her." Tommy grimaced at her sharp look. "Also named Georgie as the man that attacked her."

"Staub? What in heaven's name?"

"My question exactly." He leaned against the wall. "Once I talk to Sally, I'll get with David and we'll go have a chat with Georgie."

Jane sighed. "How a good man can go bad. What could do such a thing?"

"Based on history, many things make good men go bad."

"Not just history, life today is no better."

"Don't I know it?"

"Probably better than most."

*Friendship makes prosperity more shining
and lessens adversity by dividing
and sharing it.
-Cicero*

Jane slowed the buggy to a stop in front of Daisy's small homestead. All around was quiet. Much like when she'd visited her brother recently, curtains were drawn and there was little to no sign of life. Even the flowers in the windows were wilting under the late fall heat wave.

She hesitated to alight from the buggy. It seemed as though the doctor wasn't at home. Still, she'd not been at the clinic. According to Lydia, Charles had gone to Mike's hotel clinic to cover another of Daisy's absences there.

Seeing as she couldn't think of anywhere else for Daisy to be, outside of Mike's, she'd at least try to visit. Their last encounter hadn't been friendly, but Jane still considered the woman a friend. One that appeared to be going through something difficult.

She pulled the brake and alit from the cart. First, she gave Brag the treat of an apple, then went to the door. She knocked gently, waiting quietly for a few minutes.

No answering call came immediately. Some scuffling noises sounded through the door for a few minutes. When silence fell again, Jane knocked a few more times. This time she called out to the home's owner, "Daisy?"

A full minute passed. Jane nearly made up her mind to leave before the curtain near the door pushed open. Daisy peered out before disappearing again. The door opened to reveal a slightly disheveled Daisy. "Jane. What brings you by?"

"I wanted to check on you." A thump from the back drew her attention, but Jane restrained the urge to peek at the cause.

"Whatever for?"

"I barely see you anymore. Last time we spoke you were cross with me. Honestly, I'm worried about you."

"There's nothing to worry about." Daisy sighed deeply, but held the door open for Jane. "Come in, then."

Jane stepped inside, surprised to find the room neat as a pin. In the past when she'd visited, she'd often find every smooth surface littered with medical texts and journals. There was no sign of any of it today. "Lydia said you took the day off again, I'd hoped I'd find you here."

"There's hardly need for me to work as much any longer. Charlie has plenty of help these days. He told me he's hiring another doctor, too." Daisy's back faced Jane, so she couldn't see her friend's face. The tone with which she spoke the words was rather biting, though.

"Charles has always appreciated your presence, you know that." Jane smiled pleasant as she could when Daisy approached. She accepted the offered glass of water and took a seat. "I do suppose his ultimate reason is for there to be more time for him to spend with his family. Having a child certainly has drawn him homeward more often than in the past."

"Of course. The child." Daisy sipped her tea. "So, did you need something?"

"No. This is hardly the first time I've ever visited, Daisy."

Daisy's tense shoulders sagged. "Sorry."

"Might I ask you something? As a friend."

Daisy's gaze lifted. A calculated gaze turned her eyes dark. "A friend?"

"Yes. We have been friends, or rather I thought we have."

A light scoff turned into a false cough.

Jane frowned. "I suppose I thought wrong, then."

"You tolerated me because of Cole, then Michael."

"Hardly. You saved my life, several times. We had moments where I thought we could become quite close." Jane took a sip of a drink as she contemplated her own words. She'd thought they could become close, but there was always something impeding them reaching true closeness. "I apologize for my bluntness, but it felt as though you always kept us from getting too close."

"I don't—I mean—perhaps." The cup twirled through Daisy's fingers. "I thought there was too much bad between us."

It was Jane's turn to scoff. "Please. If I can be friends with David, I can certainly be friends with you. No, let me amend that. If I can be friends with Graham, who literally threatened to make my hanging slower and more painful, then I can certainly be friends with you after little more than some jealousy."

Daisy almost smiled at the mention of Graham. "Talk about a changed man."

"We all change. Some for the worse, others for the better. I'm glad Graham was one that changed for the better." Jane set her cup down. "Why have you not been doctoring as much? You have been a trusted physician around here for years."

"Not so much."

"You were the sole doctor when I first arrived in town. By all accounts, you were used rather often for everything from minor wounds to major ones. Cole used to complain about how it kept you from whoring—not that I believe he truly minded. It meant profit for him in the end."

"I was the sole doctor. Precisely. People had no choice. Now they do."

Jane shifted closer to set a hand on Daisy's. "You have been out of sorts for some time, Daisy. Since well before Charles brought in Andrew. Since—"

Daisy didn't lift her head when Jane's words failed her. Her thumb rubbed along the condensation on the outside of the glass.

Jane searched her friend's sullen features. The epidemic had been tumultuous for the town. So many sick had overflowed the clinic. Still, it was Daisy that seemed to suffer lasting effects. She didn't care to pinpoint the issue so bluntly, but perhaps it needed to be addressed thus. "Since the epidemic."

Daisy flinched at the word, withdrawing her hands from Jane's grasp.

"Charles lost as many souls as you did. Both of you worked so tirelessly to save as many as you could. You, yourself, fell ill but refused to stop working. I admired you for it."

"Admired? For what? Losing so many lives? So many more than…"

"The town is more populous than the first epidemic you faced. There was bound to be more, no matter what happened." Jane didn't rise to follow her friend when the woman went back to the small kitchen. "I can't begin to understand how difficult that was for you both. More so for you, after what happened the first time."

Daisy didn't respond. Her hand shook when she poured another cup of water. Several drops sloshed onto the table.

"You never talk about your husband. What was he like?"

"Emmett?"

"Yes, Emmett. I know he was a lawyer. That you came to Dominion Falls together. Other than that, I'm woefully underinformed. I know nothing of the man himself. You loved him, clearly."

"He—he was a chatterbox. Made him a good lawyer, and people liked him." Daisy remained in the kitchen, her voice shaking as her hands had been. "I think it was his talk that got me my first patients. He supported me, was so proud of me."

Jane lowered her eyes, but otherwise didn't acknowledge the sharp crack in Daisy's voice.

"It was my uncle that supported me in school. The rest of my family disavowed me for such an ill-fitting career for a woman. I met Emmett while I was in school. He charmed me right away with his talk. He was so intrigued that I wanted to be a doctor."

"Flattery is many a man's way into a woman's heart."

"He was quite good at it. With everyone he met, really. Still, it seemed quite directed at me, and we began courting right away. He refused to marry until I'd finished school. He didn't want me to be distracted. We came out here shortly after. I think he convinced Mrs. Daugherty to hire me on his charm alone."

"Lillian hired you?" This was news to Jane, but not unsurprising. Lillian had paid Reverend Greene for years, and initiated the library—keeping it alive by her own pocket. In fact, she'd bet anything that it wasn't Emmett's charms that had brought Lillian to hire Daisy.

"She did. We got the building that Cora lives in now at first. One room for doctoring, one room for Emmett to do his business. We'd pull a mattress out every night and sleep in the front room. It was small, but we made it work."

Jane smiled at her glass on the table, afraid if she looked at Daisy dead on the spell would be broken.

"After a while I got some patients, and his business picked up. He bought another building in town. A larger one I could use for a clinic, and we could make a home. He'd keep the smaller building for his law office. Then it happened. Before we'd made the first payment."

Now Jane lifted her gaze to face the woman. She turned in her seat, but didn't go to her. Daisy's eyes were focused somewhere far away, beyond the room, beyond the town.

"I did all I could. The clinic wasn't set up, but I took in as many as I could. I put the least affected in the saloon, those bad off but not near death at Martha's, the worst in the clinic closest to my medicines. Emmett insisted on helping and fell ill. He went when I wasn't there, I was at Martha's helping them. I wasn't there."

Jane's throat swelled with tears as Daisy's eyes fluttered closed, a tear slipping down her rouged cheek. "I'm so sorry."

Daisy sniffed, swiping at the tear. "It was years ago."

"Time doesn't necessarily lessen the pain—especially if you've denied yourself the freedom to feel it."

"Denied myself? I didn't—life did. Immediately his family was beckoning me home. The bank was ready to foreclose before seeing if I could make the payments."

"You didn't have time to grieve. You, instead, had to change who you were." Jane remained quiet as Daisy gulped down her water. When no response came, she pushed forward. "Why did you never go back to your given name when you left Cole's?"

"Caroline? I don't feel much like that girl anymore. You should understand that."

"I do. In more ways than most, I think." She knew Cole understood, too. He'd left a life behind once himself. Jane took a deep breath. "I imagine last years epidemic reminded you too much of all of that."

"It was years ago," Daisy repeated.

"Might I ask—are you all right?"

"I'm well enough."

"Let me rephrase. Are you happy?"

Daisy turned to look at her. For a long moment there was quiet. A small smile crossed her features, but her eyes remained dark. "I just got engaged. Why shouldn't I be?"

"That isn't what I asked. I asked if you are happy."

"I don't know what I am anymore."

"Or who you are?"

Daisy's lip trembled and she looked down. After a moment she cleared her throat. "Perhaps you should go. I have an appointment soon I need to get to."

Jane rose at the dismissal. Instead of leaving, she crossed to Daisy. She folded her friend in her arms. "If you need to talk, I'm here. I promise to keep whatever is said between us. Michael is my brother, but you are my friend. If you'll have me."

Daisy returned the hug meekly. "Thank you."

After another squeeze, Jane stepped back. "I hope you'll be at the next tea. Your presence has been missed."

"If I'm available." Daisy had already turned away, busying herself at the stove.

"I hope I'll see you Thursday, then." Jane took her leave somewhat reluctantly. She felt as though there was more she should have said. It didn't seem as though Daisy wanted to hear it, though. She only hoped that sometime soon she'd be prepared to listen, or be heard.

Perhaps Cole was the better to listen, though. He'd always had a way with his girls, and Daisy had been his favorite for three years.

Yes, she'd talk to Cole. Hopefully he'd have better luck with Daisy.

The only charm of marriage is that it makes a life of deception necessary for both parties.
-Oscar Wilde

Cole stood on the porch of The Golden Touch with Wil. The place currently sat deserted for two reasons. One, they didn't open for another fifteen minutes. For another, the cowboys were working on loading the cattle on the train for transport.

After days of the saloon being overrun, with the uptick in lawlessness from the cowboys, Cole was enjoying the quiet while they had it. By all of Jane and Tom's reports, the casino had been much the same, even with the lack of whores.

He couldn't be happier for the boom in business. He could, however, live without the amount of fights they'd needed to break up. Not to mention being away from the casino and Jane so much.

Seeing as Jane had decided they'd been too happy and calm, and not many knew of her pregnancy, she'd also decided it was time to stir up some trouble between them.

A rather public argument had already taken place. Cole had remained in the saloon to sleep rather than return home the night before. They'd also let others believe a wandering eye for both of them.

He didn't mind the game, for it made life interesting. The new brothel also afforded plenty of opportunity to make others wonder over the stability of their relationship. Never mind that every single night he was able to make it home Jane waited for him, eager and loving. He didn't care who talked so long as that's where she always was.

To further the game, he'd picked his 'favorite' of the whores. He never went to a room with her, he wasn't fool enough to try that, but he kept her close when neither of them were working.

He took a deep drag of his cigar, eyes on the smoke from the train. "You thought any more about bringing in another bartender for weeks like this one?"

"I'm considering it," Wil acknowledged. He lit a cigarette, blowing the smoke out of the corner of his mouth. His gaze settled on the main thoroughfare. "How often these trail runs come through now?"

"More and more frequent over the past year. Got good grazing land north of town, and the train gets the cattle where it needs to go." The one difference between the new saloon and the old, besides the placement of Wil's room, was that they'd built this one elevated from the street. That gave them a nice vantage point, high above the activity to keep an eye on things.

Wil grunted an acknowledgment. "Woulda been nice to know before I got here."

"We told ya we had runs. Just didn't mention how often. Slacks off in winter, of course. Still, wouldn't hurt to get an extra hand." Cole noticed Jane at that moment. Draped on the arm of Patrick, she strolled down the street without a care. Her grin was bright, and her laughter carried on the air after the man said something in her ear. "If you know someone you'd like to bring in, we'll take your input on it. Otherwise, Tom can find us someone else—but we'd run the risk of you not getting along. That would be a problem."

"I have an idea of who I'd call on, but I ain't sure he'd be interested." Wil's jaw clenched. "We didn't part on a good note. Things got ugly in the end, but he's a good friend."

"We'll leave it up to you." Cole sucked his lips in to give a sharp whistle.

Jane's gaze immediately landed on him. She stuck her nose in the air rather than respond. Together, she and Patrick continued on their way. Inwardly, Cole couldn't deny his amusement over her mock anger at him. The woman was truly determined to keep every person in town guessing as to why they'd opened the saloon.

"Jane," Cole called. He made sure to lend a dark note to his words.

Wil straightened, flicking his cigarette off into the dirt. "Fun as it is to watch the two of you go at it, I'm gonna get set to open."

"Be there in a minute." Cole hopped down the steps. When Jane excused herself from Patrick's side to saunter over to him, he lifted a brow. "What shenanigans are you up to now?"

"I've been ordered to take the afternoon off by no less than three people. Tom, Sally, and Katherine all ordered me to relax. There are no shenanigans. I am simply a woman enjoying some leisure.”

“In the company of a rake, no less.”

“Well, it is hardly fair for you to be the only one spreading rumor and scandal. I am no damsel in distress, Mr. Mitchell.” She looped her fingers into his belt to tug him close. “What’s the matter? Jealous?”

“Of him?” He nodded Patrick’s direction. “I could be, if you wanted.”

“No. I doubt you could.”

“Says who?”

“Me. You like him too much.”

“I still could.” He chucked a finger under her chin. “Did you stop by the clinic?”

“I’m fine, Cole. Tired. The baby is making me sore. Same as always, and nothing more. I did stop by the clinic, but only to visit Charles, Millie, and baby George.” She freed her chin from his light hold. “Patrick has been kind enough to offer to escort me to check on Chauncey, seeing as all my usual companions for such a mission of mercy are occupied. The poor man remains violently ill according to Andrew. Much longer, and he’ll need to go to the clinic no matter what his stubborn mule head says.”

“Chauncey ain’t been sick a day since I met him.”

“I know. They’re fearing the worst. I’m going to take him some of that vile tea I had to drink when pregnant with the twins. I only hope it helps.”

Cole didn’t miss the flicker of concern that puckered her brow. It might have gone fast, but she couldn’t hide it from him, not anymore. The mention of the extreme illness of her last pregnancy had bothered her. "Sure you won't need it this time?"

"I've had no indications of nausea with this child." At that statement, her gaze wandered down the street. Now the concern pulled her brows together without ceasing. He eased a finger over the wrinkles forming across her forehead. They soothed somewhat at his touch.

"Didn't have none the first time, neither. That's when ya had the problem, and you never got a reason for it."

Her eyes tightened, the faintest shimmer in the corner of her eyes belying the tears she was likely holding out of pure stubbornness.

"That's why you're so worried."

"Worried if I'm sick, worried if I'm not. It's of no consequence. I simply worry." She backed away without a kiss. "I'm fine. According to the doctor and midwife everything looks as well as can be expected. I'll see you in a few hours."

"Hey, now. Where's my—"

"No, sir." A sly grin had returned to replace the flash of concern. She backed up so fast, she bumped right into Patrick. He caught her easily when she stumbled. "Not today."

He did his best to appear rightfully pissed. He suspected his amusement was far too great for such deception. "You'll pay for that later, Janey."

"I'm counting on it." She draped her arm back through Patrick's and took off down the street. As she rounded the corner, she allowed him one last glance over her shoulder.

"Jezebel," he muttered just loud enough to be heard by passers-by. He just hoped his laughter wasn't heard as well as he climbed back up the steps into the now open saloon.

A handful of girls draped on the porch to entice men off the street. When he walked inside he was immediately greeted with a whiskey by Buttercup. The girl followed him to the bar where she perched close beside him as ordered. Also as ordered, she didn't dare touch him anywhere below the belt.

Wil nodded a greeting, but kept in conversation with Ben Carr, a relatively new man in town that had opened a butcher shop round the bend. Men trickled in slow so the place didn't fill up fast enough for Cole to help out behind the bar yet. Instead, he engaged Buttercup in conversation.

He'd named her for her golden yellow hair and shocking amber eyes with gold flecks. He had to admit she was the prettiest girl in the lot. That's not why he'd picked her as his decoy. He'd picked her because the girl could carry on a decent conversation.

She'd had her schooling until nearly fifteen, but then her family had married her off. Now she was on the run from the man that had beat her, and he'd been happy to add her to the flock. Out of the lot of whores Tom had found, she was the one he didn't pity one bit yet. He wondered if it would change as it did so often.

The inane conversation kept him distracted and seemingly wrapped up in her until the saloon was nearly three quarters full. At that point he shooed her off to find some paying company. A glance told him Wil still had things well under control.

Cole tossed back his whiskey. He made his way around the saloon to see who needed what, and to make his greetings to customers old and new. Though he hadn't the memory of Jane, he still liked to know the sort that patroned his saloon.

After an hour, Will seemed to still have a good handle on things. Cole stepped out onto the porch to get some fresh air. One thing about the casino that was better, was the air didn't get quite as thick with sweat and other unseemly smells like the brothel tended to.

There were still a few whores on the porch making their enticements. Cole went to the other side of the porch instead. He noticed a familiar figure wandering the street. One of his former whores, in fact. He let out another whistle to get her attention.

Daisy stopped at the sound. After a moment, she turned his direction. "What?"

He hopped down the steps easily, crossing the street to where she stood in the shade. Jane had told him to try to talk to Daisy. No time like the present, he supposed. How to broach the subject, though?

"Did you need something?" Daisy set her hand on her hip, giving him a familiar petulant look. More so, he noticed her dress was loose. One shoulder barely clung on, giving an ample view of her cleavage.

"Daisy, what are you doing?"

She quirked a brow, her green eyes focused on him. "You're the one that stopped me."

"No. I mean, this." He flicked at her shoulder where the fabric held on by sheer will it seemed. "What happened to your fancies?"

"They became uncomfortable. There's nothing improper here."

"No, but it's not…"

"What?"

He studied the woman before him. For three years he'd known her as his whore. For several before that as the town doc he helped out by letting her care for his whores and sending the men to her as well. Then after he'd sold her contract, he'd watched her change and grow back into a mostly-proper woman again.

"If you don't got nothing to say, I'm going to go about my day."

He touched her arm as she passed, unsure what to say. "Daisy."

She paused at his touch, her gaze fixed on his hand where it sat. Her free hand came up to touch it. He noticed it shaking before she set it over his. "Nothing to worry about."

"Don't seem like it to me. Seems like it's plenty to worry about."

When she lifted her gaze, a sad smile danced across her lips. "You always were good at reading us. Glad to see some things don't change."

He kept her there, not deterring her from the touch. "You aren't one of my girls anymore, Daisy. Haven't been for a long time."

"Once a whore, always a whore."

"Not always. Look at you, look at Sally."

"Sally had a soft place to land."

"So did you, last I checked."

"You'd think so, wouldn't you?"

"Daisy."

"I need to go. Thank ya for your concern." She lifted on tiptoe to kiss his cheek, then rushed away. A cloud of dust rose in her path she moved so quick.

Jane was right. There was something up. Something much more than he thought he could fix. Even if Jane thought different.

*I would much prefer to suffer from the clean
incision of an honest lancet than from
a sweetened poison.
-Mark Twain*

Cole headed back to the porch. He noticed a couple of the girls whispering to each other on his approach. Though the upswing in gossip would cheer Jane, he wasn't about to allow such a thing on his watch. He curled his lip to snarl at them. "Get back to work."

He allowed a smirk when they scrambled to do just that. Gossip was one thing, outright disobedience hadn't ever been tolerated, much. His girls had a certain amount of leeway, but he only let so much fly free.

When he turned back to the street, he nodded at the passing Sheriff. "Davie."

"Cole. Any trouble at your place?" David stopped underneath him, tilting his hat back to see him better. "I figure them cowboys will be off tomorrow. Heading back south before winter hits."

"So far it's as expected. Nothing to call ya in for."

"Good to hear. Have you seen Mike?"

"Mike?" Cole shook his head, unable to stop a glance toward the corner around which Daisy had disappeared. "Nah. Can't say I have, probably a few days since I have."

David set his hands on his hips, a frown crossing his features. "He is supposed to be on duty today. Just rode out to the hotel, and they haven't seen him. Didn't answer at the homestead, neither."

"Odd." Far as Cole knew, Mike had never missed a day of work. If he wasn't hard at work at the hotel, he was at the jail as deputy. With Tom working so much between the casino and saloon, he had reason to not work as much. "No. Last I heard of him, Jane had gone to see him, said he had a megrim. That was a while ago, though."

"Lee said he hasn't been working as much, either. Inconvenient for her. At least she can take Marjorie to work, but it's hard to work with a babe on your arm."

"She's been working more? With the baby and all? Jane'll be grumpy if she hears that."

For that, David chuckled. "Like she has room to talk. She works endlessly with babes, children, and adults all around her."

Cole laughed along with him. "Fair enough point. I'll keep an eye out. I see him, I'll let him know you're looking for him."

"Much obliged." David tilted his hat in thanks before heading down the street.

"Cole," someone called from inside.

After one glance up and down the street, wondering where Jane was, Cole went back inside. For the next hour he mingled, served, dealt out whores, and laughed with the men inside. The place now fairly teemed with life, plenty of people to keep things busy.

When he had a second to get behind the bar again, he found a surprising soul sitting there. More than that, the man was staring at the pocket of whores lounging in the corner. "Mike? What are you doing here?"

Mike peeled his gaze from the whores, his nose wrinkling as he took in Cole. "Didn't know you'd be here."

"Good to see you, too." Cole leaned on the bar, studying his brother-in-law intently. Amount of booze in the place, and Cole could still smell it wafting off the man. "You're drunk?"

"What of it?" Mike gulped down half his beer. "Thought I'd stop by. See if you've got any more whores need saving. Maybe make sure this one actually wants it."

Cole glanced around the packed place for a minute, glad to see most everyone engaged in other things, unable to hear Mike, or at the very least not paying him any mind. He wanted to keep it that way, but he also wanted to get the man out of the saloon. Perhaps into the apartment where Jane could mind him if she was back.

"She's a whore," Mike muttered.

"Who?"

"You know who."

"I don't know what ya mean, Mike. Why don't you come over to the apartment? We'll get you some coffee and a dark room to sleep this off." He circled the bar to stand next to him. "Before you embarrass yourself."

Mike violently pulled his arm away from Cole's reaching hand. "I know how to walk."

"Easy, Mike." Several heads had turned their way. "Let's talk about this outside, away from the crowd."

"Are you encouraging her?" Mike rose to glare at Cole. The runt was the smallest of the lot and had to lean back to do so. He swayed ominously, but his fists clenched.

"Again, don't know what you're talking about. Let's take it outside." Cole didn't try to touch the man again. He nudged his chin toward the door.

Mike huffed a couple more times. He turned, but grabbed his beer to down the rest.

Cole didn't stop him, just waited patiently. He glared at the nosey onlookers at the bar until they turned back to their booze. Once Mike finally started walking toward the exit, he followed suit. All the way down the steps until the man spun on him. He held up his hands to show he wasn't on the attack. "Do you really want to go shouting your business for the whole saloon to hear? Or anyone out here?"

Mike's brow furrowed. "Are you encouraging her?"

"Hardly seen her. Just saw her a little bit ago. Seems upset. So do you, though she ain't drinking her way out of it."

"No, she's whoring her way out of it."

Cole stared at him. Sure, Jane had mentioned she thought Daisy was whoring, but it was only suspicion. Neither of them had gotten her to admit it. Cole wondered if Jane knew that Mike was aware of the situation. "Getting drunk ain't gonna help nothing, Mike."

"Sure don't hurt."

"Yes it does."

Mike threw up his hands, storming off to his horse.

Cole didn't bother trying to stop him. He didn't want to be throwing fisticuffs in the middle of the street. Before Mike could take off, Cole set a hand on the horse's bridle to hold it. "I think you and Daisy gotta sit and talk."

"I don't need advice from the likes of you." Mike jerked his horses head away, then took off down the road.

Before he'd disappeared from view, he passed a wagon tearing into town. In the front seat was Jane, holding onto the handle for dear life while Patrick raced the wagon through the crowd. She half stood to follow her brother's progress before flopping back into the seat.

He followed their path, a panic inside. Jane knew better than to race like that in her condition. Something had to be wrong. He tore through the still shaken crowd to follow the path of the wagon right up to the clinic.

Neither Jane nor Patrick could be seen at first, but the door to the clinic stood open. Just as he skidded to a halt, Jane and Patrick tore back through the door with Andrew hot on their heels. Patrick leapt into the back of the wagon. With surprising strength for an apparent dandy, Patrick picked up something large from the bed.

Though wrapped in a blanket, Cole recognized it as a human. He stepped forward to help Patrick remove the man from the wagon. They carried him inside to a room. As the blanket fell back, Cole recognized the man inside. "Chauncey?"

Jane half hauled him out of the room. "Let Dr. Cross do his job. The nurse will be in soon to help. Patrick, come along."

"I'll stay here and assist until the nurse arrives." Patrick was rolling up his sleeves as he spoke.

Jane didn't argue with him one bit. Cole stared at her aghast when she shut the door behind them. "You're letting him stay?"

"Horace is our friend, our employee. Patrick has been volunteering with a doctor that helps battered women. Doesn't have experience in whatever that is, but he knows how to help." Jane spun when footsteps clamored down the steps. "Charles. Go back to Millie and George. Dr. Cross has things well in hand."

"I'll see for myself, thank you." Charlie kissed her cheek as he rushed past. The new nurse, Bonnie, right behind him.

"What happened?" Cole turned his attention back to Jane soon as the door closed.

"We found him near death. Patrick had to force the door open. I have no idea where Opal is." Jane's hands shook as she slipped them over her hair, now frazzled from the wind and events of the day. "I'm no doctor, I can't guess what it is."

"You could, you've read enough." He smirked at her cross look. "What? You named the scarlet fever that near took you."

"Anyhow." A deep sigh slipped from her lips. On top of everything else, she looked pale. Drawn. Possibly just tired, but he worried anyway.

He guided her to a nearby chair. "You feeling all right?"

"I'm pregnant."

"Doesn't answer my question."

"Drained. Between Tully, and Lucy, and we still haven't found Agnes. Now this?" She set her head in her hands. "I need to get back to the children. Sally has lessons today, and

I think she and Thomas were going to speak to Georgie Staub."

"Thought she was fighting with Molly."

"They seem to have patched things up." She lifted her gaze to his. Her normally deep blue eyes seemingly paler. "I think I want to go home and enjoy my family for a while. It won't be quiet, but it doesn't have to be."

"Then we'll go." The door to the exam room opened before he could get her to her feet.

Charles stepped out, looking a bit drawn himself. He met their gaze and shook his head.

"Oh no." Jane's hand flew to her chest. "No. Charles. Please tell me he's not dead."

"Not yet. It doesn't look good." Charlie set a hand on her shoulder. "They'll monitor him overnight to see if there's any improvement."

"What happened? Chauncey is one of the healthiest people I've ever known."

Cole nodded in agreement. "The man's never been sick a day he's worked for me. Didn't even get sick during the epidemic."

"Why don't you visit with him?" Charlie didn't bother to answer the question. "We don't know where his wife is, he should have company. He's not thinking clear enough to tell us where she's at."

"Charles Emerson." Life had flooded back to Jane's features in her indignation. "What aren't you saying?"

"I can't be certain." Charlie sighed at her continued glare. "I think he was poisoned. This doesn't seem to be a normal illness. He's hallucinating, and he's growing extremely agitated. His skin is flushed, pupils dilated."

Jane's eyes darted side to side. It was as if Cole could see her brain putting the pieces together. "Nightshade?"

Cole stared at her for a moment, trying to figure out how she got there. "Jane?"

"I've read about it."

"Of course you have." Cole couldn't help but chuckle as she proved him right.

"It seems that way," Charlie concurred. "I can't be certain, though. I mentioned it to Andrew."

Jane sighed, touching her brothers arm. "Go back to Millie and George. It seems as though Patrick's going to be here for a bit, he'll come for you if you're needed."

Cole waited until Charlie was climbing the stairs before he spoke low. "This is gonna fuel Sally's fire, isn't it?"

"And Thomas'. And mine." When the door opened again, she managed a wan smile. "Thank you, Patrick. For helping."

"Not much for me to do, but I'm happy to. You should come in, see him." Patrick held open the door for them.

Cole led her into the room, surprised to find no frantic race to work on the man lying on the table. The two medical personnel worked quietly and urgently.

Jane left Cole's side to move to Chauncey's. She took his hand in hers. "Horace. It's Jane."

Chauncey twitched, then turned his head toward her. When he spoke, his voice was raspy, hard to hear. "Janey."

"That's right. You fight this, you got it? You're stronger than whatever's got you right now. You didn't even blink at the grippe, you can handle this nonsense."

His whole body seemed to be trembling, but he managed a nod.

"Where's Opal, Horace? Do you know? We can get her for you."

"Gone. With eggs."

"Eggs?" Jane looked up at Bonnie in confusion. The young nurse shook her head in response. "We'll see if we can't find her."

"No." Chauncey panicked suddenly, lashing out.

Before Jane could react, Cole had pulled her away from the bed. "Sorry. Didn't want you hurt. Gotta think about the baby."

"It's fine. He was there for a second, then hallucinations again." Jane leaned back against Cole. "He's going to make it. Right?"

"Hope so. I'm already looking to hire more people, don't want to have to add another to the list."

"Cole!"

"Kidding." He squeezed her shoulders. "Chauncey can't be replaced. Been working for me for years. Man's an ox. This isn't gonna get him."

"Your lips to God's ears."

"He ain't got much to do with me, but I hope you're right."

Peace visits not the guilty mind.
    —Juvenal

Sally's pace slowed, her mind racing. When Cole and Jane had returned to the apartment, Jane had been visibly upset. With good reason. Chauncey's current state didn't bode well for his long-term prospects.

Longer than Sally had known either of them, Chauncey had worked for Cole. Even married a whore that used to work for Cole. Opal had been called Marigold in her hey-day at Cole's saloon. Unlike Daisy, once she and Chauncey had paid off her contract, she'd returned to her original name.

Not even Jane had known Opal as Marigold, that had happened before she'd stumbled in Dominion Falls. Though Chauncey still worked at the Inn, Opal mostly kept to herself. Sally had heard her at church talking about all the chores she had as a housewife with a large garden.

Now along with Agnes, Opal appeared to be missing, too. Jane said they didn't see her anywhere around the house or land. Patrick had gone to look while she'd tended to Chauncey.

All of it was upsetting, but it was Jane that worried Sally. Her ma looked tired, with dark circles under her eyes. She'd never been one to sleep much, but the baby seemed to be making Jane more drained. Well, that and all of the chaos happening.

"Hel-lo. Yoo-hoo." A hand waved in front of Sally's face.

"What?" Sally shook off her thoughts to find Molly grinning with an exasperated lift of her brows. She'd totally forgotten she was even walking with Molly. "I'm sorry. I got lost in thought."

"Clearly. I was nearly at the end of the street, still talking to you when I turned to find you weren't even with me any longer." Molly set her hands on her hips, her brows and lips pursing in a semblance of a stern expression. "I apologized, I thought the days of you ignoring me were over."

Sally scoffed lightly. "I wasn't ignoring you. I'm just worrying about Ma."

"Your ma is fine. Now." Molly laced her arm through Sally's to guide her down the street. "Where was I when I lost you. Hmmm."

"Don't ask me to help. I have no idea what you were talking about."

"Clearly." Molly sighed. "No matter. I was only discussing what we might work on in upcoming lessons. We've already discussed tarot, accents, and languages. Tommy's teaching you to fight, and quite well. You're already skilled in seduction."

"Not so much. I was a whore, I didn't have to seduce. Men already came with one thing on their mind."

"They always have one thing on their mind." Molly kept their pace slow. A sensual tone warmed her next words. "Well, we can work on that, too. I'm more than happy to show you some subtle tricks of the trade."

Sally did her best to keep the rising heat of a blush tamped down. "It probably wouldn't hurt. It's been a while since I've lain with a man."

"That part is easy. It's the subtlety of seduction that takes work. Your ma can do it with a look, I've seen it. Then again, I doubt it takes much to get Cole to get up and go."

"When it comes to Ma, it never did." Sally chuckled softly.

"They're upset over that Chauncey fellow, aren't they?"

"Sure are. He's worked for Pa for years. Opal did too, before they were married."

"Your Pa allowed that?"

"Of course." Sally slowed their pace a moment, thinking hard. "Actually, before Ma I doubt it was a regular thing. He kept a firm hand on his whores. He liked Chauncey, though. Probably why he allowed it. She kept working for Pa until she and Chauncey paid off her contract."

"Married and whoring. Interesting."

"They met while she was whoring, guess it didn't make much difference once they were married. I think it took a year or two for them to pay off her contract. After that, she's stayed a happy housemaker. Comes to town for shopping, church, and occasionally to visit."

"What's Chauncey like?"

"Funny. Kind. Even when I was a whore, he always had a nice word for me. A funny story. He's loyal, too. Pa said Guy tried to get him to come over to the Silver Saddle many times, offered him good money for it. He never left Pa's place, though. Ma saw to it that he got a good raise when the Inn opened."

Molly made a soft hum of interest.

"What?"

"Nothing. Just thinking your parents are good people. Treat others better than most I've seen. Funny that they've had so much tragedy."

"Yes, they've certainly had their share." Sally shrugged. "They've had lots of good happen, too. All of us kids, they're happier than I've ever seen them when the apartment's full up."

"I noticed." Molly paused now, staring at the façade of The Golden Touch. "I think I'm going in for a drink. You with me?"

"Not today." Sally actually would have liked to go in with Molly, but she knew Tommy wanted to head to Georgie's. "We're heading out to Staub's place. I thought you'd be joining."

"Nah. I don't think you need three people. The two of you know him, I sure don't. Join me when you're done if you want." Molly hopped up the steps to the saloon, greeting Wil with a warm smile.

Sally shook her head, chuckling under her breath at the bold flirtation between the pair. Far as she knew, neither of them had any interest in the other, but they sure put on a good show. She checked her pocket watch to see how much time she had.

Before she'd put it back in her pocket, Tommy himself came around the corner leading Brag and her horse, Agatha.

"I thought I saw you passing with Molly a few minutes ago. Thought I'd come to you. Where'd she go?"

Sally jerked her thumb at the brothel. "Visiting with Wil."

"I can go alone if you want to join the fun."

"No, I want to go see Georgie. I can't believe he did this. I keep hoping Lucy's memory is faulty on this one." Truth be told, she wasn't sure she was ready to be in the brothel. It was so similar to the original, and she worried some would remember too well her previous life if she went inside. She hopped into her saddle. Soon as she was settled, Tommy took off. She followed right behind, catching up easily.

They rode in silence for around ten minutes. Their pace kept them at a good enough clip to be making good time to the Settlement. Near around the lake, she slowed. For a moment, she allowed a glance back toward town.

Tommy followed her gaze, before glancing back at her. "I told you—"

"It's not that." Sally interrupted without shame. She let Agatha dance a few paces, her gaze still on town.

"Out with it, then."

"It's Ma."

His brow puckered. "What about her?"

"Baby seems to be taking a lot out of her this time. She seems so tired." She shook her head. "No. Ill."

"Babies make women ill, Sally."

"That's not what I mean." She pursed her lips, trying to figure the words. "I don't know. I was thinking about it earlier, I guess it's still in my head. When she came home from the clinic, she didn't seem well."

"Her and your pa care a great deal about Chauncey. Think she's just worried, on top of every other damn fool thing happening. It's no worse than she's lived through before, only this time she's got a babe adding to it."

"I suppose." She shook her head of the thoughts. One flick of her wrist turned Agatha back to the settlement.

"Trust me. A good night with her family, another with Cole, and some deep sleep and she'll be back in fighting form by the morning."

She smiled at his words, despite her doubts. "You have a point."

"Good. Let's get this over with and get back home."

"Sounds like a solid plan." She clicked her tongue to get Agatha moving again.

They entered the settlement another ten minutes later. The once small neighborhood had grown considerably in the past few years. Though the wreckage of several homes lost in the tornado still marred the landscape, the line of simple homes still nestled nicely in the little dip in the valley they'd landed.

Sally nodded in greeting to the few people milling about as they made their way toward Georgie's homestead. She frowned slightly. "Do you think he'll even be home? It is the middle of the work day."

"Hammy said he hasn't been in for a couple of days. Hope he didn't pack up and skip town. Townsfolk won't be happy we let a potential murderer out of our grasp."

"He didn't kill Tully, he was busy on Lucy – if her memory is correct."

"Don't matter. He was there, and can name others that were." Tommy pulled Brag to a stop. The look he gave Sally was hard. "It's part of the job, Sally. People you like can turn. Doubting their guilt doesn't take it away. In our line we've got to assume the worst."

"But hope for the best. I can hope a man I once knew, one that was kinder than others, couldn't have done this."

"Hope is hard fought in this business. Your ma raised you right these past couple of years, but you'll find it harder to keep."

She raised her chin stubbornly. "I'm not you."

Before he could answer, she urged Agatha on toward the little Staub homestead. Nestled in between two homes packed with kids, it was a simple, small home. No garden out back, no friendly flowers in front, nor even curtains in the windows. It was the same with most of the bachelor's homes, unless it was a group of miner's. Still as unfriendly, but bigger than this.

She dismounted, tossing Agatha's reins over the small hitching post. She'd knocked on the door before Tommy caught up with her.

The door opened suddenly, and Georgie stared at them both. His eyes wide in his pale features. The man had shaved his long beard off, and his features were sunken. As though he'd been starving for days.

Sally stepped forward slightly. "Georgie?"

"Miss Pansy."

"She's Sally now, Georgie." Tommy's harsh tone made the man back up a couple steps.

"Tom," Sally chided. She held out her hand. "Georgie. We were hoping to talk to you. Do you mind if we come in?"

"I—" Georgie gulped as he kept a fearful gaze on Tom. Then his shoulders slumped and head dropped. He bobbed his head once in agreement before returning to his table. Only thing on it was an empty bottle of whiskey, and a gun.

Sally set her hand on Tommy's when he reached for his own weapon. She studied the man quietly. After a minute, she turned her back on him to face Tommy. She whispered, "It's not meant for us."

Tom's brow furrowed, his jaw working in silent protest.

"Trust me." At his nod, she moved to the table with Georgie. She took the seat beside him, not even acknowledging the weapon right in the man's reach. "Georgie. I remember you well from the saloon. You were always kind to us. We liked you more than most."

A little color flooded to his cheeks, but he didn't look at her. He stared out the window, tears shimmering in his eyes.

"I heard you liked going to Tully's after Ma closed the brothel. The girls there like you, too." She gingerly set a hand on his. Now both their hands were awful close to the weapon. Still, she ignored its presence. "Lucy always spoke kindly of your visits."

Georgie shuddered at the name, his hand convulsing under hers. When he spoke, the word carried so low under his breath she almost missed it. "Temptation."

"Can you tell me why you hurt her?" She knew now, without a doubt, he'd done it. The single tear that tracked down his weathered cheek was proof enough.

"Had to."

"But why?"

He met her gaze finally. "I'm so sorry. She was a good girl. Not good enough."

Sally shook her head. "What do you mean?"

Georgie pulled his hand free of hers.

"What about Tully? Who hurt him? Who was with you Georgie?"

"No. No." He shook his head fitfully, finally grasping it with his hands. "I can't."

Before she could say more, Tommy clasped the man's shoulders. He hauled Georgie to his feet. "Georgie. You—"

"Stop." Sally pushed to her feet, shoving the men apart. She held Tommy at arm's length. "I told you to trust me. Trust me."

Tom glared at her.

"It isn't always about brute strength." She turned to face Georgie. The man had backed against the wall. If anything, he looked paler after Tommy's attack. "I know you feel guilty about it. I know you liked Lucy. One way to make it right would be to tell us who else was there. What they did with Agnes."

"I can't. I—I…" He gasped, his body going rigid.

"Georgie!" Sally rushed forward as he collapsed to the ground. She rolled him over, taking in his pale appearance. "We need to get him to the doctor. Get a wagon."

Tommy's footsteps pounded out the door, shouts rang through the Settlement.

She brushed back Georgie's hair, searching his terrified features. He gasped slowly for air for several minutes. "Georgie. Stay with us. We're going to get you to the doc. He'll fix you right up. Keep breathing."

He didn't listen. With one last agonizing breath, the light left his eyes.

It is not much for its beauty that makes a claim upon men's hearts, as for that subtle something, that quality of air that emanates from old trees, that so wonderfully changes and renews a weary spirit.
-Robert Louis Stevenson

Cole drew the wagon to a stop and set the brakes. The chatter in the back didn't cease. In fact, the volume increased exponentially. Jane didn't scold a single child as they cheered and clamored from the wagon, even though the hounds howled along with the excited children. Her gaze remained on the nearby trees, a peaceful smile on her tired features.

He was loathed to interrupt the peace she currently felt. Gently, he ran a finger along her hand.

She turned to face him, bemusement flickering across her features. "What's so funny?"

"Not funny." He chuckled despite his protest. "Just wondering how you can look so peaceful with all that racket going on."

"It's the racket that brings me peace. Nearly all of our children are being loud and obnoxious. And the blasted dogs."

"Glad my idea was a sound one."

"It certainly was. The children will freeze in the swimming hole. It's already October, and the temperature has already dropped a couple of nights."

"Them boys don't care. Neither do Lizzie or Cindy, and Alma don't swim. We'll keep the twins to the shallows."

"Fair enough." She leaned in to give him a kiss. "We'd best get out of the wagon before they all jump into the water fully clothed."

"Let's get to it, then." He hopped out of the wagon, managing to make it to the other side before she got out. After he'd helped her down, he turned to grab the picnic basket.

Jesse, Jay, and the two hounds came tearing around the side of the wagon so fast, they knocked Jane clean off her feet.

He didn't know how he did it, but Cole managed to snag her before she hit the ground. He whistled sharp and hard, and both hounds stopped. The boys stopped a second later, then turned with wide eyes. Cole raised his brows. "You boys about knocked your ma clean off her feet. You'd best apologize."

"Not my ma," muttered Jay.

"No matter, you still apologize."

"Sorry, Ma." Jesse appeared properly abashed. "We thought you was still sitting in the wagon. Didn't mean to."

Jane's features had paled slightly, and her hand shook as she brushed back a loosened lock of hair. She managed to find a smile for the boys. "I'm fine. Go slow, please. That could have been the twins or Alma and our afternoon would have been ruined."

"Sorry." Jay hung his head, plodding toward the swimming hole now.

Jane sighed heavily. "Well, that put a damper on things."

"You all right?" Cole chucked a finger under her chin. "You're pale."

"I thought I was hitting the dirt. You caught me. No harm done."

"Ya sure?"

"Quite certain. Go on, mind the boys while I get the girls ready." She gave him a kiss before heading to the back of the wagon where the girls were stripping down into the swim garments Jane had had made for them.

Cole hefted the picnic basket out of the wagon. With one sharp whistle, the dogs fell into line beside him for the short jaunt to the creek. He heard a squeal behind him and spun to find Colton barreling toward him at breakneck speed.

He scooped up the child before he tumbled over the bank. Laughing, he gathered the jabbering boy closer. It was rare that Colton was this talkative. Colton pointed at the trees, talking about the birds he could see now that the leaves were gone, and then at the creek.

Colton clapped his hands happily. "Swim!"

"Wade," Cole corrected. "No deep water for you, young man."

At the creek, he set down the basket, but not Colton. Both Jesse and Jay were already swimming in the deep waters. Though Colton might not be the daredevil Clara was, he couldn't be sure he wouldn't try to get in the deep water. Thankfully, the girls didn't take too long coming along behind the boys. Willow actually held Clara's hand, the pair laughing together on their haphazard path to the water.

"Cindy." Cole beckoned his oldest. "Get Colton for me, would you? I'll see to getting our picnic set up for when you're too cold to carry on."

Cindy stopped in front of him, her strawberry blond waves barely restrained by a leather strap. She held out her hands to her baby brother. "He'd better behave. I wanna play, too."

"I think it's Clara you need to worry about there, not Colton." He chuckled as he handed Colton off. "Keep the twins in the shallows. Don't need Jane panicking about them drowning or nothing."

"Yes, Pa."

He grabbed the blanket from on top of the basket. By the time he had it half-unfolded, Jane had the other end. Together they stretched it over the ground. He let her take her seat while he went back to the wagon to pour them both a glass of lemonade from the bucket in the back of the wagon. The moment he settled onto the blanket, Jane scooted close to him. He wasn't about to argue her proximity. Her soft sigh grabbed his attention, though. "You good?"

"Quite."

"Good."

She chuckled softly. "I know the water's likely freezing, but the day is so nice and soon we'll all be shut in for days at a time. I don't even know if Jaybird and Willow will be able to always go with Black Moon. The weather being so unpredictable in the winter."

"We'll keep them going long as we can, and start again when we can. Nothing else to be done about it."

A warm smile lit her features. Her eyes softened with love, sparkling clear blue at him. "I love how you can always cut through the clutter of my thoughts with plain logic."

"Gotta be good for something."

"You, sir, are good for a great many things."

"A great many?"

"Oh yes."

"You'll have to show me all of them later."

"I plan to."

He rumbled his approval of her statement. A squeal from the swimming hole pulled his attention from Jane. The kids splashed each other with aplomb. "I should get a fire going so they can warm up when they're done."

"Good idea." A kiss brushed his cheek in the moments before he rose.

By the time he stood, she lay flat on the blanket, her gaze on the sky. He couldn't help but stare for a few minutes. The peacefulness she carried seemed a rare treat. From the time they'd found out about the baby she'd been worried over it taking. She'd done the same with the twins and all had worked out in the end, but this time seemed more like the first, when they'd lost the baby.

"Hey." Her soft voice broke through his dark train of thought. "What's wrong?"

He shook his head to clear away the dark thoughts. Jane still lay on the blanket. She'd propped herself on her elbows to study him. The peaceful expression had gone in a pucker of concern across her brow. He leaned down to wipe the worry away with his finger. "Nothing. Mind wandered. Never used to do that. You're a bad influence."

"I disagree."

"You think you're not a bad influence?"

"With that, too. I'm talking about your mind wandering. Always has, only now it's of things you aren't trying to force yourself to forget."

"Sometimes they are," he admitted.

She offered an understanding smile. "This is one of those times?"

"For a second. I'm gonna get back to the fire."

"You mean start on it. You hadn't lifted so much as a twig as of yet."

"Good point." He tapped her nose gently. Soon as she lay back down, he set to work to build the fire. Nothing too big, just enough to warm the children when they got out of the water. Easy to put out soon as they were ready to leave.

The second he stretched back out on the blanket, Jane curled into his side. He tugged her as close as she could get. Her soft sigh drifted across him, sinking right into his own contentment.

"It's a shame," she broached their silence in a whisper. Close as she was he heard it easily, even with the kids squealing and dogs barking.

"What is?"

"If we'd thought further ahead we could have brought supper, blankets."

He pursed his brow up at the sky, contemplating her words. They didn't make sense. "We got a picnic, and we're on a blanket."

"More blankets, and dinner. The picnic is a light dinner." Her gaze remained on the sky even when he tilted his head to focus on her. "We could have camped under the stars. Away from the street lamps I bet we'd see every star in the sky."

"Street lamps aren't so bright you can't see them."

"They're bright enough that you can't see them all."

He chuckled softly. "Greedy."

"With you, children, and stars."

His laughter faded as hoofbeats reached his ears. They both turned to see who was coming to interrupt their picnic. The figures drew near enough to recognize Tom and Sally.

Jane perched on her elbow, studying their approach. She rose before they got close enough for conversation without yelling. Cole took her lead. Though the pair rode toward them almost casual, an uneasy feeling settled in the pit of his stomach.

She must have felt the same, for Jane's hand clasped his. Soon as the pair got close enough, she called out, "What is it? What's wrong?"

Sally grimaced from her saddle. Rather than answer, she glanced at Tom.

Tom alit from Brag to approach. His face half-hidden in shadow, he didn't give away much. Never had. Still, Cole had known the man long enough he could see a certain tension in his gate. "Didn't say anything was wrong."

Jane flinched away from the kiss to her cheek. "What's happened?"

"Georgie confessed." Sally's hands twisted in Agatha's reins as she drew close. The horse followed her sedately, unimpressed by the tension of the moment.

"And died," Tom added.

"What?" Jane's hand clenched in Cole's. "What do you mean he died?"

Sally answered the question. "Andrew thinks it was a heart attack."

"Guilt, more like," Tom contradicted.

"Perhaps. He looked set to off himself when we got there. Gun on the table and all. I managed to get him to confess to hurting Lucy." Sally grimaced. "Then he…"

Jane swayed so violently, Cole snatched her close. "Jane!"

"Ma!"

"Lou?"

Her hand to her head, she didn't speak a moment. "Sorry. I got so dizzy."

"I'll take you to the doc." Cole bent to scoop her off her feet.

"No. No." Her hand settled on his, and she lifted her gaze to meet his. Though pale, her eyes held his with a familiar strength. "It only lasted a moment. I think it was the shock."

"Shock don't do that to you. You've had plenty of it." Cole kept a firm hold on her. No matter her legs seemed to be holding her strong.

"Really. I'm fine. I believe it was the shock. The baby makes me handle things different is all." Despite her reassurance, she didn't fight his hold. "Let's sit and let Sally and Tom tell us what happened. I'll finish my lemonade and have something to eat. If I feel poorly after that, you can take me to the doctor."

He hesitated a moment, but her smile reassured him. "Promise?"

"I promise." She tapped his hand gently where it lay on her waist. "Now, Thomas, Sally. Join us."

Tom wasn't right in front of them anymore, though. He leaned into the back of the wagon.

"Thomas?"

He emerged with a cup nearly spilling over with lemonade. "What? You said lemonade."

They all laughed as he drank the cup in one large gulp before grabbing more.

"The children will want some, too. Don't go drinking it all, you swine."

Can any man or woman choose duties?
No more than they can choose their
birthplace, mother, or father.
-George Eliot

Jane did her best to not react to the man huffing at her from across the counter. She poured a bourbon for him while he ranted.

"Why you didn't immediately go to the clinic is beyond me." Charlie set down his hat on the bar. "I can't believe Cole didn't bring you in."

"Every single one of our kids was at the creek, and the moment passed quickly." Jane urged the bourbon across the bar. "It was the shock of the situation, learning of Georgie's passing. Cole, myself, and the children were enjoying a peaceful afternoon. I saw no reason to mar it because of a brief spell."

"Jane." His next scolding cut off when she pressed the bourbon in his hands.

"I went and saw Bonnie this morning. She said everything still looks perfectly fine. She agrees it was likely the shock."

"Oh." Charlie sipped his bourbon. "I didn't know."

"I'm aware. Thomas likely told you in passing and you got all up on your doctorly high horse, refusing to listen to me and instead began ranting the moment you saw me."

His cheeks darkened at her scolding. "I was worried for my sister. It's allowed."

"I'd prefer if you showed your concern with quiet appeals rather than sharp scorn in the future." She tapped his finger. "I am not an idiot, after all."

"I know you aren't." He grimaced. "I don't like hearing these things second hand."

"I haven't seen you, and you aren't my doctor for my pregnancy. Daisy is, or was. Now it's Andrew and Bonnie. I'm quite happy with their care." She leaned closer. "Be glad I let you care for my injuries after Mac's attack. I still don't care for your medical nosing."

Finally, he allowed a smile. "You've never forgiven me for treating your scarlet fever."

"For your hounding when I was in recovery, you mean." She laughed with him. "And no, I didn't care for it. I got bored of your bossiness quite quickly. Unfortunately, you let Daisy tend to the rest of the town so you might hover and boss me around."

"That wasn't entirely my intention."

"Entirely." She poured him another bourbon. "Drink your bourbon and leave me be. I'm a grown woman who isn't nearly as stupid as she was. I've learned from my mistakes. If something is wrong, I will report it. Trust me for once."

"I'll do my best. Past behavior lends to the belief you won't."

"I have more to live for than I ever have." Her gaze drifted toward the Faro table where Cole sat playing with Bernie to try to help the man win back some of what he'd lost at poker. She then turned her attention to where Sally stood at the roulette table with both Patrick and Molly threatening her attention to the game.

"Thomas also told me he's been urging you to get yourself a governess." Charles caught her gaze when she leveled it his way.

"He has mentioned it a time or two. I'm loathed to do it."

"You've taken the world on your shoulders. You should ease your burden. It'll be better for you and the children."

"Then I shall ease it by abandoning something else. I will not abandon my children to another person."

"You wouldn't be. It would be assistance to care for them so you might have more of a life than only them." He studied her quietly. "You are about to have more children than you'll know what to do with, and Sally is branching out on her own."

"She's been marvelous about helping with the children, but I'm loathed to ask assistance now that she's finding herself," Jane admitted. "Still, I can manage."

"Where are they now?"

"Jay is with Jesse and David at the jail. The twins are right where you'd expect."

"Scamming cookies off of Cora in the kitchen."

"Precisely. Willow and Alma are at the meadow picking flowers with Cindy, Lizzie, and Katherine." She frowned slightly.

"And who is manning the library, seeing as Kat is playing in the meadow?"

"It's closed," she admitted. "I'm going to head over soon. I haven't been able to find someone to see to the place while I'm otherwise occupied."

"The library you pushed for years to have built and it isn't even open."

"If I can't find someone good enough to watch my books, you honestly expect me to find someone capable of caring for, and teaching, my children?"

He chuckled under his breath. "I guess you have a point there."

"Damn straight, I do." She looked over when someone sat beside Charlie. "Graham. How are you holding up?"

He shrugged, rubbing a hand over his scalp. "Exhausted. Can't wait for this election to be over. I'll know one way or the other and can stop galivanting around the valley."

"Doubt that'll stop when you're elected mayor." Charlie smirked at the large man beside him. "Might get worse, because then everyone'll be wanting things done."

"He's not wrong." Jane set a mug of coffee in front of him. "Having second thoughts?"

"No." Graham shook his head. "Maybe. Linh's not happy how much I'm gone. I try to take Joshua when I can, though."

She patted his hand sympathetically. "It'll be good in the end. How is she enjoying your new home? Is everything set up?"

"Still waiting on some furniture." Graham's nose wrinkled. "I swear Callahan messed up our order. Only half arrived."

"I wouldn't put it past him. I know Cora laments selling to him. He's never kept it up to standards like her Kelly did." Jane ran the towel over the top of the bar as she took back Charlie's empty glass.

"Not sure why he's even bothering."

"He's selling." Charlie frowned slightly. "The whole thing, including the stock. I heard Norman talking about the notices he sent as far west as Chicago."

"Well, hopefully whomever takes over runs a better business than Callahan. We've had trouble getting supplies ourselves. Thankfully we were able to contact some suppliers directly when Callahan failed to deliver."

"Callahan's worthless." The familiar baritone of Jane's husband rumbled nearby. He reached around her for a mug to fill with coffee.

"Charles said he's selling." Jane met his passing kiss. "We were speculating if the new owners would be any better."

"Gotta be." Cole nodded in turn to Graham and Charlie. "Gentlemen. Can't stay long, have to set up for tonight's games in the silver room."

"Might not make it tonight. Linh would like me home for a change." Graham drained his coffee. "Speaking of, best get home. I told her I'd bring dinner so's she wouldn't have to cook for a change."

Jane waved him off, turning to Cole. "Did you get Bernie square?"

"Only let him win back half, as you've ordered. He's not gonna learn, you know." He drew her close. "You think too highly of people sometimes."

"I call it hope. Now, unhand me. It's time for me to head to the library. Katherine will be dropping off Alma soon, and Cora will be dropping off the twins shortly after."

"Don't know how you can work with that little monster hanging around."

"Don't speak of Alma like that."

He smirked. "I meant Clara, and you know it."

"She takes after my sister." Charlie smirked. "Clara the original was every bit of a wild child as your Clara. Into everything we were. Drove us mad."

"I've heard as much thanks to all of your stories." Jane smiled at her brother. These days talk of her former self didn't seem to hurt as much. Perhaps it was that they were all finally accepting she was a different person. "She's a lovely, intelligent child. Only a bit…precocious."

"She's a monster," Cole repeated. "Tearing up everything nice, including her brother's books. Can't have anything nice."

"You be nice. Or I'll let her into the liquor storage."

"You wouldn't dare. That's half our profits right there."

"Fair point." She gave him another brusque kiss, then allowed a kiss to her brother's cheek on the way past. "I'll see you both later."

She made her way through the pit, greeting guests as she passed. Near the stairs she was stopped by Jake for several long minutes as he went on and on about the cowboys letting their cattle eat their way through his small field of corn.

When she got to the apartment finally, she was surprised to find Sally there. "Oh, hello. Your time at roulette over?"

"Yes. Edgar got in."

"What are you up to now, then? Going with Molly somewhere?"

"No. She's going to the brothel." Sally became intensely interested in tightening the fastenings of her knife cuff. "I thought I'd go see how Andrew is doing with the autopsy. He's supposed to be working on it this afternoon."

Jane studied her ward for a few minutes. "You haven't been to the brothel since it opened."

"Not really, no."

"No interest? Or something else? I've seen Molly go in there often. I bet Wil would be a good person to help Molly with teaching you German. He's fluent in it, you know. Raised in a German family, more a town, really."

"I know." Sally adjusted her blouse. When she lifted her gaze, a small grimace crossed her features. "It's really like the old place."

"I see. Well, you aren't a whore any longer, Sally."

"I know."

"I'd ask if you'd like to come to the library," Jane changed the subject rather than berate her charge. The young woman would get past her turmoil on her own time. "However, I have no doubt you'd rather attend an autopsy."

Sally's frown cracked into a grin. "You sound rather disgusted, Ma."

"To each their own, Sally. I've seen enough death to last me a while. If it gives you happiness, I'll not fault you." She moved toward the door. "I'll be at the library until it closes if you need company."

"Thanks, Ma."

Jane stepped out into the brisk air, crossed behind the barn to get to Second Street. She waved to Archie at the livery on her way to the library.

The light from the sun bounced off the windows, setting the building in a warm glow of sunset. She'd need to light the lamps shortly after opening. In the valley such as they were, the sun disappeared behind the mountains much earlier than it would in the plains out east.

"Miss Jane!" An eager voice practically shouted behind her.

In her startle, the keys hit the porch in a clatter. Jane turned in surprise to see a doe-eyed young woman grinning at her. "Emmeline. You startled me. Where did you come from?"

"The tea shop. I was waiting for you to come." She waved the Falls Report in her face. "I saw your ad. I'd like to apply."

Jane's heart sank slightly. Emmeline certainly had the ability to read and write, and a modicum of intelligence. She was scatter-brained, though. Using the moment of grabbing her keys to gather herself, she rose and nodded. "All right, come in. We'll talk about it."

"Thank you. Pa said I gotta get a job. Ma said I'm not allowed to help with the young'uns anymore ever since I near burned down the house."

Jane swallowed her groan, following the exuberant young woman inside. Politeness would have her give the interview, but then she'd have to figure out how to let her down easy. Then again, there hadn't been many applicants.

She needed to find someone to fill the spot, and fast. Last thing she needed was something to happen to the library she'd worked so hard to build.

*If you are distressed by anything external,
the pain is not due to the thing itself, but to
your estimate of it; and this you have
the power to revoke at any moment.
-Marcus Aurelius Antoninus*

Jane settled in the chair next to the stove. Clara lay at her feet, bent over the paper before her. Her tongue poked out; brow furrowed in concentration. Unlike her brother, she wasn't attempting to read or make letters. She was drawing something.

Content they were handled for the time being, she rested against the back of the chair with a soft sigh. The simple act of opening the library and starting the fire had tired her. That afternoon she was due to have tea with the ladies, too. By then she hoped Sally would be done with her lessons and ready to watch over the twins. Not that Lillian would find them a nuisance. She treated the twins as her own grandchildren.

Clara slammed down her pencil. With a few grunts and an awkward lift of her behind, she got to her feet. She toddled over with the paper aloft. "Mama, look. Horsey."

Jane took the paper, smiling at it. The drawing was impressive for such a young one. The lines of the horse were clearly laid out. The head, body, and legs all in surprising proportion. "Very good, Clara. Which horse is it?"

"Gatta."

"Agatha," Jane corrected. "Very good. You should give it to Sally when you see her next. I bet she'd love to have it for her room. What about Tempest? Can you draw her?"

Clara nodded enthusiastically, heading back to her paper.

The water bubbled merrily in the pot on the stove. Jane almost didn't want to stand, but the allure of a nice, hot tea was too great. Before she'd finished preparing her tea, the door opened. She did her best to erase any trace of tiredness to greet the patron, but when she turned her smile faltered in surprise.

Daisy stood there, unwinding the muffler from her neck. Her gaze rested on the children for a moment before she grimaced Jane's way. "Is it a bad time?"

"Not at all. The children are quite skilled at entertaining themselves. Clara has a delightful imagination that takes them on journeys far beyond these walls and the conversations they contain." Jane stepped forward to help Daisy out of her coat. "The tea isn't for a few hours. I wasn't expecting company."

"I doubt I'll be at the tea. I just—I hoped we might talk." Daisy met Jane's eyes, and concern flickered across her brow. "Are you well?"

"The baby is making me tired is all. I'm well enough for tea and talk. Come in, please. Have a seat. You like two sugars in your tea, yes?"

"You remember, you don't have to ask."

"I do have a modicum of propriety which lends to me acting as though each time is the first." She smiled Daisy's way before returning to the stove. "Now, you don't take milk every time. Is today one of those?"

"Yes, please." Daisy didn't precisely sigh, but the breath she released was audible.

Jane took her time preparing the teas to allow Daisy a moment to compose her thoughts. Likely she'd been pondering a visit for a while but being in a situation you'd only thought about could make all previous thoughts dissipate. Jane was familiar enough with the sensation to know.

Daisy gathered her mug close the moment Jane sat. She cradled it in her hands as if to warm them. After a sip, her gaze drifted out of the window to the passersby.

Jane was loathed to push the woman, but she also didn't know when they were likely to be interrupted. After a sip of tea, she leaned forward. "How are you doing?"

"Everything is so discombobulated. I don't know anymore how I'm doing. It ain't—" She closed her eyes as though to gather herself. "It isn't what I imagined. None of it."

Jane fought the urge to reach out to her friend. Daisy still sat hunched and closed off. It wasn't yet time to approach. Instead, she spoke quietly. "Your life has changed drastically many times over. It can be overwhelming, I know."

Daisy released a snort. Something akin to a smile twitched her lips. "You'd know."

"I would."

This time an actual chuckle emerged from Daisy. "I don't know what to do."

Jane studied the woman across the table. Despite the moment of brevity, a darkness kept her closed off. Like a great weight settled on her shoulders pushing her into the ground. "Then let's begin with a simple question."

There was no denying the note of suspicion in the green eyes that lifted to face her.

"I ask with no ulterior motive, and with love." Jane tilted her head. "Do you love my brother?"

"I...do. I think." Daisy's brows knit together. A grimace creased the pretty features back into a deep frown. "You must think me awful. I should be happy. We're supposed to be engaged."

"I think no such thing."

"But he's—"

"You are my friend. For the time being they are two separate matters."

Daisy grimaced at her tea, expressing the doubt she didn't voice.

"You met Emmett so young. You were idealistic, I bet. Despite most of your family urging you to not be a doctor, you did anyway."

"I wonder what happened to me most days. I'm not the girl I was."

"Life turned you on your head. In mourning, and desperation, you took Cole's offer to be a whore. A life like that, when unwanted and unexpected—even in a place like

Cole's—can break a person. Cole always said he got annoyed when you went doctoring. Said you got too full of yourself and bossy."

"The only time I felt like I knew more than anyone in the room. Now…"

"Now there are two more doctors with equivalent knowledge."

"And everyone else is getting smarter. Even Cole."

"Much to his chagrin, I assure you."

Daisy's visage twisted in a mix of amusement, and upset at her own laughter. "I shouldn't laugh. He'd not like it."

"There's a great many things Cole doesn't like. To avoid them all is tantamount to insanity. I once tried, and it did me no favors. Now we live with each other's idiosyncrasy's rather than suffer the consequences of accommodation."

Daisy half-grimaced an acknowledgment behind her cup.

"Besides, long gone are the days when you had to accommodate Cole's particular's."

"His particular's were easy comparatively."

Once again, Jane caught a glimpse of something in Daisy's gaze. A something she didn't dare name, not for her own fears, but Daisy's. Jane took a sip of her own tea. There was no time like the present to address the matter most worrying her. "Daisy."

"Never thought I'd miss it."

Taken aback by the abruptness, Jane fell silent.

"Such a ridiculous thing to miss."

Assuming Daisy meant working in the saloon, Jane ventured a guess. "There is a certain comfort in knowing where your head will lie at night, and that your food and health are going to be there. Then again, there was the threats of losing the contract."

"He never meant it, until he did." Daisy's shoulders sagged.

"Might I ask—" Jane hesitated again, but there was no dark look from her companion. "With no judgment at all. Are you whoring again?"

Daisy's lips disappeared between her teeth. Her gaze stayed hard and long on the street outside the large window. "What if I was? Would you think less of me?"

"Do we not have a whore at our ladies' teas? Did I not take in and raise a whore as my own? Am I not friendly enough with Leanne's whores?"

"But not your own."

"I must maintain a separation with them, but I don't think any less of them. I've offered them all a chance for better, or if this is the life they prefer, I make it as comfortable as I can. For some women whoring is their only option. For others, it's a choice. They go into it to put food in their children's mouths, or their siblings, or they go into it because they can make decent money, one of the few areas a woman can."

"But I—"

"Have doctoring, which you have turned your back on for the time being. That's your choice, Daisy. I think no less of you. You've been through something terrible a few times." Trying her best to be delicate, she posed her next question. "Have you tried talking to Michael about any of this?"

Daisy snorted. "Sure. If he would sober up for more than a few minutes."

"Sober—what?" Jane took in the comment, confused by its implication. If there was one thing the Young's all knew, it was their limits with alcohol. Not one of them had crossed it to her knowledge, with the exception of her own foray into too much consumption a few years prior.

"I should go."

"No, wait." Jane shook off her surprise to focus on the woman in front of her. "I just—Daisy, I'm worried."

"I can take care of myself, Jane. Been doing it for a while." Daisy was already halfway to the coat rack. "I shouldn't have come."

"Daisy. There's someone out there hurting whores, and former whores. It isn't safe to be meeting these men alone. Would you consider—"

"A brothel?" Daisy flung her muffler around her head. "In case you hadn't noticed, that's where the whore that got killed was. Didn't matter none, did it?"

"Daisy." Jane's words disappeared into the gust of wind that came through the open door. She stood on the threshold as Daisy disappeared into the crowd.

What had she meant, Michael needed to sober up? Had he been drinking that much? Come to think of it, when had she seen him last? It had been a while.

"Mama." Colton tugged her skirt. "Mama, look."

Jane closed the door on the chilly day to face her son. She admired the letters he'd drawn before ushering him back to the fire. Colton got back to his writing quickly. Jane set about cleaning up Daisy's cup.

No sooner had she cleared the table of the excess cups when the door opened again. Leanne breathed out the cold air, a bright smile on her features. "Good morning."

"Good morning." Jane moved forward to help her remove her coat. "You're nearly two hours early today."

"I was with Tommy last night. The big dope had to do something called work, and I do hate wiling way my time in his cramped little room."

"Don't blame me for the size of his room. I offered him a full apartment with water closet. He poo-pooed it."

"He would. How did I end up falling for such a duff of a man." Leanne flopped into a chair. "Oh, look at you, Colton. I swear it's like seeing your pa every time. At least, I imagine that's what he looked like your age. I sure didn't know him then."

"There isn't a soul alive that did."

"Well…" Leanne gasped over the pause where neither of them spoke of Cole and Leanne's pa. She picked up her nephew, nuzzling him close. "Oh, you are such a dear."

Clara slapped her leg. "I am!"

"Well, of course you are." Leanne managed to gather Clara into her lap as well. "You both are perfect darlings."

"Don't encourage them," Jane chastised quietly. "They're spoiled enough."

"As one of your closest friends, it's my job to spoil them." She smooched them both soundly on the cheeks. "The oddest thing happened the other morning."

"Is that so?" Jane split an orange into sections. With a delicate hand, she sprinkled some white sugar over the top of them until they glistened in the light. She held it out to show the children, who scrambled free of Leanne's lap to pounce on the plate she put on the floor. "What oddness occurred?"

"I thought I saw Opal." Leanne accepted the cup of tea Jane offered.

"You what? Did you sound the alarm?"

"I'm afraid not. It was so brief, and I wasn't even sure it was her. It might have been a miner making a constitutional in the woods. They were filthy. For a moment, I thought…but then they disappeared into the trees. Buck naked and all."

Jane's brow furrowed at this news. "Did you at least inform Thomas?"

"I did. Told him last night. Might have distracted him rather thoroughly after, though."

"I have no doubt you did."

"Well, when you're good at something, you must do it with aplomb. You understand."

"I certainly do. I do it as well." Jane winked. "It's the best way to distract a man, after all."

"Best for the man, and the woman."

"So long as the man does his duty."

When men are pure, laws are useless;
when men are corrupt, laws are broken.
—Diogenes the Cynic

Sally tucked Jane's list into her reticule so she wouldn't lose it. Pulling the basket higher on her arm, she ensured the items inside were secure before setting off for her tasks.

Soon as she rounded the corner a whistle sounded. It took her hardly a second to find the source. Wil leaned on the railing of the saloon. At his side stood Molly with a drink in her hand. Both were hidden in the shadow of the porch, but Sally approached.

Not yet certain she wanted to go inside, she merely stopped beneath them. She nodded to Molly before turning her attention to Wil. "There are better ways to get a person's attention."

"Worked, didn't it?" He winked. "Come on up. We're just chatting. Nothing like a pretty pansy such as yourself to worry about."

Sally quirked a brow at the use of her former whore name. "I'm afraid I haven't the time nor ability to lounge about as you do, Mr. Karlson."

"Ya make time for what's important."

"That should tell you how I feel about you." Sally smiled her sweetest and curtsied low and slow to give ample view of her cleavage before she rose. As expected, the man was chuckling. "If you'll pardon me, I have errands to run."

"Look forward to the day you got time and inclination, Sally." He nodded again, turning his attention back to the street.

Sally turned back to her day, but quick footsteps caught up to her. Molly's arm laced through hers. A bright laugh flittered from her friend. "That was very good. Subtle, and yet quite an attention grabber. Perhaps you've learned a thing or two from your ma about the way to subtly seduce."

"Ma is quite good at it." Sally flushed slightly. "I wasn't, though."

"Oh, don't lie. You were, and you know it very well."

"Perhaps a little. His use of my whore name set me off worse than the whistle, though."

"Why don't you join me at the brothel? I promise you'd have fun."

"I don't know." Sally didn't want to discuss her reasons right then. Perhaps she'd find the courage soon. Until then, she'd go when she was ready. "Why do you spend so much time there, anyway? Don't you have anything better to do?"

"Not particularly."

Sally snorted. "Please. You're an intelligent woman, there has to be something."

"Sally, dear. I was brought here to teach you."

"You're a Pink. There's mysterious deaths and murders to examine."

"And we have. Ad nauseum. There's only so many times I can go over the same facts before it becomes little more than drivel."

"You're an outside, objective, soul. You can be getting to know the people in town. Nosing around, finding out information. Tommy and I, well, we know these people. Have a hard time imagining any of them harming someone else. Well, most of them, anyhow."

"You got Staub."

"All the while hoping Lucy remembered wrong. If she hadn't, we never would have suspected him, and he'd have taken his own life, or died of a heart attack, without us knowing." Sally blew out a breath.

"Well, if you must know, why else would I be spending time in the brothel?"

"Fun?"

"Sure, and to get to know some of these ruffians. Still, outside of our lessons which are a few hours a week, I have little to do. You are always on some task or errand for your ma or Tommy. Tommy's working all the time, or with his friendly blonde."

"Well, I suppose the brothel is a good place to get familiar with a good portion of the town." Sally paused at the porch of the general store to peruse the fruit on display. She grabbed an apple and tossed a couple pennies into the basket for it.

They continued wandering down the street toward her destination. Several loud yells emitted from the new, and hastily constructed, saloon across the street. Right behind the shouts came several gunshots. It sure hadn't taken long after Tully's death for another saloon to spring up. This one was even seedier. Sally knew her parents were annoyed by its presence, but it had gotten a fast following from some of the miners.

"*Get out.*" A large man's shadow blocked any light from outside. "We don't want your preachin' ya fool. Get out of here."

Molly sidled next to Sally, her gaze on the group of men that were unceremoniously shoved from the saloon. "My, my."

At the front of the group of about six men was Pastor Eckles. He wore a smile despite the guns trained on him, and the weapons discharging inside the saloon. Whatever he was saying, or likely preaching, was lost to the ruckus. His gaze fell on Sally briefly before the group headed east up the road toward Main.

Sally shook off the chill down her spine. "Ugh."

"What?"

"I swear his eyes are dead. No wonder ma doesn't like him." She turned away from the departing group to resume her path. After a wave to the passing sheriff, she ducked into the leathersmith's. "Mr. Kilmurry."

"Miss Sally. Miss Molly. How are ye?" Mr. Kilmurry smiled at them both.

"I'm well. Ma asked me to bring by some of Willow's work for you to look at." Sally reached into her basket to pull free the five pieces of beaded work Willow had created. "Ma said she'd spoken to Mrs. Kilmurry about them."

"That she did," the woman herself emerged from the back. "Afternoon to ye both."

Molly nodded, drifting away to study the wares. Sally spread the pieces on the counter. "Willow said she didn't know what to ask for each."

"I bet your ma had an opinion, though." Nessa smiled brightly before leaning over to study the pieces. "Oh, these are as lovely as Miss Jane said. Let me see."

While Nessa studied the pieces, Sally's attention wandered as well. Spotting a lovely embroidered coin purse, she pulled it down. Bright colored threads decorated the leather as beautifully as Willow's beads did. She recognized the style as being similar to Jane's favorite reticule. While Sally had a perfectly acceptable coin purse, she knew Willow had no such thing. If she was to earn money, she'd need somewhere to keep it.

"Four dollars for the lot," came Mr. Kilmurry's voice.

"No," his wife objected. "Five. A dollar a piece. We'll be able to get good profit no matter what we put them on. Is that acceptable?"

Jane had told Sally no less than three dollars, so it clearly was. "I believe that will be acceptable."

"Miss Jane's the one that told me to know the value of my own pieces, I'm not going to short her ward for more profit." Nessa nudged her husband in the ribs, even as he chuckled.

"I know better than to argue with my wife." Mr. Kilmurry patted her hand. "Five dollars, it is. Let me get that for you."

"And I'd like to purchase this for Willow. With my own funds. She'll need somewhere to keep her money." Sally set the bag on the counter. Within a few minutes, both exchanges were complete and Sally headed back outside with Molly.

Molly sighed softly, continuing the lazy stroll. "I'd have more fun if you were available more. You're always working or doing things for your ma and pa, watching the little brats."

"It's called being part of a family. You should try it some time."

"I have. Didn't care for it much. Most of us don't. That's why we are what we are." Molly followed her up the steps to the mercantile. "Besides, you're an adult now."

"Or so we believe," Sally muttered under her breath. She still had no idea how old she truly was. Her ma sure didn't care to celebrate birthdays for the daughter she never wanted. Only reason Sally thought she might be an adult was based on when she'd been sent to school. Of course, she'd also lost track of time after she'd run away. How long had it been before Graham had found her?

"Sally?" Molly's brow pursed as she stood in front of Sally.

"Hm?" Sally shook off the memories to face Molly. "What?"

"You were awful lost in thought there. What was that about? Your ma again?"

"No. She's doing better. Tired, but her mood's much improved. It was…nothing." Sally brushed off the memories best she could. No reason to reveal them, not to Molly anyhow. The woman was an expert at hidng her true self, no reason to reveal her own past.

Fortunately, distraction arrived in a very attractive package that emerged from an aisle ahead of them. Instantly upon seeing the handsome form of Patrick, the familiar tingles of a blush flittered across Sally's chest.

Patrick caught sight of them, and a smile creased his features in a most inviting way. His eyes sparkled as he held out a hand to take Sally's. "Miss Spencer. What a delight."

"Mr. Warner." The heat hit her cheeks as his lips brushed the back of her hand. Excitement tingled through her when he kept his gaze firm on her, even as he greeted Molly.

"Miss Malone. It's a pleasure." His hand hadn't released Sally's yet. "What has you lovely creatures out an about today?"

"Errands for ma." Sally couldn't explain the breathless whisper of her voice.

"Then I shouldn't keep you, but I do hope you will be at supper tonight? Your enchanting Ma has invited me to join your family to dine." He offered a small wink. "I haven't yet said yes as I wasn't certain the guest list included you, or if you had other tasks set upon you."

"Oh. No. I mean, yes. I mean—" she took a deep breath, "I'll be there."

"Wonderful. Then I won't keep you from the rest of your day." He kissed the back of her hand again, before offering a kiss to the back of Molly's as well.

While he paused to pay for his purchase, Sally kept her gaze on him. Molly did as well, moving close enough to whisper. "According to research, that man rather enjoys teaching young innocent women the ways of indecency."

Sally's insides quivered at the idea. "I'm aware. I've heard Ma speak of it."

"Of course, his isn't the only way." Molly's gaze cut to Sally. "It all depends on your preferences, I suspect."

"I haven't the faintest idea of my preferences. Except that his flirtations flummox me."

"You need more flirtations, then." Molly's fingers laced with hers. "For you shouldn't be flummoxed at all. You should want to learn all the ways of wickedness."

"I'm beginning to think I do."

All excess is ill, but drunkenness is of the worst sort. It spoils health, dismounts the mind, and unmans men. It reveals secrets, is quarrelsome, lascivious, impudent, dangerous and bad.
-William Penn

Jane didn't look up from the newspaper when someone sat across from her. It was easy to tell by the grunt it was her brother. She continued reading the story she had almost finished. Tommy took a coffee from the waitress, sipping at it while she read.

The second she shifted the paper, he spoke. "Lucy arrived safe."

"Good." They'd seen to sneaking Lucy out of town in the middle of the night the week before. She'd initially been terrified of leaving with an unknown element, but then Tommy had snuck in another of his specially trained friends and she'd gone willingly. "That's that mattered settled, at least."

"Cole's friend in Chicago feels she can find somewhere suitable for her, so she'll be off with a new name and location after a time."

"Wonderful." She set aside her paper. "Was there something else?"

"Nope. Just wanted to sit with my sister."

"I'm honored. Leanne busy?"

He offered a dramatic gasp. "You insult me."

She merely raised a brow.

"Yeah."

"I thought so." She laughed softly. "I'm afraid you won't be with my company long, though. I, myself, need to get to work quite soon."

"I figured as much. I gotta head to the saloon tonight. Think Wil's gonna cave on getting some help. Hope he does it before winter fully sets in."

"It would be rather helpful if he did. You'll do your customary nosing, I assume?"

"Always."

"Good. Now, what did you find out about Leanne possibly spotting Opal last week?"

"Did a little searching. Asked Black Moon. He said there's been someone around the foothills. He's seen them once, but they act crazy and he avoids them. Can't rightly tell if it's man or woman, but said the hair is long."

"Then it could be her."

"Could be." He studied her long and hard before leaning forward. "What about Daisy?"

"Avoiding me again. I wanted to suggest Leanne's for her, but she's skittish. Can't say I blame her after what happened to Emily." Jane sighed heavily, finishing off her tea. "Speaking of, have you seen our brother recently?"

"Which one?"

"I said 'speaking of' as we were talking about Daisy. Which brother do you think I mean? Don't be deliberately obtuse."

"Well, you've been awful attentive of Nick lately."

She narrowed her eyes. "Jealousy doesn't suit you. You practically live in my home, and you have Leanne. He, however, lives alone and doesn't deal with his wounds like you and I do. He needs more attention. You get too much."

His brows rose, a smirk tugged the corner of his lips with his nod. "Fair enough."

"Then answer my original question, please."

"Haven't seen Mike in a couple of weeks. Last time I saw him was at the brothel."

"At the what?"

"Now who's being obtuse?"

She stared at him for several long minutes, waiting for the inevitable laughter to show it was a joke. It never came. "Why on God's green earth was he at the brothel?"

"Drinking, and pretty far in the sauce so far as I could tell, too. Why?"

"Why? Are you seriously asking?"

He leaned forward on his knee. "I seem to remember a time when you got pretty drunk when your relationship was having troubles."

"That was one time. I've not done it again. Based on several things I've heard, it seems that our brother is often drinking. I mean, has he even been working? Has he done anything to research the land behind his hotel to see if it would work for a ski resort?"

"Have you asked him?"

"I haven't seen him," she admitted. "Last time I did he claimed a megrim, but now I wonder if it was the ill-effects of alcohol. I'm worried. I need to make more of an effort to see him. I never seem to have time, but for important things, I need to make it."

"Gee, why wouldn't you have time?" He pursed his lips. "I'm telling you, Jane. A governess would help."

"I hate to think of such a thing, and you know it."

"There is such a thing as too much pride, Jane. Where are the children now?"

"Here and there." She adjusted the newspaper so it lay square to the edge of the table. "Mostly at Lillian's. She had Cindy and Lizzie over, and it turned into most of the children."

"You're already relying on other people all of the time, what's the harm in paying someone that you know can reliably be there so you aren't scrambling to find someone to watch the children when you need to work, or are otherwise occupied?"

"How on earth could I ever find someone I'd trust enough with my children?"

"Is that a yes?"

"No."

"You are an impossible woman."

"So I've been told." Jane sighed and pushed herself to her feet. "I'd best get to work. Stop trying to push me into getting help, and go push Wil into it."

"I'll stop for now, but I'm not done with you. It's an argument I'll win, especially seeing as your man agrees with me."

"You'll certainly try." Truth be told, she was already mostly convinced. Perhaps it was just how tired this child had made her, or knowing her brother was annoyingly right. Either way, she had half a mind to tell him to look for someone for them. She was loathed to let him know he was right so quick, though.

"I'll succeed."

She waved him off, rather than admit any such thing. After spending most of the day at the library, she wondered how the casino looked. The weather outside had been cold, but bright and sunny, so she hoped for a busy night.

The moment she stepped through the door, she was pleased to see her hopes were met. The floor bustled with activity. Cole was behind the bar, but he didn't give her a smile upon seeing her. Instead, he wore a deep frown. Confused, she scanned the pit. Not seeing what had him upset, she made her way toward the bar. Along the way she exchanged greetings.

Though Cole gestured her closer, she didn't rush herself. When she made it to his side, she searched his features. "What has you so perturbed?"

He nudged his chin behind her. "You didn't notice?"

"Notice what?" She turned to scan the length of the bar. Only a few scruffy miners alongside some higher class patrons. Nothing out of the norm. Halfway back around to ask him again, she paused. When she looked back down the line of patrons, the man on the end caught her eye. At first she'd thought him a miner due to his rough state.

A scraggly beard covered the normally infinitely familiar features of her younger brother. He drank down a whiskey fast, following immediately behind with a beer. "Michael?"

"Been here a couple hours. Keep trying to get him to slow down, but he gets belligerent."

"But…" She turned to face Cole.

"Thought you'd want to see him. Only reason I haven't kicked him out. We can try to get him somewhere quieter." Cole pulled her close. "You try. He seems perturbed with me."

"He's been avoiding me, I'm not certain I'll have any more luck than you." She moved down the bar, pouring another beer on the way. The beer was set in front of Jake Bosen, who happened to be sitting next to him. She didn't miss the way Mike glanced at the beer.

Mike didn't meet her gaze when she approached. "Another whiskey."

She wrinkled her nose against the smell of alcohol wafting from him. "I think you've had more than your share, Michael."

"Didn't ask your opinion."

"No, but when have I ever avoided giving it?" She circled the bar to get to his side. A gentle touch to his shoulder had him tensing. "Michael. What are you doing?"

"Don't start with me, Clarabelle."

"Why don't you come with me to the apartment? We can have some coffee, and talk."

"I don't want coffee. I asked for whiskey." He glared over his shoulder at her. "Sure don't want to talk to you."

"Michael, please. I only—"

"I said I don't want to talk to you." He jerked his hand back so fast; she didn't have time to react or move away.

The blow to her cheek hit so hard, a small shriek left her before she could contain it. Her hand went to the injury as she stared at her brother.

Rather than appear reticent, his features were twisted in anger. "Get the hell away from me."

"Michael." She was bustled out of the way as several people moved forward to usher her brother from the casino.

Cole's intense gaze replaced the scene as he pulled her hand from her cheek. "We should have Charlie check you out."

"I'm fine. I, ow." She blinked a few times as the pain of the impact actually hit her. "I'll be fine. It's him I worried about."

"Jane, he hit you." Cole tucked a finger under her chin to keep her from craning to watch her brother being escorted from the building. "He didn't even care he hit you. You get that."

"He's drunk. Not thinking clearly," her words died on her lips at his low grumble of disapproval. She sighed softly. "You're right. Sorry. I just never imagined Michael would do something like that. This isn't him. He's wearing his wounds like a shield."

"Doesn't give him the right to hit you with them."

"I said you were right." She did her best not to wince as he pressed his fingers to her cheek. "Stop. Please."

"Let's go see Charlie."

"No. My brain isn't rattled, it's just a bruise, I think."

"You think."

She smirked at him. "Maybe I don't want a similar lecture from him that you're giving me right now. Besides, I mean it. My brain doesn't feel rattled, I'm only sore. Like the black eyes I give you when I have nightmares."

His eyes narrowed. "It's not funny."

"I know it isn't, but you're fussing. I'm fine. I promise. If I feel a headache or dizzy or muddled in any way I'll report to a doctor. I promise."

"I suppose that's acceptable."

"Damn straight it is." She tilted her head back to accept his kiss. "Get back to work."

"Fine. Don't go after your brother."

She narrowed her eyes. How he'd known she was thinking that, she didn't know.

"I mean it."

"Fine. I won't. I promise." She crossed her arms until he went behind the counter again, calling for order by offering a free round to the men that had escorted Mike out of the casino.

She turned to scan the floor for someone that could assist her. Spotting Teddy at a nearby table, she rushed over. With a promise of a couple of free whiskeys, he agreed to go fetch Nick for her. She climbed out of the pit, feeling Cole's eyes on her the whole time.

When Nick and Teddy entered, she immediately looped her arm through her brother's and led him from the room.

"What is going on?" Nick studied her profile as they walked. "Teddy only said you insisted on seeing me."

"I made a promise I must keep, but you are my loophole."

"I'm not certain how I feel about being your loophole."

"Never mind that." She turned to face him. "Someone must check on Michael. He was just escorted from these premises for hitting me as well as being drunk."

"He did *what*?"

"I'm fine." She swatted away his hands. "I don't think he meant it."

Nick's expression didn't change, but his eyes glinted with anger. "He didn't mean it?"

"Please." Jane exhaled slowly. "I promised I wouldn't go after him, but I still think someone should check on him. I should have gone to see him sooner, but I tried to believe he and Daisy could maybe be adults and talk."

"It took you years to figure that out with your man, why shouldn't it take Michael even longer?"

"Touché." She allowed a small smile. "Make sure he's all right. Don't scold him too harshly until he sobers and realizes what he's done. That's all I ask. If you can get him to talk, all the better. Then again, you don't know the whole story."

"I'll do my best, but I can't promise I won't flatten him if provoked."

"I'd expect no less." She kissed his cheek. "Let me know how it goes. I'd like a chance to talk to him myself if we can get him in his right mind."

"Love makes a fool of all the Young's at one point or another."

"I know all too well."

"You should. I was mostly talking about you."

There is no past we can bring back by longing
for it. There is only an eternally new now
that builds and creates out of the past
something new and better.
—Johann Wolfgang von Goethe

Cole leaned on the porch railing of The Golden Touch next to Wil. With fifteen minutes to go before they opened, he was content to enjoy the quiet while they had it. The nice weather would bring a good crowd in quick, especially seeing as it was Saturday.

From his vantage point he could see most of the town, including Jane and Kat on the porch of Kat's place. The pair were laughing together quite boisterously. When Patrick stepped out of the house to join them, the laughter grew in volume until he could hear it over the usual sounds of the town.

He wasn't about to complain, it was good to see Jane in good spirits. He knew she'd sent Nick after Mike. From what she'd said, nothing much had come of the meeting. Jane would bide her time before confronting her brother. Cole was determined to be there when she did. He didn't know what had gotten into the man lately. Then again, he did. Alcohol. Ruined a great many men before him.

Hammy started up the steps. Ten minutes early, which was normal when he came to the brothel. Halfway up the steps the man seemed to forget what foot he was on and crashed to the steps.

"Hammy." Cole rushed to help the carpenter to his feet. "Ya alright?"

"Fine, fine." Hammy blinked as though dazed, staring at his hands still planted on the step above him. "Tripped is all."

"Hell of a trip." Cole did the heavy work of lifting Hammy to his feet. "Let's get ya inside. Maybe just one beer before you get back to work today."

"I'm fine." Hammy waved off the reproach, shuffling into the saloon.

Cole narrowed his eyes as the man disappeared into the shadows. Wil flicked his cigarette aside before he joined Cole to follow the man's progress up to the bar. Buttercup had taken the initiative to get Hammy's beer for him.

"Want me to restrict him?" Wil glanced Cole's way. "Why ya look so worried? It's Hammy. Probably had a few beers before work."

"Yeah, sure. Don't restrict him. We'll keep an eye on him, though." Cole returned to the railing to look over the town. "Trail runs are winding down now that the winter's set in proper."

"How early in spring do you think they'll start?"

"Soon as the first chinook blows, I imagine." Cole kept his gaze on the street, searching for familiar faces.

"I've decided to call my friend to help out. He'll have the winter to settle in before the runs start again."

"Glad to hear it. My woman will be happy to have me around more."

"Are ya sure about that?"

Cole chuckled softly. "Yeah. Pretty sure."

Wil stretched, then sighed. "Here comes a few. Best get inside and get to work. You coming?"

"In a bit. I'll wait until it gets a little busier." When Cole turned back to the street, he spotted Jane heading his way. He hopped down the steps to meet her. "Thought you were having a good time. Did ya just come to see me?"

"I came to check on Mr. Hamm. I saw his little tumble." Hands on her hips, she appeared annoyed with him. "Amusing you, Mr. Mitchell, is not on my list of things to do today."

He frowned down at her. A whisper of a smile tugged the corner of her lips. "What's so funny?"

"I sometimes forget you haven't got the memory I have. No matter. Mr. Hamm?"

"Said he tripped. Seems fine. You worry too much. About everyone." He tugged her close against him. "Now about amusing me."

"Oh, no sir." She set her hand against his chest. "You have work to do. I, on the other hand, have been having a delightful time and have no plans to interrupt it."

"You interrupted it for Hammy."

"Mr. Hamm is worth it."

He tucked a finger under her chin. "You'd rather spend time with the Nancy boy?"

"I assure you Mr. Warner is no Nancy." She winked and stepped back. "Ask me how I know."

He caught her wrist and spun her back into his arms. "Not funny."

Despite his words, a bright grin met his harsh tone. "Jealous?"

"No."

"Oh, that's right. You actually like him." She pushed out of his arms again. The woman was bound and determined to make people think were fighting.

He didn't want to let her go that easy, though. "Hey, where's my—"

"No, sir." She backed up fast from his reaching grasp. "Not today."

He did his best to appear rightfully pissed, but he suspected his amusement was far too great for such deception. "You'll pay for that later, Janey."

"I'm counting on it." She strode back toward Kat's with a little skip in her step.

"Jezebel," he muttered loud enough to be heard. He only hoped his laughter wasn't heard as he climbed back up the steps to the saloon.

He settled in to have a few drinks. Buttercup didn't join him this time as she circled the floor much as Jane used to, serving and socializing with the patronage.

She handled herself well, and he again considered that she'd make a good replacement for Jane as madam one day when Jane got tired of it. If she wasn't already.

He moved behind the bar to pour himself another drink, then circled back to his seat. Hammy sat close by, and appeared to be asleep on the bar. Cole poked the carpenter in the arm. "Hammy. You asleep?"

"Huh?" Hammy's head popped up. "What?"

Cole chuckled low. "I asked if you were asleep. Why don't you head home, let Teddy take care of the rest of the jobs today? You look tired."

"Nah." Hammy rubbed his hand over his face. "That nap's all I needed. Back to it."

Cole chuckled as the man polished off his half-full beer in two gulps before hopping off his stool. Wil moved closer, one eye on the door. "Fell asleep halfway through his beer. Didn't have the heart to wake him up."

"He's getting old. Can't keep up as much. If I tell Jane she'll pester him to rest more." Come to think of it, Cole figured he'd tell her anyway. Might do Hammy good to think about retiring. No better way to be happy than to not have to work. Then again, Hammy loved his work.

Wil had already made his way back down the bar and entered a spirited discussion with a handful of men.

Cole nursed his whiskey, keeping an eye on the floor from where he sat. A hand tickled along his thigh, making him freeze in place. He didn't know who dared touch him so intimately, but he'd bet the saloon and Inn that it wasn't Jane.

Right before the hand reached his cock, he snatched it tight. "What do ya think you're doin'?"

When he turned to glare at the whore, he dropped the hand in total surprise. Daisy's sparkling green eyes met his, a cockeyed smile on her pretty features. "Though you knew. Has it been that long?"

"What in blazes?" His body numb with shock, he stared at the woman in front of him. He had no idea what to say or do. He knew Jane had suspected, and even confirmed what Daisy'd been doing, but this was too much.

She took the advantage of his surprise to slip between his knees, her hands skimming along his thighs. "Perhaps you need reminder of how helpful and profitable I can be."

Cole jolted out his shock. He flew to his feet so quick she stumbled backward. He grabbed her upper arm secure enough that it might have looked rough to the patrons, but he knew it wouldn't hurt her. Over her protests, he dragged her from the saloon into the seclusion at the end of the porch. "Daisy. What in hell are you doing?"

"I already told you—"

"No. What are you doing?" He gripped her shoulders to give her a firm shake. "What in hell has gotten into you? Wil's said you were propositioning the customers. I'm guessing you were entertaining men at the clinic before ya stopped going in, and Jane says you're doing it at your house. You're using Mikey until he can't think straight just so's he won't kick ya to the curb. Now this, and ya know Jane'll break your fingers if you try again."

Daisy's eyes widened under his tirade. Tears sparkled at the edges of her eyes. "I…"

Cole cursed when a tear slipped down her cheek. With trembling lips, her head dropped to rest against his chest. "Damn it, Daisy."

"I don't know."

He squeezed her shoulders. "Epidemic messed ya up something fierce."

She nodded against him, her hands braced against his stomach. "I don't know where I belong. Nothing's felt right since—since you sold me to Guy."

"Seemed like it was right for a while. You were actin' the part real good, anyhow."

"I thought it could be. I tried so hard."

"You should try talking to Jane again."

"No." She sniffed, backing so suddenly she hit the railing.

"She's worried 'bout ya. And I ain't good at the words."

"Never needed them," she muttered. A laugh fluttered out after.

Cole chuckled along with her. "No, guess I didn't."

She wiped at the tears on her cheeks, leaving streaks of charcoal and rouge in the process. When he raised a handkerchief to clean them off, she lifted her face to accept the help. "Would you take me back? I mean, in house."

"You'd do better at Leanne's if that's what you want." He made a last dab at her cheek before he handed her the handkerchief. "She's got better stock there. You always were top-notch."

A flush filled her cheeks. Her head ducked for a moment as she dabbed at her own cheeks. She lifted her head, a warm smile making her prettier despite the smudges of coal still present. "You were always worth it. Even after Jane, you know. Iris was wrong when she said you weren't worth anything other than a good screw once a week. Or twice, in my case."

"Good to know." He leaned on the railing next to her. "You finally gonna talk to him? It's been a long time coming."

"It's embarrassing, and I'm still so confused."

"Jane's good at knocking sense into my thick head. Probably handle you just fine."

"She possibly hates me. Or she will, once you tell her about what just happened."

"Nah." Cole draped his arm across her shoulders. He knew above all else—jealousy, worry for Mike—she was worried about Daisy. "I told ya. She's worried about you. Only reason she didn't use you for the baby is because you got mad at her, and then stopped working."

"Charlie's probably ready to fire me anyhow."

"Nah. He thinks you're a good doctor. He's complaining you're gone."

She sagged into him, her hands wrapping around his waist. "Sorry."

"I know. Sorry I sold ya to Guy. Didn't think I had much choice at the time."

"I guess in the end it got me freedom, with my coffers still full. I just wasn't ready for it."

"You were ready, just scared." He straightened, pulling her into a hug. "Just when you were ready to stop being scared, everyone got sick again."

She accepted the hug for a long minute. Small sniffles shook against him, but when she pulled away from the hug, her eyes were dry. She cleared her throat, brushing her hands over his shirt. "I've gone and gotten charcoal and rouge all over you."

"I'm used to it. Even when I'm not working with the whores, them burlesque actors get it everyone." He chuckled, pulling on the shirt to check the damage. "Good thing I'm working here tonight. I don't gotta change."

"Guess not." A warm smile returned, almost teasing like the Daisy of old. She poked his stomach. "Unless I got you so excited you have to go find your woman."

"Skilled as you are," Cole leaned close to mutter in her ear, "nobody gets me excited like her. Not ever."

"We haven't for a long time." Her lips brushed his cheek before she pulled back. "This is why we liked you, Cole—at least your favorites."

"What in *hell* are you doing?" Mike stood at the top of the steps, his face twisted with fury.

Daisy tensed so fast her fingers clutched his holster.

"Shit," Cole muttered.

Indulge not thyself in the passion of anger, it is whetting a sword to wound thine own breast, or murder thy friend.
—Akhenaton

Cole pushed Daisy behind him. The man looked ready for a fight, and he wasn't going to give him a go at a woman. Cole strode toward Mike. "Mike. It ain't what you—"

Wham.

White spots burst across his vision. The solid right hook to his nose left blood pouring free. He gripped his nose. "Son of a bitch, Mike. It ain't what you think."

"How could you?" Mike ignored him to storm toward Daisy.

A towel was shoved into his hands. Cole took it to press to his nose while Mike and Daisy bickered in undertones nearby. "Thanks."

"No problem. Should I break them up?" Wil stared down the couple arguing a few feet away. He folded his arms across his chest, eyes narrowed at Mike as he grabbed Daisy by the shoulders.

"For *months*," Mike snarled. He'd released Daisy to gesture wildly around.

"No. Get the customers drinking. This has been a long time coming. I'll keep an eye on it." Cole could have cursed ten times over at the fresh break to his nose, but did his best to remain calm as possible. He didn't dare look away from the pair to see if Jane had spotted the incident. Last thing he needed was for her to get in the middle. Well, that, and he couldn't let things get out of hand between the two.

"With that nose?" Wil snorted.

"Shut it."

"Got it, boss." Wil saluted. Without another argument, he disappeared inside.

"Mike." Cole moved toward the couple. "This ain't the place."

"You son of a bitch. My sister know what you're up to? I'll kill you for what—"

"Your sister is going to be plenty mad you broke my nose." Cole used Mike's ire at him to urge Daisy away. He pushed her behind him toward the steps in hopes she'd make a quick escape of it. "You ain't gonna talk calmly right now. Leave her be, you can talk tomorrow."

"Not a chance in hell." Mike managed to catch Daisy's arm before she made it down a step. "Tell me, my *darling fiancée*. How long have you been propositioning Cole? I thought Jane was your friend?"

Daisy seemed too stunned to speak. Her hand flexed in his grip.

"Don't you have anything to say for yourself?" Mike shook her arm.

Cole moved forward to break them apart, but Daisy came to herself. She straightened against the assault, tugging on her hand. "I'm not happy, Mike. I haven't been for a long time."

"You seemed plenty happy to screw me often enough to shut me up at every opportunity. Whenever I wanted to talk, you were more than happy to splay your legs. At least I didn't have to pay for it with money. Just all your manipulation."

"You're hurting me," Daisy tugged her arm.

"Mike. That's enough." Cole grabbed the man's arm hard. His own tight grip freed Daisy's wrist from Mike's. She stumbled down a couple steps at the renewed freedom.

"Hurt you a fair lot less than you hurt me," Mike growled. He followed her down the steps.

In the distance, he could see Jane heading their way. Following right behind were Kat and Patrick. Jane didn't run, but she was moving fast enough.

"I can't believe I ever thought I loved you." Mike leaned so close to Daisy, she bent over backward. "You're nothing but a *lying whore*."

"Michael Jacob Young!" Jane skidded to a stop several feet from the stairs.

"Shut up, Jane." Mike stormed down the steps. "I found her and Cole all over each other just now. Maybe you should learn to keep your man in check, or set him loose."

Jane barely glanced Cole's way at the accusation. Rather than address him, she turned a dark scowl on her brother. "Don't worry about me."

"That bitch has been lying—"

"Stop." Jane remained remarkably calm, though her cheeks darkened with anger. "Temperance of thought, Michael."

"Says the queen of public displays," Mike spat at her. He turned to glare at Daisy, who remained frozen where he'd left her on the steps. "Go back to your brothel since you love being a whore so much."

Shockingly, Daisy took off after him when he turned on his heel to leave. Her loose hair flew behind her as she charged toward him. "You don't get to scream in my face and walk away. I'm not the only one at fault here."

Cole grabbed Jane's arm before she could race after the pair. "Don't you dare. Not with the mood he's in."

"But he's…" Jane stomped her foot in frustration. The pair were yelling in the street a few feet away. Cole knew all too well her first instinct would be to break up the scene. That's how he'd knocked her out once. She yanked her arm free from his light grasp. "Damn it."

"You never once bothered to think if everything you were offering to *save* me was what I really wanted! You just assumed it's what I wanted. You never bothered to ask." The regretful, embarrassed Daisy of minutes ago was long gone. "You were so busy saving me you couldn't see how *miserable* I was. You didn't even care!"

"I loved you!"

Jane turned her gaze up to Cole. Surprisingly what she said wasn't about the fight, at least not exactly. "You and Daisy?"

"She made a pass. Then asked to come back under contract." Cole kept his tone low under the yelling of the nearby lovers. "Your brother walked up when she was thanking me for shaking sense into her."

"I see." Jane's brows furrowed. "You're a bloody mess."

"Manipulative bitch!"

"Michael!" Jane straightened when her brother grabbed Daisy by the shoulders.

Mike shoved Daisy away from him hard enough to make her stumble. "Get the hell away from me. Go back to your john's beds. You disgust me. If I never see your face again, I'll be a happy man."

Before he could stop her, Jane took off after her brother. With handfuls of skirt, she tore down the street after him until she managed to get right in front of him. She stopped short to make him stop. Cole moved to follow, unable to hear what she said to him.

When Mike grabbed Jane much as he had Daisy, Cole burst into action. Too slow, though.

Patrick broke the contact between the siblings. Jane tumbled back onto her rump. Patrick blocked a punch from Mike, then managed to flip the man on the cobblestone. He tugged his lapels to straighten them, staring down at Mike. Mike appeared to have had the wind knocked out of him as he made a few fish-like gasps for air. Patrick shook his head. "I think it's time we think about our actions, Mr. Young. You've already assaulted one woman. I wasn't fast enough to stop that one, but I won't allow you to injure a pregnant woman."

Cole pulled Jane close while Mike scrambled to his feet. Mike glared at Jane. "Leave me *alone*."

Daisy rushed forward to Jane, "Are you all right?"

Cole got to his feet when Mike took off. A firm hand on his arm made him stop. He glanced over to find Graham shaking his head. Cole narrowed his eyes. "That bastard."

"Got his business handed to him. Worry about your woman." Graham nodded down to where Daisy was looking Jane over.

Cole turned his attention to Patrick. "Thank you. You were quick on your feet."

"I've partaken in some fighting. I know how to handle a man who's not thinking." Patrick tipped his head. "Kat and I will await word on Jane."

"I'm fine," Jane grumbled.

"Is the baby hurt?" Cole moved closer, kneeling beside Jane.

"I don't think so." Jane's voice was tense, stilted. "Ow."

Daisy cast Jane an exasperated look. "If you were fine, you wouldn't be saying ow, now would you?"

"Fine. It could be worse. Just my wrist and my derrière." Jane winced when Daisy moved her wrist.

"I think it's merely sprained." Daisy tucked a lock of hair behind her ear. "Jane, I'm so sorry."

"You should be, canoodling with Cole." Jane grabbed Daisy's hand when the doctor pulled away. Her smile broke free, and she chuckled. "Sorry. Horrible time for teasing. It distracts me from the pain."

"Well, I'm certain Bonnie will want to check the baby." Daisy didn't pull her hand free from Jane's. Her brows creased. "I'm truly sorry."

"I wish you'd both done this far sooner, it might not have been quite so violent, or public." Jane leaned in to hug Daisy with her free arm. "Cole, will you help me up? I feel a bit stiff."

Cole helped her to her feet, concern growing with every wince. "Looks like Patrick's interference wasn't quite in time."

"It was, I just got jolted on landing. We'll go slow. Daisy, will you come?" Jane met the doctor's gaze.

Daisy cleared her throat. "I—I think I should head home."

Jane nodded quietly. "I understand. May I visit you tomorrow?"

"I don't think it's a good idea."

"Please."

Daisy lifted her gaze to Cole instead of Jane. He nodded to reassure her. "I told ya, she ain't steered me wrong yet. She's good at knocking sense into people when she isn't getting knocked around herself."

"Which happens far too often," Jane concurred. When Daisy finally nodded, Jane hugged her again. "I'll see you tomorrow. I should get to the clinic and make certain everything is as it should be, and perhaps get this wrist wrapped. Rest tonight, Daisy. Please don't try to go talk to him on your own. You both need time to cool down now."

"Don't think I care to do anything of the sort." Daisy slipped away into the lingering crowd.

Jane leaned into Cole on their way toward the clinic. "I've never seen him like that. He scared even me. I don't scare easy."

"Then why did your fool ass chase after him?" Cole clucked his disapproval. "I told you to stay put, didn't I?"

"I think everyone agrees I'm not that great at listening. Besides, I never dreamed he'd do anything to hurt me. He nearly flattened you for hurting me."

"He wasn't going to flatten me," He protested.

"Oh, right. Of course not. No man could flatten the great Cole Mitchell."

"Nah. You could, though."

"You bet your ass I could."

Since love and fear can hardly exist together, if we must choose between them, it is far safer to be feared than loved.
-Niccolo Machiavelli

Jane remained quiet patiently while Bonnie washed her hands. Cole, on the other hand, fidgeted endlessly beside her. Jane knew he was nervous about the baby, but she honestly wasn't as concerned. Her wrist, on the other hand, had swollen some in the time it had taken Bonnie to complete her exam.

Cole glared at the young woman's back. Her lingering silence appeared to be working his last nerve.

"Bonnie." Jane moved to sit, unsurprised when Cole practically lifted her into a seated position. "I apologize for Cole. He's being an impatient brute."

"You got knocked around, I'm allowed to worry." He narrowed his eyes on her. "You landed hard enough to hurt the ass I like so much, maybe it hurt the baby, too."

"I landed on stone, of course I have a sore rear." Jane smirked his way.

Bonnie laughed softly as she returned to the table. "All the rumors I've heard about the two of you appear to be true."

"The baby," Cole interrupted.

"Appears to be fine. There's no sign of bleeding. Everything appears to be as it should be." Bonnie turned her attention to Jane full on. Her expression had become serious, but amusement still danced in her mismatched eyes. "I would suggest you rest for a couple of days, and report any change in your condition to myself."

"I will. Thank you."

"I would normally say I'd like to see you next week, but I'm afraid I'll be out of town. I have to return to Denver for another delivery, and to gather the rest of my things."

"Oh, I thought you'd seen to the last of your deliveries before you arrived in town." Jane sighed softly. "Well, I'll just hope that nothing comes up while you're gone. Unless I can convince Daisy to look things over for me."

"Hopefully I'll only be gone for a few days, but it could be as long as a week." Bonnie looked up at the knock on the door. "Come in."

Charlie entered the room, immediately taking in Jane's wrist, then Cole's still bloody face. "I'd heard there was an incident. Michael did this?"

"You're interrupting. Bonnie, when do you leave?" Jane turned back to the midwife. "Should I come see you before you do?"

"I'm leaving in five days. I was just going to suggest you stop by in four days. Like I said," Bonnie said when Cole opened his mouth to interrupt. "Everything appears fine. It doesn't hurt to check a few days after. We all know aches and pains can take a few days to show."

"Thank you. I'll see you in a few days, then." Jane turned her attention back to her brother. "See to Cole's nose first, please."

"What? No." Cole frowned down at her. "You're more—"

"You're still bleeding. Daisy seemed to think my wrist was only sprained. Besides, the sooner you set that nose, the better." Jane didn't waver from staring him down, despite his dark glare. "We checked the baby first, the was the most important. Now, it's your turn."

Cole grumbled his way down into a chair. "Fine."

Jane nodded to her brother. "Go ahead, Charles. I'd be prepared for a yell, though."

"I always am when setting noses." Charlie stepped over to Cole, examining the nose. He ignored the grunts of complaint. "Now, would you care to explain to me what happened here?"

"I would if I could." Jane sighed. "I mean, I can, but I don't know all of it. From what I understand, Cole tells me Daisy propositioned him."

"She did, did she?" Charlie planted his feet.

"Yeah. Turns out she has been whoring like Jane—" Cole's words cut off in a yell when Charlie made a quick shove to the side of his nose. "Damn it."

Jane waited quietly while Charlie pressed a clean towel to Cole's nose. "As he was saying, as I'd suspected, Daisy's been whoring again. I saw the pair of them come onto the porch of the brothel, but didn't pay them much mind. Apparently Michael spotted them as Daisy was thanking him with a hug and assumed the worst."

"Tried to talk him down, but he wasn't hearing it." Cole pulled the towel away, opening and closing him mouth, swirling his jaw. "Still feels off."

"Looks it, too." Charlie studied him, then shifted again. "Obviously, this was the result of him trying to talk you down."

"Sure was." This time Cole didn't yell at the adjustment, just grunted. "I hate it when they break my damn nose."

"Get some fresh water and clean it up." Charlie moved in front of Jane. "Now, what about you? Did Michael do this to you?"

"Not directly, though it might have been worse." She winced when he began to move her wrist about. "Patrick stopped him from grabbing me, but I got bumped to the ground in the process. At least it's my right wrist this time instead of my left. I'd hate to have to write with my right hand again."

"Your writing was plenty legible. Don't forget, Clara was right-handed."

"But I'm left-handed. It's not comfortable for me. Ow." She released a breath when he finally let go of her hand. "Was Daisy correct?"

"Yes. Just a sprain." Charlie moved to the cabinet to get some supplies. "I can't believe Michael would do this."

"It wasn't intentional."

Cole cut her a glare, his gaze dark. "You just said it could have been worse. He wasn't thinking, and I'd bet he was drunk. I'm gonna kill him."

"No, you're not." She clamped her hand over Charlie's mouth when he opened it. "And neither are you. I can handle the runt."

Charlie peeled her hand from his face. "Clearly, you can't."

"This isn't the first time, neither. He just hit you last week." Cole leaned in. "You aren't dealing with no one. 'Specially not someone with his temper unchecked."

"He wasn't drunk this time, I smelled no alcohol." She stopped her argument immediately when both men stared her down. With a small sigh, she looked down. "Fine. I just believe he'll be full of regret soon, and last thing he needs is one of you ready to kill him."

"The runt is not your problem." Charlie began to wrap her sore appendage. "The baby is. Rest as I'm guessing you've been instructed to do, and leave Michael to us."

"I left him to Nicholas and it did nothing."

"Jane." Cole set his hand on hers. "Stop trying to fix everything."

"I can't help it," she admitted. "I was worried about him before, now it's even worse. I don't want either of them to continue this suffering. He's acting so out of character."

"Remember what I once told you about logic not being your strong suit when it comes to matters of the heart?" Charlie set a hand on her shoulder. "Michael was even worse. I'm honestly surprised he hasn't been married multiple times, he used to fall in love very easily. I suppose he had his heart broken too much and gave up until Daisy."

"Now both of their hearts are broken. He's acting an idiot." Jane smiled weakly at her brother. "Thank you for your assistance. I believe Cole and I will head home."

"Good idea. Take it easy the next couple of days, both of you. Cole, you likely have a concussion, no sleeping." Charlie helped her off the table.

"Aw, darn. I guess Jane's just gonna have to help me stay awake all night." Cole's grin had returned full force. "What a shame."

"Goodness, whatever shall we do? We have to take things easy, although that can be fun if done right." Jane chuckled at Charlie's grumble. "Hush you. I'm allowed to lust after the man I love, aren't I?"

"I'd prefer to not hear about it." Charlie nodded to them on his way out the door.

Cole pulled her close, his brow pursed once again in concern. "You gotta be more careful. Promise me."

"I promise. I won't go chasing after any other angry men. Then again, I didn't know Mac was quite so angry, nor did I chase him."

"Jane."

"I promise." She tilted her head to meet his gaze. He leaned down to grant her a kiss. She smiled softly. "I love you."

"Love you, too." His forehead rested against hers. "You know it wasn't nothing. I was trying to figure out what was going on with her."

"Don't you worry. I trust you completely. I never doubted for a second that there was anything untoward."

"Too many games lately if your brothers doubt."

"Michael is in torment, has been for months. He is not the yardstick by which to measure the others." She set her hands on his chest. "Let's head home."

"Good idea."

Jane frowned down at her injured wrist on her way out the door. "Goodness. How am I ever going to be able to handle Clara like this?"

"You won't." He chuckled low. "You're gonna need some help."

"We're too busy to pull anyone from the floor. I've abused Sally's kindness too much as of late. There is no help to be had."

"What about Tom's suggestion?"

There it was again. The damn governess argument. She'd end up losing in the end. They were right. The time had not yet come, though. "I couldn't foist my children on a governess. I want to be involved."

He stopped her in the middle of the street. In one step he blocked her path, his intense icy blue gaze on her. "You are. In everything. You need to breathe, too. We got all them kids and you hardly go to the library anymore, you and Kathy don't have your teas near as often, you've cut back on your mercy runs to the settlement. You haven't rested since we got the new strays."

"Our life is such that I cannot afford rest."

"Jane."

"Cole."

"I hardly see you. You don't got all the distractions you had before. It's all the Inn, the brothel, and the kids."

"Then we hire more help for the Inn and brothel. I won't get a governess." She straightened her shoulders. "Clara's ma raised seven children and ran a farm without a governess, and she educated them all."

"I'm not saying she'd gotta be thre all the time. They'd be your problem for a chunk of the day. Then you could stop using Cora, Kathy, Sally, Leanne, and Lillian to keep an eye on the lot."

"No."

"Stop being stubborn."

"I'm not."

"Then stop being prideful."

"I…" Well, fine. He had her there.

"Think about it, anyway."

"I'll think about it. Happy?"

"I'll be happier when we get home and relaxing."

"There are children at home." She smirked at the pout he gave at that news. "Oh, stop pouting. Don't forget, I must keep you awake tonight."

"That's right. Bully for me."

24

One of the surest evidences of friendship that one individual can display to another is telling him gently of a fault. If any other can excel it, it is listening to such a disclosure with gratitude, and amending the error.
–Edward G. Bulwer-Lyton

"Let me drive you." Cole held onto the side of the cutter.

Jane kept close to the side, though she could hardly block him from jumping over her if he got such a notion. "No. You put River on the cutter, and she's the easiest to steer. She listens to the slightest tug on the reins."

"It's not you being able to drive I'm worried about. I don't like what you're planning."

"I'm going to see Daisy."

"Then trying to see your fool brother after, you can't tell me you're not. If it was just Daisy's, you'd walk. She's close enough to town."

"I do plan to swing by Michael's. I doubt he'll even see me if he's upset." She set her hand on his. "I told you I'm not going to go chasing after another angry man that has no desire to speak to me. I'll check his mood before I ever get out of the cutter."

"Don't you lie."

"I beg your pardon." She narrowed her eyes at him. "I've already promised, and now you accuse me of lies."

His ferocity cracked. "I don't like it, is all."

"I promise to be careful."

"You got a tendency to get yourself injured. I should go with you."

"I always have, the entire time you've known me and I've known myself. You do love to tell me this frequently as though I'm unaware. I'll be fine. Daisy's isn't far, and Michael's place is only a few miles outside of town." She set her hand on his. "You need to get to work looking for more help for the saloon and casino, and you also have to work today. Even if you do look like a racoon with those bruises."

"If we aren't gone long, it won't be a problem."

Jane sighed heavily. "Cole, you can't come. I need to speak to Daisy alone."

"I'll stay outside."

"What's more, Michael isn't happy with you. If you show up with me he's far more likely to be reactive and angry than if I arrive alone. Please. Trust me."

"I do, but your wrist. The baby."

"I'll be back in a few hours." She pushed him back a step. "Stop hovering and fussing."

"Take it easy. I want to enjoy some hovering and fussing."

"That's not hovering and fussing." She offered him a wink. With the reins in her left hand and a click of her tongue, the cutter took off. Thanks to snowfall overnight and a freezing morning, the cutter slipped cross the snow easy as anything. Within minutes she'd arrived at Daisy's small home near the southern edge of town.

Jane slid from the cutter to set River up at the hitching post. After a pat to the horses nose, and the offer of a carrot, she made her way to Daisy's door.

One knock was all it took for Daisy to answer this time. Though she offered Jane a wan smile, she appeared very tired, as though she hadn't slept all night. "Morning, Jane."

"Didn't you sleep at all?" Jane stepped inside at Daisy's invitation. She shed her cape and followed the doctor to the table.

"No. Your wrist, was it broken?"

"No. Charles agreed with your assessment. A sprain that should heal quick enough. Clara is quite displeased with my restrictions, as is her pa."

Daisy flushed. The mugs she set down clattered together. "Again. I'm sorry."

"Daisy, that's enough. I've told you I don't believe anything untoward happened. I trust Cole completely."

"But I did make a pass at him."

"You're going through something very difficult. Have been for some time. Perhaps you haven't handled it well, but the good Lord knows I've not always been great at handling my difficulties either. You're human, just as the rest of us are."

Daisy didn't respond. Throughout the course of preparing the cups of tea, she maintained her silence. When she finally took a seat, her long, drawn-out sigh broke the silence. "I should be happy. I keep telling myself that."

"No one can tell you to be happy, even yourself. If you aren't, you aren't." Jane set her hand on Daisy's. "If finding that happiness takes you on a road you didn't expect, then that's what happens."

"What person in their right mind would go back to whoring after winning freedom?"

"Plenty of sane women choose whoring, and rather enjoy the career. Look at Buttercup. A beautiful young woman, and quite intelligent having had much schooling. She wants to work in the brothel and cares not to leave. I don't fault her for it. A woman deserves a right to choose."

"It feels as though I haven't had a choice since Emmett died." Daisy played with the handle of her mug rather than meet Jane's gaze. "You probably think differently."

Jane thought back over their first talk. "No. I don't know that I do. Your first choice after his death was an impossible one. To give up the one thing you'd worked so hard for and enter a life of propriety and society, or to keep being allowed to doctor. Of course, Cole himself often makes that decision seem easier. At least back then when he took the whores on and trained them himself."

The tiniest wisp of a smile crossed Daisy's features. "It wasn't an unpleasant way to begin my life as a whore."

"I imagine not. It certainly wasn't unpleasant for myself, either." Jane took a sip of tea, her gaze drifting around the small home. Once again, she was struck by the missing medical texts that had once littered every surface. "If for you returning to a life in the brothel is what you want, I wouldn't fault you."

"When you first pushed Cole to sell my contract to myself I found it exciting." Daisy bit her lip, shaking her head. "Then I was terrified."

"I apologize if you ever felt I pushed you into something you didn't want to do. It was never my intention. I truly only wished for you to be happy."

"In a strange way, I think I was happy. I had clients that weren't so good, but I was able to do my medicine and not worry it would all fall out from under me again."

"Life as female doctor can't be easy, especially without support around."

"That's what scared me. When we first came, I had Emmett. Then, after I joined the brothel I had Cole. I was his favorite, because of my doctoring. It wasn't so bad knowing that. Then you came along, and I didn't have him so much."

"Cole is worth quite a bit," Jane acknowledged.

"He certainly is. He might have owned our contracts, but he was always kind. Not just in bed, but in everyday life. He didn't take any guff, but he was funny and…he was a really good listener. He listened to us. A lot."

Jane smiled. It had been Cole she'd felt safe enough to talk to for months before they ever ended up in bed. She completely understood. "He's a wonderful listener. That's how I fell in love with him myself."

"Yeah." Daisy's gaze drifted off beyond Jane. The look Jane had seen a few times in their recent discussions softened Daisy's features. Wistful, longing. No, more than that. "I don't even think he knew he was doing it."

For a few moments, Jane found herself unable to speak. Now that it lingered, she could place the expression. It could only be described one way—love. Not jealous in the slightest,

Jane kept her voice soft and kind as she could. "Daisy. Are you in love with Cole?"

"What?" Daisy started from her reverie to face Jane dead on. Pink flooded her cheeks as she shook her head vehemently. "No!"

"Were you?"

"I—"

Jane set her hand on Daisy's, keeping her gaze steady. She'd once suspected love when Daisy's first bits of jealous reared their head in her first months with Cole. Still, no flicker of jealousy flared in Jane herself. For it wasn't about that, not any longer. "You were."

"Perhaps. I might have been. It was so soon after my husband died, and I'd lost everything. Cole took care of me, he allowed me time to grieve. Gave me near six months with only a couple select men and himself before he left me to the wolves and my wiles. Got the stuff I needed to keep doctoring on the regular."

"Then I came along."

"Messed a lot of the things up. From the second you showed up dead, and it only got worse when you woke. He stopped making time with all of us from that first night."

"So I've heard." Jane squeezed the hand she still held. "Are you still in love with him?"

"I don't think so." She smiled weakly at Jane. "Not that it would matter."

"Of course it matters."

"He never looked at none of us like he looks at you anyhow." Daisy lowered her gaze to stare at her tea. "With the way you first suggested, paying off my own contract, it was going to take me near a year to build up the money to buy out my own contract. I had time to adjust."

"You weren't being thrown to the wild with no way out."

"Right. It was taking some getting used to. Some days I wanted nothing more than to stay right where I was."

"Cole told me he thought you were trying to get your contract back quite a bit back then."

"I was. Then I wasn't. Then I was again." Daisy chuckled softly. "Right as I started to get used to the idea of doing this thing, the saloon blew up. Cole sold me to Guy and there was once again no way out. Guy wouldn't have ever let me buy my own contract."

"No. Guy Forrester wasn't the type to give his whores freedom." Jane pondered as she sipped her tea. "You had to go back to what you knew, and what was comfortable for you by that point."

"Then Guy got murdered and suddenly everything was up in the air again."

"And Michael bought the place, offering you a glimmer of hope. The whore part of you was stripped away without so much as a bye or leave."

"It was just…gone."

"Michael was kind, and flattering. You thought you were in love."

"I did. More and more it feels like he only wanted to save me."

"I can understand how you'd see it that way, even if it wasn't the intent."

"I wanted to believe it was love. I still do. I just…I don't want to be loved, or to love him, because he saved me. I don't feel very saved some days anyway."

"You need time. Both of you do after this. I don't know if it's salvageable, if either of you would want it to be. It can't be decided in a day. There's months of pain for both of you." Jane released a small sigh. "Besides, you need to figure out what you want to do first. Who you want to be going forward."

"I don't know what to do anymore."

"Do you wish to remain a whore?"

"I honestly…I don't…I don't know anymore."

"It's not anything you have to answer right this second. Let me say this, and please do not interpret as anything other than words of support for whatever choice you make. Cole was right that you'd do better at Leanne's. Her contracts are fair and generous. I'd wager a bet she'd allow time for doctoring. She would even offer you a short contract if you only wanted to get your feet wet and cease the sneaking deceit to get yours."

Daisy frowned. "Would she care to have me?"

"Leanne takes only the best, and you certainly qualify." Jane smiled warmly. "If that's what you choose, you're welcome to it. Heaven knows I won't judge you for it, not that you care much for my opinion in the matter."

"Being a whore is—"

"A career choice for some. Women have so little options, some of them prefer it to the life of a wife or maid or whatever limited options they have, most of which offer them little power. While you have a career as a doctor, perhaps you weren't ready to let go and need more time to adjust. You've spent the better part of four years trying to move beyond a life you didn't hate as much as others told you that you should."

"I didn't hate it," she admitted quietly. "Even after Cole."

"Then the decisions is yours."

"I'll think on it."

"Of course. When you have made a choice, you know where to find me. Or Leanne. We'll let her know privately so she might prepare."

"Thank you." Daisy rubbed her hands along her thighs. She closed her eyes. "Mike will never forgive me."

"Don't underestimate the Young capacity for utter fury at those we love that only leads to pure forgiveness. Goodness, just look at Cole's and my entire relationship." Jane smiled at Daisy's sobbing chuckle of a response. "Question is, could you forgive him?"

"I think we might be broken beyond repair after this."

"Your relationship may be. A broken trust is hard to repair. I can only suggest that when tempers ease you both talk, truly talk. With someone there in case of further tempers. You both saw fit to avoid everything rather than face it for a long time."

"If tempers were to ever ease, I would consider it. Once I've had time to think for myself, and my future, for a while."

"Fair enough." Jane squeezed her hands. "You are my friend. We weren't great shakes at it when we first tried for friendship, but you are a friend. I care about what happens to you. I only want for you to be happy."

"I think I forgot a long time ago what that means."

"What?"

"Being happy."

Mutability of temper and inconsistency with ourselves is the greatest weakness of human nature.
-Joseph Addison

Cole stepped onto the porch of the saloon to check if Jane had returned yet. There was no sign of the cutter behind the Inn. "What's taking you so long?"

He considered going to Mike's against Jane's wishes to make sure the man hadn't lost his temper again. Sure he trust Jane, but given Mike's recent displays of temper, Cole sure as shit didn't trust him.

Right as he made the decision to go after Jane, the man in question came around the corner of the Inn. Mike's gait was a bit unsteady as though he'd been drinking too much again. If Jane was right and he'd been sober the day before, the same sure couldn't be said today.

Mike strode right up the saloon, appearing to not have spotted Cole where he stood at the edge of the porch. Mike quickstepped up the stairs and moseyed his way into the saloon without ever paying one bit of notice to Cole.

"Well. I'm guessing that means Jane couldn't find him." Cole followed Jane's brother into the bar.

From behind the counter, Wil cast the youngest Young a dark look. Cole knew little about the bartender, he liked to keep things close to the vest as most brothel managers did. What he had noticed was that despite his cool demeanor, he didn't care for men that hit women. Still, he didn't kick out Jane's brother, just moved in front of him. "What'll it be?"

"A bottle of whiskey." Mike slapped the counter. "I'm starting to sober up. Can't have that."

"Maybe coffee would be better," Cole suggested.

Mike turned on the stool so fast the seat almost toppled right over. "Didn't ask you. Get the hell away from me. You bastard."

"You came into my saloon. Who were you expecting to see?" Cole leaned on the bar near Mike. Not close enough for the man to get a swing in-he wasn't stupid-but near enough.

"Was hoping you'd be over there." Mike jerked his thumb across the street.

"Too bad. Think you've had enough sauce, Mike."

"Not nearly. Give me a bottle, Wil."

A whore drew close to distract him as they'd been told to with customers that got riled. Cole shook his head firmly at her. No reason to get anyone else involved. Lily backed off, returning to her perch by the stairs.

Cole turned back to his brother-in-law. "No, Mike. Jane's out there looking for you. She went to your house to talk."

"And yet, I'm not there." Mike glared his way. "Unless she's coming to tell me she left your sorry, lying ass finally, I don't care to hear her nonsense."

"Never gonna happen."

"It sure as hell should." Mike leapt to his feet, fists clenched at his side. "She always loved you. That's why she wanted it back. Why I wasn't enough. Why she went looking for you."

Cole held up his hands. "You've got it all wrong, Mike."

"Do I?" He took two steps closer to Cole. Despite the proximity, Cole didn't back off. Last thing he was about to do was display weakness in his own saloon.

Cole leaned closer until he stood nose to nose with the shrimp. "Get the hell outta my saloon before I do something Jane'll never forgive me for."

Before Cole realized he'd gotten close, or could stop the man, Carl Denner set a hand on Mike's arm. "Come on, Mikey. There's a—"

Mike went on the attack quick as anything. He landed a solid punch to Carl's chin, and the approaching assistance of Noah Bryant was met with a elbow to the nose.

Cole managed to grab Mike's arm. The little shrimp slithered an arm free at the same time as Hammy went to help Noah to his feet. The old man caught a fist to the eye.

"*Michael*!" Jane's voice echoed through the saloon the second Cole caught the arm again.

Cole's arms wrapped around Mike's until he lifted the man clean off his feet. The man kicked and fought. "Damn it, Mike. Stop."

Jane rushed to Hammy's side, tears in her eyes. She got his head settled in her lap. "Mr. Hamm? Gilbert? Are you all right. Wake up. Michael Jacob, you should be ashamed."

"Shut the hell up for once in your damned life!" Mike continued to fight Cole's hold. "Let me go."

Hammy stirred in Jane's arms. Slowly, his eyes blinked open. When he realized where he was, he offered a goofy grin. "Lady Jane."

"There you are. I'm so glad you're all right." She kissed his forehead. "I want you seen by Dr. Cross to ensure no damage was done, and to get that cut cleaned up."

"Aw, Lady Jane. No need. It ain't nothing."

"I insist, Mr. Hamm." Jane gingerly extricated herself so she might stand. "Mr. Goodell. Would you fetch Dr. Cross for me? I would like Mr. Denner and Mr. Bryant seen to as well."

Mike had finally mostly stilled, but Cole didn't dare release his hold. He didn't trust the man for nothing. By the Colt Dragoon in Wil's hand, he didn't neither.

"Michael." Jane moved in front of her brother, glaring him down. "You're coming with us right now. Cole, can you get him to the apartment?"

"Are you kidding?"

"Fine." Jane gestured to one of the ground floor rooms to her right. "In there, then."

Cole carried Mike to the room. When he released him, he shoved him away. The door clicked shut behind him. Mike made a dash for the door where Cole suspected Jane still was, so he clotheslined Mike when he tried to pass. The man dropped for a second before hopping back to his feet.

Mike glared between the two of them, stopping on Jane. "I don't need your damned high horse right now."

"What high horse?" Jane almost sounded calm, but a tremor in her voice belied her anger. "What on earth were you thinking? You could have killed that dear sweet man because you feel like an incompetent man and a fool."

"Don't you—"

"Enough." Jane's fingers brushed Cole's arm before she stepped in front of him. He didn't like her putting herself in the line of fire like that, and braced himself to move at the first sign of trouble. Jane set her hands on her hips. "Do you realize how you could have hurt me yesterday if Patrick hadn't intervened? You could have hurt the baby."

Mike's anger faltered. "I didn't."

"No. If you had, Cole would have shot you dead on sight."

"Well," Cole hedged. "Maybe not dead, just shot."

Anger ratcheted Mike back into tension. "You know what he did!"

"Nothing." Jane didn't react to her brothers anger. "He did nothing."

"Says him. I know what I saw."

"No, you don't. All Cole did was talk to her, which is more than you've done in months. That is likely what makes you maddest of all." Jane stepped closer to her brother. Cole grabbed her arm to stop her, but she slipped right out of his grasp. She set her hands on either side of Mike's face, then pressed her forehead to his.

Cole couldn't hear whatever she said to Mike, but his shoulders sagged. The change in his mood didn't lessen

Cole's tension. The way Mike had been acting, who knew when he'd flip back to anger again.

"Cole, leave us alone for a few minutes."

"Not on your life," Cole all but snarled.

"Please. Trust me."

"It's not you I don't trust."

"Please." She turned to level her gaze with his. "He'll never remain calm if you're in here. You can be right outside the door. Trust me."

The last thing he wanted to do was comply, but at one last nod from her, he stepped back. "Fine. I'm leaving the door open."

"Just a crack, but that's acceptable." She edged her brother to the bed and sat beside him.

Cole stepped outside, pulling the door until only several inches were left to close it. He opened his holster, hand on the handle of the Walker should there be any sign of trouble from within the room.

While he waited, Andrew showed up to attend to the injured men. Noah would have a face bruised as Cole's currently was. The others were deemed clear, though Andrew tried to urge Hammy to rest at the clinic for the night.

Slowly the saloon activity returned to normal. There was not a hint of any violent activity from the room behind him. It was almost to quiet.

Right before he could burst into the room the check on them, the door slammed open. Mike glared hard at him before he stormed from the saloon in complete silence.

Jane emerged a moment later, frowning at the door where he'd disappeared. "Above all, he's the most angry with himself. I wouldn't be surprised if he went to Buffalo for a while."

"Being mad at himself don't excuse none of this." Cole gestured to her wrist, his nose, and Hammy sitting at the bar.

"What did you do when your heart was broken?" Jane lifted her gaze to his. She set her hand gently on his where it lingered on the Walker. "You dug up a grave, you tried to hurt me deeply on several occasions, you stole the sheriff's position, and you beat up Graham a few times."

"Graham deserved it. Hammy don't."

"Fair enough point." A warm smile lit her features. "They will heal. In time."

"How was your talk with Daisy?"

"Enlightening." She wrapped her arm around his waist. "I believe I've talked about them enough for today, though. Perhaps we should go home. I'd like to spend a few hours with you."

"What about business"

"It can wait. We have staff."

"Yesterday you said we needed more."

"We do. And a governess."

Cole paused. He used her chin to search her features. "Really? You agree?"

"With another little one on the way, yes. I may be exceptional, but even I cannot do it all."

"You're exceptional, eh?"

"Wouldn't you agree?"

"I'd be a fool not to."

The less routine the more life.
-Amos Bronson Alcott

Jane's even breath brushed across Cole's chest. Cole was relieved that she finally slept quietly. The past several nights she hadn't slept well at all. Worry over her brother, and everything else, had left her restless. She'd spent most of the previous day concerned that she hadn't seen Daisy since their meeting several days ago.

Seeing as she finally seemed in a good, deep sleep he didn't want to wake her. With slow, careful movements he slipped from the bed.

At the very least she'd done as ordered and kept close to home. She'd even spent more time at the library again. Busy as they'd become, he almost regretting opening the saloon. Almost, but not totally. The rush of trail runs that had come through town had their profits seeing a marked jump. A big enough increase that the storm that had hit two days prior didn't bother him in the least.

He expected that the tracks would finally be clear that day, and that meant the arrival of guests. A glance at the bed where Jane slept had him pausing with his trousers half on. One milky white leg had kicked free of the sheet, which now draped along the curve of her hip. The softest swell of her growing belly showed, as well as the plump mounds of her breasts.

Her features were relaxed, a hint of a smile on her pink lips. Golden curls skimmed her shoulder. Cole let his trousers drop to the floor again. He leaned across the bed, ready to capture a nipple in his mouth. One of the bells above the bed rang before he reached his goal. "Damn."

Jane blinked awake at the intrusion, her eyes still hooded with sleep. "What"

"Nothing. Ignore it." Cole shifted to hover over her.

A coy smile lit her features. "Gladly."

The damn bell rang again, and again, and a fourth time. Cole groaned. "I'll go see what the problem is. You wait here."

She stuck her lip out in a pout. "I'd much rather you stay."

"Bell won't stop ringing if I do." He captured the puffed out lip to nibble it until she groaned. "Be right back."

The bell rang again as he tossed on his trousers. When he threw open the door, Jane stood behind him with her robe on.

"I thought I told you to wait."

"Curiosity won over sleep."

Cole tried to glare at her, but the fact she hadn't bothered to don a chemise gave him hope their return to the bedroom would be swift.

"Thomas Eugene. How dare you disturb my morning repose." Jane kissed her brother on the cheek, then paused. "What's this?"

Cole moved out of their room to figure out what she stared at. A young woman around Alma's age stood behind Tom. She seemed slightly familiar to him, though he couldn't place how or why.

"I believe you know Ada." Tom urged forward the stranger.

"Oh, yes. Of course I do. Miss Pine, I can't tell you how disappointed Jesse, Cindy, and Lizzie were to hear you were not returning to teach this year." Jane shook the woman's hand.

"I was supposed to be married this fall." Pink swept across her cheeks as the looked from Cole to Jane, then back again. "I'm sorry we interrupted."

"Nonsense." Jane ignored the woman's embarrassment to focus on her brother. "Why, may I ask, are you introducing me to a woman I've known for several years?"

"I thought you might like to meet someone who could be an option as a governess. I thought you'd prefer someone you knew over a complete stranger." Tom draped his arm across Jane's shoulders. "Ada's fiancé up and took off with a whore while he was in Pueblo on what was supposed to be business."

"How horrible. I suppose it's best that it happened before the wedding rather than after, though." Jane elbowed her brother in the ribs. "Don't be so uncouth, Thomas. Miss Pine."

"Ada, please." The young woman continued to blush.

Jane glanced down to take in her robe, then to Cole in just his trousers. "Well, I suppose there's no better way to get this handled quickly. Ada, if you do decide to work for us, you should be aware that Cole and I have no qualms about being comfortable and rather loving with each other in our home even more so than in public. You will often find us in such a way. If it embarrasses you, this may not work."

"I'm unaccustomed, is all. I believe the town is quite aware of yours and Mr. Mitchell's comfort with affections." Ada blushed even deeper at her own comment.

Cole laughed outright. Jane joined him with her own amusement. He moved to Jane's side to nod at the young teacher. "You've got that right, Ada."

"Please, come in and have a seat. I'm uncertain what Thomas told you about what we are looking for in a governess."

Cole held back with Tom, eying his brother-in-law. "Couldn't have waited for a decent hour?"

"The pair of you never have a decent hour." Tom chuckled low. "I ran into her at the mercantile and we got talking. You know she was living with her brother in the settlement. Lost him and his wife in the tornado. When her fiancé took off, she took a job at the laundry. The woman's smart, and Jane already trusts her seeing as she was her boy's teacher."

"Good point. Jane might've finally agreed to this, but she was nervous about bringing in anyone she didn't know."

"Plenty of experience in having her trust broken."

"Too much. Speaking of—did you look into that bartender Wil suggested?"

"Looks clean. I'm waiting on word from a couple more contacts, but Wil wasn't lying. The two of them worked together out in Abilene." Only years of working with the man helped Cole notice the faintest twitch of a brow that showed he was hiding something.

"What is it?"

"Hm?"

"You got that look like there's a secret hiding there."

"Alma." Jane rose from the couch. "Would you like to meet Ada? She's a new friend."

Cole glanced toward the stairs. Immediately his tension rose. His sister was hunched at the shoulders, her fingers plucking at the sleeves of her blouse. Her gait stilted, slightly rocking. "Uh, Jane. Right now may not be the best time."

"Oh dear." Jane scrambled for the blanket draped across the back of the couch. She headed toward the young woman. "It's all right, Alma."

Cole remained where he was so Alma wouldn't be too crowded. Jane rubbed her hands along Alma's arm, speaking in low tones to her. In a fluid motion she threw the blanket over Alma's shoulders.

Without a clue what could have triggered Alma's current fit, Cole knew Jane would pull out all of their tricks to calm her down. She'd call on him if the simple matter of wrapping her tight in a blanket didn't do it.

Jane fumbled with the blanket when she tried holding it in place with her bad wrist.

"Want help?"

"No." Jane grunted, but finished wrapping the blanket around Alma. She urged her to sit on the end of the settee. She held the young woman close and tight as she turned her attention back to Ada. "My apologies, Ada. It appears Alma is having a difficult morning. Please, continue."

Before Ada could say a word, more footsteps echoed into the apartment. Sally emerged in a bright mood, which immediately faltered at the sight of Jane and Alma. She rushed over to take posision on Alma's other side. "Good morning."

"Good morning," Jane responded. "It seems everyone is waking now."

As if on cue, the twins' bedroom door opened. Clara rushed out at top speed, cheering as she dragged a paper bird on a string behind her.

"Clara," Cole warned.

Under his words a high-pitched keening filled the air. Clara stopped dead, turning toward Alma. The paper bird dropped to the ground, the stick shortly after. The child rushed forward, only to slow a few steps away. She leaned her head on Alma's knees, patting her legs and making soothing noises.

"As you can see," Jane spoke in low tones. "Things can get hectic around here. This little spitfire is Clara. She is a handful most days, but has the sweetest heart. And this young man is Colton. He's begun reading already."

"Already? They aren't yet three, are they?" Ada studied the young boy who had snuck in quietly to his ma's side.

"Not yet. We have a few more months before they turn three." Jane smiled down at her son. "It seems he's beginning earlier than I did by all accounts. Isn't that true, Thomas?"

"Not entirely. I think you started early as him. You stuck to Ma like glue whenever she had a book in hand. Much like Colton is with you now." Tom grinned her way. "There's a reason you started teaching at the age of fifteen. You were too smart for your own good"

"Perhaps with books." Jane's happy countenance flickered a moment before she managed to overcome the mention of Clara's inadequacies. "Shivering Willow and Jaybird will round out the charges that live with us. Of course, you already know Jesse, Cindy, and Lizzie. There are times they stay with us for a night or two. About once a month, in good weather, Willow and Jay retreat to the woods with the Sage Brush's Cheyenne guide for a couple of nights, wherein Jesse joins them."

"They were raised by Indians, yes?"

"The Ute, to be specific. They've been with us about a year and a half now. There are still struggles, but fortunately Jay hasn't run away since he started going with Black Moon once a month. I do allow them to wear what they wish at home, and their clothes for going out are simple for their comfort. Should the day arise that they wish to dress more like us, we'll adjust."

Ada's brow furrowed. "But they are white."

"That may be how they were born, but it isn't how they were raised. I wouldn't be so cruel as to expect them to be what they've never known. In Jay's case, he was an infant. He only remembers the way he was raised. Willow was likely the age of my twins when the Ute took them in." Jane sighed and shook her head. "I know the town expects us to make them fit in, but that would be far worse for them."

"Interesting tactic. Is that why you haven't sent them to school?"

"They don't have the learning to be at the level of children their age, plus there have been some incidents with other children who are not so accepting. It's led to some fights." Jane glanced at Alma. Any remaining tension Jane had carried seemed to ease away from her shoulders. "Are you feeling better, Alma?"

Alma nodded slightly. "Chickens."

"Sally? Would you be so kind as to assist Alma with the chickens this morning? Bring in the hounds when you're done. Bourbon and Whiskey could use some time warming by coal instead of horses." The run they'd had Hammy build for the dogs opened into the barn so the pups could be near the body heat of the horses on colder nights. At least until Jane allowed them to sleep in the apartment, which had yet to happen.

Cole stepped aside when Sally dashed past him. She greeted someone on the steps, which had him turning again.

Leanne emerged from the stairwell, a huge yawn splitting her face. Her own robe barely closed as she rubbed her eyes. "Did I hear Tom? Oh, goodness. Hello."

Jane chuckled when Leanne tugged her robe further closed. "Ada, this is Leanne. She's considered part of our family as well. So she'll make an appearance now and then."

"What is this?" Leanne nodded to Ada. "Not that it isn't nice to meet you, of course. It's awful early in the day."

"It's near nine," Tom corrected.

"Pardon me. My waking hours differ from the average person." Leanne nudged him. "Plus I was kept from sleeping well."

"Ada will be, we are hoping, stepping in as governess. Of course, we must discuss salary and living arrangements. I'm assuming by the loss of your brother's home you'll need a place to stay that is not the boarding house."

As Jane moved closer to Ada again to discuss the details, Cole turned his attention to Leanne. "Have you heard from Daisy?"

"No. I expected to after I talked to Jane the other day. I've not seen her, though." Leanne leaned into Tom as another yawn interrupted her. "I expected at least an inquiry as to terms, but perhaps she hasn't yet forgiven me."

"You didn't do anything." Tom rubbed her shoulder. "Maybe she still isn't sure."

"How can she be sure without terms?" Leanne glanced at Cole. "Why?"

"Jane's fretting because she hasn't seen her since they talked. Maybe we ought to go check on her." Cole glanced Jane's way. "Don't tell her, she'll get mad if we don't invite her."

"She'll be madder if we lie," Tom pointed out.

"Damned if I do. Damned if I don't."

*The death of a beautiful woman is unquestionably
the most poetical topic in the world.
-Edgar Allan Poe*

Kat laced her arm through Jane's as they strolled down the street. "She really said yes?"

"She did. After some discussion, Ada has decided to take one of our staff rooms until she can afford a home. At least living at the Inn, she won't have to pay to live there." Jane smiled happily over the news. "I'm so glad Thomas ran into her this morning. I'm pleased to have a governess who is not a complete stranger."

"It's wonderful Miss Pine will remain here to be your governess. Cindy will be delighted."

"As will Jesse. He laments daily that Miss Thompson isn't up to snuff in her way of teaching. He whines that he's quite bored." Jane laughed along with her friend. "I believe that's why he and Lizzie continually get in trouble for talking during class."

"As I point out to Miss Thompson, they aren't disturbing a soul. After all, their conversations are quite silent, and often held below desk level." Kat shrugged. "If they were falling behind in class, I'd be more upset over the distraction. However, they're both quite ahead of the rest of their class. Though I can't imagine why, *Jane*."

"I have no idea what you could mean." Jane feigned innocence, but it only sent Kat into another fit of laughter. "My wonderings revolve around the mercantile these days. When are the new owners finally going to arrive? I believe Mr. Callahan has grown rather impatient to depart from our little town."

"The rumor is they plan to take over in the new year. I imagine they'll arrive next month to facilitate the change. I've heard little about them otherwise. They bought the place sight unseen, *and* paid in full for the contents along with the building."

"They did? That's good to know. It means they're keeping it as a mercantile. I'd hate to lose it. The Turner's kept a wonderfully supplied store, and that new general store over on Second Street is lacking in stock."

"There's also less places to hide for tawdry deeds."

Jane didn't try to deny it. A pleasant flush warmed her cheeks. "I can't say you're wrong. Although that isn't the only reason I frequented the mercantile. Don't paint me quite so wicked."

A high, sharp whistle cut through town. On instinct, Jane lifted her gaze to locate the source. All of her brothers, as well as herself, tended to use such a whistle as a signal of trouble. Sure enough, Tom stood at the end of the street. As she watched, he issued another whistle.

In quick order Charles and Nick appeared. Right behind were Sally and Sheriff Schaffer. All four souls beckoned by the call took off down the road toward the man making the whistle. Panic gripped Jane's heart. Tom hadn't even looked at her, which meant the call wasn't meant for her, but it also meant some form of emergency.

Jane turned to apologize to Kat, but her friend was already shooing her. "Go."

Without further ado, Jane gathered her skirts to run down the street fast as she could. By the time she rounded the corner, the group was already well off in the distance. She skidded to a full stop when she realized where they were headed. "Oh no."

Jane stood stock still for a long minute as she watched them all disappear into a small house right at the edge of town. The same house she'd been to mere days ago to visit with Daisy. "Daisy."

Her heart lodge firm in her throat, Jane pushed forward into another run toward the homestead. When she hit the door, Cole stood there to block her entrance. "You don't wanna go in there, Jane."

"What? I—What happened?"

"She's gone."

A million words caught in her throat. Jane shook her head against the hundreds of scenarios racing through her mind at his words. Her worse imagining couldn't be reality. It simply wasn't possible for there to be a darker meaning behind them. She refused to believe it. "Where did she go? Did she leave a note?"

"Jane." His hands settled on her shoulders, strong and warm. The normally sparkling ice blue of his eyes were dulled. "She's been killed."

"No. No, no, no, no." She couldn't sink into the comforting embrace he wrapped her in. That would make it real, but it couldn't be. She braced her hands against his stomach. "What do you mean, killed?"

"The way she died, it's not natural. Someone killed her."

Jane stumbled away from his embrace, her gaze shifting to focus inside the house. She noticed Sally's gaze pouring over the entire room before she disappeared into the bedroom. "Let me inside."

"It's best you don't. The baby."

"Cole. I know death. I've shaken his hand. I will be fine." She had no doubt he'd argue, but he stepped aside. Jane edged though the living room. Her gaze drifted to the table she'd sat at with Daisy a few days before. Two cigarettes floated in a mug there, and Daisy's purse rested at the end of the table, untouched.

"Someone should get Graham, tell him to bring the wagon." David's voice was gruffer than usual.

"On it," Nick offered. He paused outside the room soon as he saw Jane. After a moment of studying her, he stepped forward and squeezed her shoulder gently. Then he took off out the door on his errand for the undertaker.

Cole's warm body pressed against hers from behind. The warmth of his presence showed how cold shock had made her. "You don't gotta."

"I do." She squeezed his hand in appreciation before walking the last few steps to the bedroom. In the doorway she paused to take in the scene.

On the bed lay Daisy, flat on her back, eyes wide open to the ceiling. Her chemise was torn half off. Bruises dotted her face, arms, ribs—and most prominent was the ring of bruising around her throat. Jane's own throat closed at the sight, all too familiar with what it meant.

"Strangled," She managed to gasp. Every head in the room lifted at her voice.

Sally's brow furrowed. "Ma, you shouldn't be here."

"I just saw her a few days ago." Jane took a shaky breath. "We agreed to talk again soon. Why didn't I check on her sooner?"

Cole's hands settled on her shoulders. "It's not your fault."

"I hate to ask." David cleared his throat. "When was the last time any of you saw Mike?"

A cry of protest emerged from Tom and Sally. Jane let her own denials be heard with them. "No. There's no way."

David flushed under the anger, but didn't withdraw the question.

"Michael couldn't have done this." Jane met David's disbelief head on. "You've known him for years, David. Longer than me. You know he couldn't."

"The past few months he hasn't been the same, and you know it. Look at what happened a few days ago to Hammy, and he nearly hurt you." David's tone was kind even as he argued his point. "I have to at least talk to him. You know I do."

Sally shook her head firmly. "No. I don't. He didn't do this. He doesn't smoke."

David's brow furrowed as he turned to Sally. Tom, on the other hand, almost beamed with pride.

"The cigarettes in the mug out there in the kitchen. There's also one here on the floor. Right here." Sally pointed with her finger. "Uncle Mike doesn't smoke, and he'd never do this. This was intentional. What he did a few days ago was blow his stack in anger. It was disorganized and reckless. This is the opposite of that."

"He's had a lot of incidents with blowing his stack in anger lately." David no longer met Jane's eyes. "I've got to at least talk to him. I'll talk to whatever john's she's been entertaining, too, if you know of any it'll help."

Jane turned away from the sight of her friend lying dead. After that, she found herself unable to move. Thoughts spun in a tangled mass, emotions blowing through so fast she couldn't keep track of what was happening.

An approaching wagon stirred Cole to life. He gently urged her toward the door, to the cold, fresh air. Outside the house the hum of conversation couldn't breech the buzzing in her ears. Her throat tightened. Even her nose seemed to squeeze itself shut.

A sharp shake to her shoulders reintroduced air to her lungs.

Cole's brow rose as he stared her down. "You back?"

"She didn't deserve that. Her last moments must have been so horrifying. Just like every other soul that's died recently. I just...I can't..."

"You can. You've been through worse."

"She was so close to figuring things out, or at least she was trying so hard to. Who could have done this to her?" Tears spilled over as the emotions crashed to the surface.

The sanctuary of Cole's arms encircled her, allowing her to release her grief without disturbance. She didn't know how long they stood there, but when she finally found some semblance of control, the sound of the wagon creaking away was the first thing she heard.

"Ma?" Sally and Tom hovered at the edge of her vision. "He didn't do it. He'll be fine."

"I know." Jane swiped at her remaining tears. "But Daisy won't."

Cole used his thumb to brush away another tear. "She was a good woman. We'll see she's taken care of right."

"We had our problems, but she was my friend." Jane blew out a gust of air to try to regain control before she wept again. She turned to Sally and Tom. "You two need to find out who did this. You must."

"We will, Lou." Tom squeezed her hand. "I'll let Leanne know when we're done here."

"I'll, um…" Jane sniffed against the renewed lump in her throat. "I'll tell Katherine and Cora, then."

Sally hugged her tight before rushing back into the house.

Tom cleared his throat. "I'll stick with the kid until she's done doing what she's going to do."

"Thank you." Jane lifted her chin to face her brother with as much strength as she could muster. "Tom."

"Yeah?"

"Chauncey. Keller. Ellis. Emily. Sally. Now, Daisy?"

"We're already on it. Let us worry about it. You worry about that kid you're carrying."

"I'm pregnant, not incompetent." She pun on her heel to storm back to town. She didn't make it ten yards before the flash of anger dissipated as quick as it had come.

Cole's arm slid around her waist. "Let's take it easy."

"I'm not a weak, broken creature." She sobbed over her own anger, stomping her foot in frustration. "Stop treating me as if I'll wilt."

"Let's go home. Word'll spread on its own. Kathy and Cora will hear."

"I should be the one to tell them." She shook her head. "I don't know whether to weep or scream. I can't decide if I want to be angry or sad."

"It's probably both. She was your friend."

"She was Kat and Cora's friend, too. That's why I need to tell them. No matter what's happened in the past year, we were all her friends."

"Fair enough. Then we go home."

"I don't need to be coddled, Mr. Mitchell."

"It's not coddling I'm after."

She laughed despite her continued tears. "Boor."

"Got ya to laugh."

"It did. Thank you."

*I love you the more that I believe you
have liked me for my own sake
and nothing else.
-John Keats*

Cole closed the bedroom door behind him. After Jane had met with Kat and Cora, he'd insisted she refresh herself. He'd hoped she'd take a nap, but instead she was simply cleaning herself up from her tears.

He'd had Ada take the children to the restaurant for some food. Willow refused to join them, and sat in her room sulking. Cole hadn't the foggiest idea what had the girl so upset, but she'd been in a foul mood since Ada first arrived as governness.

At least the former teacher had agreed to begin work straight away, which gave him time to make sure Jane was all right.

The back door opened to reveal Sally, grim faced as she stepped inside. When she spotted him, she grimaced. "Hey, Pa."

"Any word?"

"Nothing yet. Uncle Mike wasn't at his homestead, which David took to mean he might be on the run." Sally frowned down at the floor. "We gave him the name of some of the men she's been entertaining to distract him a while. Tommy's out looking for him."

"Good. Tom'll see that things are handled right."

"I guess. How's Ma?"

"Jane's gonna be fine. She's getting herself cleaned up now." Cole sat heavily in a nearby chair. He still couldn't believe Daisy was dead. The sight of her dead body sent a chill through him he hadn't felt in years. Not as numbing as when Jane had been hanged, but an ache none-the-less.

He knew Jane was concerned about him as well. After all, Daisy had been in his favor for three whole years before Jane arrived.

"I only ever knew her as a doctor," Sally said quietly. "And even then, not much. Even though she did our checks, she didn't like conversing with us much."

"She didn't like being reminded of what she was back then. Guess that changed." Cole ran his hand over his face in hopes of erasing some of the melancholy that stole over him. "Before your ma came around, she was my favorite. I kept her there mostly because of her doctoring. It's what kept me from pitying her."

"Three years? Iris always said you didn't keep favorites longer than a few months." Sally frowned. "Another lie she told, I guess."

Cole chuckled darkly. "One of a great many. I liked Daisy. She was smart, sometimes even funny. Never quite made me laugh like your ma can, but she had her moments.

Annoyed the hell outta me when she got to doctoring. She'd boss me around, and I didn't like that none."

"We all know you hate a bossy woman," Sally's voice tremored with her laughter.

"Until your ma, I did." He laughed along with her. "Daisy was a good woman, just got lost at the end there. She didn't like losing patients, and them epidemics made her lose a lot."

A knock on the door drew his attention away from Sally. He spotted Jane in the doorway of their room. Before he could read her expression, she'd headed for the door. When she opened it, she stepped back immediately. "Nicholas? I wasn't expecting you."

"I wanted to come by quickly before word and rumor spread." Nick kissed Jane on the cheek. Jane's brother had cleaned up as well, back in his suit, with his attaché in hand. "Cole, I hope you don't mind the intrusion, but I need to meet with you."

Jane glanced at Sally, frowning as if contemplating. "Sally, would you mind going to the restaurant and make sure Ada isn't drowning in children? It's her first day with our bunch."

Cole furrowed his brow, confused as to why Jane would be shooing off Sally. For that matter, what Nick wanted with him was something else he wasn't sure about. He knew Ada didn't need the help, she'd been in bright spirits when she'd left with the kids. "I—sure, Nick. Come in and have a seat. Want a drink?"

"No, I'm fine." Nick took a seat on the couch.

Jane finished whispering whatever she was to Sally, then shooed the girl from the room. She swept across the room.

"Nonsense, Nicholas. The hot water is ready if you would like coffee, or we have some brandy tucked away in here. Leanne enjoys it."

"Coffee will suit me if you're insisting." Nick set his attaché on his lap, then propped it open. "Normally I would wait a while to see to this matter, but I thought it best we got it out of the way quickly so it wasn't seen as a motive."

"How could it not be seen as a motive? Unless…" Jane's words trailed off as she stared at her brother. "Nothing?"

Cole looked between the siblings in utter confusion. "What in blazes are you two talking about? I don't speak Young, remember?"

Nick pulled some papers from his case before he set it aside. "Daisy didn't have much in the way of her name, but she made a will some time ago. Before the epidemic. Afterward, she approached me again, but changed very little."

Cole still wasn't sure what was going on. "What's that got to do with me?"

Jane sat beside Cole, setting her hand on his. "Because you're in the will, Cole."

"Daisy left her medical texts to the clinic, and some personal books for the library." Nick fixed his intense gaze on Cole. "Everything else was left to you."

"What?" Cole shook his head. "That makes no sense. What do you mean, everything?"

"She had some savings put aside, which is all yours. Then there's the homestead." Nick flipped through the paperwork. "When she purchased the home, she managed to pay in full. It left her with a little savings, which she's been adding to."

"Why?" Cole shook his head. "You're talking crazy. Daisy had to have—"

"She loved you." Jane's voice was quiet but seemed to echo through the room.

Cole turned toward her, expecting echoes of the jealousy she'd once showed. Instead, he found tears shimmering in her eyes. "No. She loved Mike."

"She did, in some ways. He was too wrapped up in saving her for her to love who he was. She couldn't separate the two." Jane lowered her gaze. "Before I came along, she was in love with you. It didn't matter if you wouldn't love her back. She admired the way you cared for the whores, the way you listened, even if you took no guff, you showed caring."

Cole stared at the papers in front of Nick. "It doesn't make sense."

A soft laugh from Jane knocked some of his shock free. "You're easy to love, and not so easy to shake. She didn't think she loved you any longer, but still admired you."

"How do you know?"

"She told me when we last spoke. I'd seen it on her a few times, and that last time I asked." She brushed some tears from her cheeks. "It's a big mess, but it means Michael had no motive except his embarrassment. That's why Nicholas presented you with this immediately. He's hoping to protect Michael."

"Not protect him, clear him." Nick flipped a few pages. "I'll need you to sign, Cole. To claim the house. I imagine Thomas and Sally would like access to it for a while should they need it for their investigation."

Cole stared at the pen for a long minute before he reached for it. "I don't need her house."

"We'll deal with selling it once this matter is cleared up if that's what you wish." Nick slipped the papers back in his case. He turned to his sister. "Same with the library books. When they're done with the house we can remove them. She'd already left her medical texts at the clinic a few weeks back."

"I noticed they weren't cluttering her living room as they once had." Jane rose with her brother. Her hand rested reassuringly on Cole's shoulder. "If you hear anything, please let me know. When Andrew is done with the autopsy, I'll speak to Graham about the arrangements. Cole and I will see she is taken care of the way she should be."

Nick leaned over to kiss Jane on the cheek. "I'll keep you informed. Cole."

Cole barely nodded to the man. After he left, Cole shook his head. "That didn't just happen. You didn't just tell me Daisy loved me."

"You aren't truly surprised." She lifted his chin with a touch of her finger. Her bright blue eyes had darkened to slate in her mood, but he still didn't detect anger. "I think we both always knew. It was easier to deny when she was no longer under contract to you."

He couldn't take his gaze from hers. The emotions he'd been battling aside for so long welled. "She was a good woman. I won't deny it. She didn't deserve what she got. None of it. Not even my version of saving her."

"No, she didn't." Jane settled into his lap, her arms circling his neck. "Life dealt her some terrible blows. Unfortunately in the past year she didn't feel she had the support to manage them. When she lost her husband, you became that. She told me how you kept her from servicing the masses for nearly six months."

"Don't make me sound better than I was."

She smiled sadly, "For a woman with no prospects, you were better. You always kept your girls safe. You did more for her, you kept her doctoring when she thought she'd lose it all."

"In the end she wasn't doctoring anymore."

"No, she wasn't." She settled against his shoulder. "She was confused. I tried to help, but I may have been too late. One thing she never forgot was what you did for her, though."

"I did more for you than I ever did for her."

"Because you didn't love her like you love me." She lifted her head, a sad smile on her features. "It doesn't make you bad because you didn't love her when she loved you. You respected her. You said yourself it's what kept you in her favor for so long."

"I did."

"That's more than she got from most people for a long time."

The truth is rarely pure and never simple.
-Oscar Wilde

Sally paused at the door of the Inn. She turned back at Cole's laughter. For a few minutes she watched him playing with Clara. Jane held Colton in her lap while she carried on a bright conversation with Ada.

When her parents had joined them in the restaurant, Jane had pulled Sally aside to let her know what Nick had wanted, on the chance it would be relevant to any investigations. Then Jane had shooed Sally on to do what she needed to further the cause.

Sally couldn't help hanging around as the family sat together. Cole interacted with Clara and Alma as though nothing had happened. Though Sally detected something when he and Jane locked gazes. They were both troubled by what had happened to Daisy. Yet they still were able to act like everything was fine.

She turned away, quietly wondering at how they managed it. Perhaps it was the children. Or just because they'd been through so much already, they'd learned to handle things better.

The town bustled about its business as though nothing had happened. A few people stood together in whispers, but those could easily be any gossip. Everywhere she looked was a face she knew, a person she'd come to know. Not a one of them showed any sign of guilt.

She paused on the porch of the clinic to let her gaze wander the streets again. The outside world acted as though it were a normal day. As though a soul they'd known for years, whose doctoring services they'd used, didn't lie dead behind the doors of the clinic.

Then again, for most of them it wasn't their family, their friend.

Sally sighed, pushing open the door of the clinic. Charlie sat at the main desk, though not facing the door. Nor did he turn at its opening. He sat motionless, a heavy tome in his hands. His gaze remained fixed on the bookshelves lined with similar books.

"Uncle Charlie?" Sally drew close to set a hand on his shoulder.

"Sally." He actually shook his head before he turned to face her. His eyes were rimmed red, features drawn. "Is something wrong? Is Jane all right?"

"She's fine. I came by to join Andrew for the autopsy."

"Right. The autopsy." Charlie gave a sharp sniff, the book in his hand shutting with a sharp slap. "I don't think he's begun yet."

"How are you holding up?" Her question was little more than cursory. She could tell he wasn't doing well.

"I'm not quite certain, truth be told."

"You don't look like you're doing well with the news."

"Shock. I'm struggling to believe it's true." He set his hand on the medical text. "Daisy brought her books in a few weeks back. I thought, perhaps, she needed a break."

"Ma said the epidemic brought back bad memories for her."

"It did. We talked about it some, but I had no idea it was so painful for her. She was a great partner in the practice before that. She often impressed me with her skills."

"Ma always liked her as a doctor."

"A fair sight better than she liked me." He chuckled quietly. "That might have something to do with being her brother, of course."

"Probably," she agreed. "We tend to get annoyed with family before others, after all."

"I don't think there's a member of the Young family that isn't well aware of that fact." He blew out a long breath. "This is going to take getting used to. I'd already been sending out adverts for another woman doctor. I suppose now I'll have to look for two."

Sally smiled sadly. "I'm really sorry for your loss, Uncle Charlie."

"Worry about Michael, not me. I'll get through this. I don't know how he'll do."

"We have to find him before we can worry about how he'll get through." She squeezed his shoulder. "Which we'll do. Soon, I hope."

"I only hope one of you finds him before the sheriff. David is a good man, but I'm afraid assumptions will win, especially with Michael's mood of late."

"That's what we're hoping, too." She sighed. "I'll go see what Andrew is up to. Ma's across the way if you need anything."

"Thank you, Sally."

She left him at the desk, not feeling as though she'd helped him much. At the door to the room used for the autopsy's and testing, she inexplicably paused. Her hand hovered over the knob, unable to make the short distance.

It was only Daisy. She'd not been close with the woman. Not like her Ma, or Pa, or even Charlie. It was another unfortunate soul is all. Nothing she couldn't handle.

After repeating those thoughts several times, she walked into the room. She grabbed the sleeve covers and threw them on. With the apron in her hand, she turned. The sight of Daisy on the table caused her to freeze.

Her brain battled with her limbs to move forward. In the end, her limbs won, keeping her frozen as she stared at the table.

"What do you think you're doing?" Andrew put down his pad, circling the autopsy table. His movement briefly blocked Daisy from view, allowing Sally to move again

"I'm joining you. It's not the first time." She held the apron in her hands still.

The apron slipped away into Andrew's grasp. He shook his head. "No. Not this time, Sally."

"What? Why on earth not? I've stood in on several—"

"Not of a friend, you haven't."

"She wasn't my friend, she was Ma's," Sally protested. "I hardly knew her, mostly."

"Sally." He set his hands on her shoulders. "You haven't been able to bring yourself to even look at her."

"You're blocking my view."

"Am I?"

She realized then if she simply lifted her gaze she could actually see Daisy lying there. Auburn hair slipped over the end of the table like a waterfall. "I, um, I was there after they found the body. I examined her."

"You examined her, but didn't cut her open. You're trembling. Sit." Andrew settled her on a stool. "As your friend, I suggest you don't join me for this autopsy. The method of death seems pretty clear at first glance. I'm only confirming. You don't need to see this."

"She's just another—"

"She's not."

Her eyes fell shut, and she knew he was right. Though she hadn't been very close to Daisy, something about this one felt different. "Fine."

"How about this? I have some tests to run on some of the samples coming from that mine in Cripple Creek. They should arrive on this afternoon's train. We'll run them together in the morning."

She opened her eyes to meet his. "Samples from Cripple Creek?"

"Some of the miners over there have been getting an unusual sickness. I certainly couldn't have them come here in case it's contagious. I gave explicit instructions to their doctor on what to get for me, and we're going to see if we can find the cause of the illness."

She sighed, casting another glance toward Daisy. Tears sprang to her eyes without a logical reason. "I don't know what my problem is. I've been friendly with others we've done."

"Perhaps you considered her more of a friend than you realized."

"She was courting my uncle."

"And you wouldn't want to affect any interpretation of the findings."

"Tommy's in the investigation, too—and he's his brother."

"Sally."

"Fine. Fine. I'll go to her place and see if I can find anything new there."

Andrew smiled and nodded. "Good idea. I don't expect this to take long unless I find something unexpected. Perhaps we can have supper and go over the results."

"I'd like that. Thank you." Sally peeled off the sleeve covers. With a sigh, she got to her feet. "You promise you'll tell me everything."

"I'll bring my notes."

Knowing how meticulous his notes were, she nodded. "Good. I'll see you then."

Sally rushed from the clinic, mildly embarrassed at the way she'd frozen. On her way past the desk, she noticed Charlie no longer sat there, but didn't want to think on it too hard.

Why had she frozen at the sight of Daisy? The woman hadn't even been cut open yet, if Andrew would in the end do so. As he'd said, the cause of death was pretty plain in the bruises on her neck, the pops of blood in her eyes.

Daisy had done Sally's exams when she'd been a whore, but those were cursory and no pleasantries exchanged. She'd also been one of the doctors that had tended to Sally after the fire in which she'd saved Tommy.

In the years since Jane had taken Sally in, she'd seen more of Daisy. Still, she was Jane's friend. Honestly, what was her problem?

She came to a stop a few yards from Daisy's home. Clearly she'd been walking faster than normal to have arrived so quick.

Two horses sat outside, and the front door stood open. Both horses belonged to the Hangman's Inn, and she knew Jane and Cole wouldn't have come by so quick. Not with most of the family gathered around them. That meant Tommy, and perhaps Molly.

She knocked on her way inside so as to not startle the pair of Pinkertons, both of whom were probably armed. "Hello?"

"Sally." Tommy emerged from the pantry, nodding her way. "I figured you'd be at the clinic for the autopsy. Molly and I thought we'd look over the house again."

"Anything new?" Sally chose to ignore the comment on the autopsy to focus on the point at hand. "What are you looking for?"

"We thought, perhaps." Molly appeared on the steps to the attic-loft. "Being a doctor and all, Daisy would keep a record of her clients out of habit."

Sally glanced upward into the small loft where she knew after the previous days events held many drying herbs. "I didn't see anything up there yesterday. Did you find anything?"

"She's got some dangerous plants up here, but otherwise, no." Molly kept down the stairs.

"Dangerous?"

"Foxglove, for one."

"Digitalis," Sally supplied. "Used to treat some heart conditions."

Tommy brushed his hands on his trousers. "There was nothing in the cellar."

"If there was a book, whoever did it probably took it." Molly shrugged. "If he knew of its existence, that is."

"Or destroyed it. Much better than having evidence in hand." Sally glanced between the pair. "Did neither of you check the stove?"

"No. We were hoping it was still here and hidden." Tommy shrugged. "Help yourself. Not much anywhere else to look in here. We already thoroughly searched her bedroom."

Sally crouched in front of the stove and pulled it open. The fire had long gone out, and ashes scattered the bottom. She grabbed a poker to move some around. "Nothing in here."

Tommy paused in his search of the desk. "Check the bedroom, then. I've looked at this a few times, but I'll give it one more try."

Sally carried the poker into the bedroom with her. The room was darker, set against the hill as the house was. Evidence of Tommy and Molly's search scattered about the room in a drawer not fully closed, a shoe poking out from the curtained area that hid Daisy's clothes.

She turned slowly to take in the room, pausing at the bed where Daisy had been found. The bed had been remade, which made her think the others had already looked under the mattress. Hopefully they'd looked in it as well.

After a glance at each of the obvious places, she moved to the stove to pull open the front. Inside were the same sort of ashes you'd find with charcoal, but something else as well. She set aside the poker, afraid to disturb the delicate remnants.

Biting her lip, she searched the room again. On the dresser sat two pictures and a silver-handled brush. She rose in hopes of finding the matching mirror. Luck presented her with it, and she snatched it up.

With a gentle motion, she slid the mirror under the evidence she'd spotted. Careful as could be she lifted it onto the stove top before leaning over. "Tommy."

"Yeah." He entered without hesitation, leaning over the crumbling pile of leather and paper. "Not much we can use there, but it was definitely a book."

"The paper is almost all gone, but there's a few edges along the spine that didn't burn as well." Sally tilted her head to try to make out anything. "Only a few letters I can see, though. Could be names, might not be. If this was her records, it won't do us a lick of good."

"Guess we find out the old fashioned way."

"Seek out the rumors Ma tries to avoid."

"Precisely."

The loss of a friend is like that of a limb;
time may heal the anguish of the wound,
but the loss cannot be repaired.
–Robert Southey

The four women sat solemnly around the table in Cora's kitchen. The table pressed against the window where they could view the town while they chatted, and the kitchen could still function to make meals for the patrons.

A fifth chair sat conspicuously empty.

Jane couldn't stop staring at the void where Daisy had once sat, even though Daisy hadn't occupied the seat in months before that day.

Cora dabbed her eyes with a handkerchief. Even though the bustle of cooking and plating going on nearby, her sniffle was audible.

Leanne drew her own handkerchief through her fingers. The seam trembled its way through her forefinger and thumb. She flipped the fabric and did the same with the next edge. "Murdered? Is it true?"

Jane jolted when Cora sobbed at the word. Kat squeezed Jane's hand gently. "It must have been an upset suitor. Who else would do such a thing?"

"It's overstating matters to call them suitors, don't you think?" Leanne shook her head. "They weren't out for love, save for one, they were there for one thing only."

"Don't lump Michael in with them," Jane snapped. She snatched her hand back from Kat's. She didn't miss the way the women glanced between each other. "He loved her."

"Perhaps, once. The last few months, though." Leanne's voice remained soft, kind.

"He's been heartbroken. It's ridiculous for David to believe Michael could murder her." Jane blinked against the burning tears. When her friends again exchanged glances, her breath caught. "You don't believe it either, do you? Not Michael."

"I believe we can all see why David would think so." Kat tried to grasp Jane's hand again, but she moved it away too fast. "Jane. If he wasn't your brother, you'd be able to see it as well. We all know Michael has been a good man, but the past few months things have gotten…"

In the lingering silence, Jane frowned. "What, Katherine? What have they become?"

"Complicated."

Leanne set a warm hand on Jane's. "Only a few days ago he got into a drunken fight in your saloon. You told us yourself. He hit Hammy, of all people."

"He—He wasn't…" Jane's words choked in her throat. "He wasn't thinking straight."

"Exactly." Cora offered a smile marred by sadness. "He was angry."

"But he wouldn't kill someone!" Jane flew to her feet. How could her friends be saying such things? How could they not know? "I can't—how could—how dare—"

"Jane!" Kat raced after her all the way to the porch. "Jane, please. Come back. We must discuss this with level heads."

Jane backed away from her friend's grasping hands. "I don't want to hear it. I don't care what you all say. Michael wouldn't kill a soul, certainly not the woman he loved."

"You're probably right."

"Probably." Jane laughed bitterly, turning away.

"I'm sorry." Kat set a hand on her shoulder. "Jane, come back. We shouldn't be fighting. We met to mourn Daisy, not toss accusations."

"Go back inside, Katherine." Jane shrugged off Kat's hand. "Please. Go away. Leave me be."

Kat folded her into a tight hug. Then, she did as Jane asked and went back inside.

Jane tried to keep her tears from falling as she watched the activity along the street in front of the Inn. A few glances were cast her way, then people would return to their business. Whispers and talk she was used to. She couldn't bother to worry over what they all thought. That her on friends would doubt Michael's innocence—and David, who had in truth known him longer than she had thanks to her amnesia.

She turned on her heel to head toward the library, only to find Cole there.

"Thought you'd be in with the hens." His thumb brushed along her cheek. Concern lined his brow, though he didn't speak to it. Perhaps he was avoiding it. "Clucking away and all you do when you get together."

"I can't be around them. They believe Michael capable of—I simply can't." She released a long breath between pursed lips. "I thought I'd go to the library. There I'd have some peace and quiet."

"You don't got a coat on or nothing." He tucked a finger under her chin. "Why don't you come back inside?"

"No. You have to go to the saloon. It's your night. I'll go to the library and gather myself there. Please don't fuss."

"Not fussing." When she cut him a sharp look, he grimaced. "Much."

She allowed a small smile at the admittance. "Perhaps I'll come by the saloon after a spell."

"Or I can come by the library. That way I can make sure you're good and warm." He pulled her close against him. "Or for whatever you need."

She closed her eyes when his thumb brushed away another escaped tear. "Thank you. Some days I wonder what I ever did to deserve you."

"Oh, I ain't that special. I'm more a punishment."

She chuckled low, poking his stomach. "You always know how to make me laugh."

He kissed the top of her head, enveloping her in his strong arms again. "I'll get your cape. Walk ya to the library. Don't argue. I'm walking you there."

"Yes, sir." She shivered when he released her, the cold air making its presence known in the absence of her anger, and his arms.

Hammy climbed the steps to the Inn. "Mrs. Mitchell."

"Mr. Hamm. You're late today." Jane walked over, granting the man a warm kiss on the cheek. For once, she didn't correct him for calling her Mrs. Mitchell so publicly.

Even though the old man had no idea she was married, he'd been calling her Mrs. Mitchell since before she and Cole had been married. "Did you get wrapped up in business?"

"Something like that." He collected her hands in his. "Y'all right, Lady Jane?"

"I will be. Soon as they find who did this to Daisy."

"Them that's saying it's Mike ain't right in the head, Janey."

"Thank you for saying so, Mr. Hamm." She planted another kiss to his cheek. "Why don't you get a bit of stew to go with your beer today? You're looking a little peaked."

"It's the cold. Ain't good on these old bones." He nodded. "I'll get some stew if ya insist."

"I do." Jane lifted her gaze when her cape draped over her shoulders. "Thank you, Cole."

Hammy tapped his hat on the way inside.

Jane sighed softly. "I worry about him."

"He's a tough old goat. He'll be fine. You got enough to worry about without worrying over Hammy." Cole squeezed her shoulders. "Let's get you to the library."

She didn't argue, wrapping her arm around his waist as they started around the corner. "How are you doing?"

"What?"

"You heard me. How are you doing?" She turned to face him, meeting his gaze.

"I'm fine. We talked plenty last night. No need to drag out the dirty laundry for everyone." Cole's gaze flicked around them to see who could hear their conversation.

"All right. Let's go, then." Before she could turn he grabbed her shoulders almost too rough to hold her in place. "Cole."

"Let's get back inside." His fingers tightened on her shoulders when she struggled against him. He wasn't looking at her, but over her head.

"What? No. I told you I wanted to go to the library."

"Just go back inside." He pulled her hard toward the door.

She pulled back strong enough to land on her rump for his efforts. "Damn it, Cole. What…"

He was already pulling her to her feet, half dragging her to the door. Then it hit her why he'd want her to go back inside. Cole's features twisted in concern when she managed to pull herself free again.

Backing away so quick she hit the railing, she stared at him. "No."

"Jane. You should go inside. Wait for Nick or Tom."

"No." She raced down the steps into the street. To the south where the new jailhouse stood she spotted two figures on horses drawing closer. "*Michael.*"

Jane took off down the street at a dead run. She darted in between the crown until even her own breath hurt. At the jail she skidded to a stop right near where the men had halted. "David, don't. Don't do this. He didn't do it. You know he didn't."

"I'm sorry, Jane. I really am." David helped Michael on his descent from the saddle.

"I don't remember." Michael's words slurred with alcohol. "Don't remember."

"Michael, stop. Shut up. You didn't do this. You couldn't." Jane cupped his face in his hands. She forced him to meet her eyes. "You would never kill someone you loved."

"Jane, I have to put him in a cell." David touched her elbow gently. "You and your brothers can visit in a bit."

"He's drunk. He's not talking straight. Did you even bother to question anyone else, David?" Jane shoved him off of her. Tears streamed down her cheeks, anger heated them. "How could you?"

"Jane. I'm sorry, he said he might have done it."

"He's so drunk it's coming out of his skin, you can't believe anything he says!" Jane fought when someone pulled her away from the door. "David, don't do this. No, Michael."

"You're not helping him, Lou." Tom grunted when she swung her elbow into him. "Come on. Go with Cole. Let Nick and I take care of this."

"He didn't do this, Thomas. I don't care what—"

"I know. But if he admitted he could have, David had no choice. Let him do his job."

Jane stared at her brother, unable to find words. "I thought they were my friends. They all think he did this. All of them."

Tommy pulled her close at her sob. His hand ran along her back. Under the murmur of a gathering crowd, he spoke soft as anything. "He won't swing. He didn't do it, and we'll find a way to prove it. Now go with your husband. Go home."

Cole's arms replaced Tom's before she even knew what happened. She was guided across the street on numb legs, her hands ice cold as they grasped Cole's. The second they were inside, she was scooped off her feet and carried to the solace of their room.

Once he set her down, Jane stood there, still and silent. Her cape was peeled from her shoulders, and warm hands rubbed over hers.

She finally lifted her gaze to his. "Do you think he did this?"

"I've seen men do worse drunk as he is."

She took a step back, yanking her hands free of his. "Do you think he did this?"

"No. Only because I saw the two of you in that room."

"You believe him capable, then?"

"Of killing? Yeah. Any one of your brothers is capable." The man had a fair enough point with that. "For that matter, so am I, and I have."

"I remember. That wasn't my question. Do you think he could murder the woman he loved?"

"No. But…" Cole grimaced, pain creasing his features.

Jane tensed at his pause.

"When things get heated, sometimes things happen on accident."

She released her breath when the truth of his words sank in. He wasn't talking about Mike, he was talking about his own past. "Oh, Cole. This is different. Yours was an instant, a heartbeat. Choking someone to death takes a long time. You have to look into the eyes of the person and watch their life fade away by your own doing."

His hands unclenched. A long breath that seemed to come from the depth of his soul released. "Then no. Even drunk, he couldn'ta."

"Thank you."

"Thank you."

"For what?"

"An instant. A heartbeat."

She set her hands on his, moving closer. The reminders of his late wife were few and far between, but when they happened his guilt always lingered deep and true. "It was. You were defending your life."

"Shoulda been defending hers."

"You were doing that, too."

"I failed."

"But you've not failed me. Not ever. You saved me."

"You saved me right back."

No one feels another's grief,
no one understands another's joy.
People imagine they can reach one another.
In reality they only pass each other by.
-Franz Schubert

Cole stood closer to the grave than he had at any funeral that had ever happened in camp. Right next to the hole, with the mound of dirt to be tossed back in on his other side. Jane leaned into him, but otherwise remained still. Charlie stood immediately to his right, his head lowered, hands clenched in front of him.

Reverend Lyons finished his prayer. A murmur of 'amen' went through the gathered crowd. Reverend Greene stepped forward to hand the shovel to Jane. She didn't reach for it. Instead, she turned her gaze to Cole. She couldn't mean he should go first. Her nod and subtle shift to the side indicated that she did, in fact, think he should go first.

Cole grabbed the shovel, digging into the dirt to toss onto the coffin. When he'd finished, he handed it to Jane. She did the same, if with less strength. After she'd handed the shovel to Charlie, she turned and walked away from the grave.

He noticed that as she wove through the crowd, she brushed off every attempt at comfort or conversation. Cole took off behind her, not surprised when Charlie came up on his side.

"I'm going to head back home to Millie and George." Charlie paused to eye his sister's departure. "Take care of her. I'll visit tomorrow."

"Always do." Cole jogged after Jane, catching her arm before she could make it around the corner. "Jane."

When she turned to face him, her eyes shimmered with tears that refused to fall. "He should be there. He loved her, no matter what was going on, he loved her. Now he can't even say goodbye. He's locked in that cell and can't say goodbye."

Cole had no idea what to say or do to help. "Sally and Tom'll fix it."

"It'll be too late by then." Her gaze swept back to the funeral. "Not one soul has bothered to support him, or believe in his innocence. He might as well be as lowly as Guy or Jackson for all they've bothered to care."

"Jane." Cole groaned when she took off like a shot. A quick glance behind him revealed the reason for her haste. Kathy, Leanne, and Cora headed straight for him. When Leanne called after Jane, Cole moved to block their chase. "Don't."

"We need to talk to her." Leanne focused behind him toward Jane's departing form. "She shouldn't be dealing with this alone."

"What am I, then?" Cole folded his arms across his chest, glaring at his half-sister.

"Cole, please." Kathy set a hand on his arm. "She's refusing to listen to any of us. You know she's being stubborn."

"She's hurting," Cole corrected. "And if none of you can say you know her brother didn't murder Daisy, then don't bother even trying."

Kathy sighed. "It isn't that simple."

"It is to her." Cole took a step back, ready to go after her. "Believe me, I'd rather let you all help me help her, but all you're gonna do is upset her more."

He turned away from their protest to return to the apartment. When he entered, Jane sat at the desk writing a letter. Clara curled in her lap, patting Jane's arm in a soothing fashion. Whiskey curled around Jane's feet. Ada was on the couch with Colton, a worried gaze on Jane.

Cole crossed to her side. Rather than rile her immediately, he brushed his fingers along Clara's curls instead of Jane's. "Who are you writing?"

"I'm finishing my letter to Al. I'd like you to drop it at the depot for me, if you don't mind."

He felt a measure of concern for her avoidance of the depot where Kathy could usually be round. "You won't even go to the depot?"

"No. I don't feel much like going anywhere."

He couldn't help himself, he leaned down to kiss the top of her head. Not even his usual jealousy of any mention of Al flared through his concern for her spirits. "If you want me to drop it off, I will."

She folded the letter with care, sealing the envelope with some water. "Mike's parent's will be arriving next week. We'll need to arrange a room for them near Tom's."

"Of course." He chose not to comment as her referring to them as Mike's parents instead of her own. Instead, he knelt beside her. "What can I do? I don't have a clue here."

"You're already doing it." Her hand settled on his cheek. For the first time in days, a soft smile graced her features. "There's nothing else you need to do. I apologize if that makes you feel useless, but I promise you are more useful than you know."

He brushed his lips across hers. "So long as you tell me if there's more I can do."

"I will. Now, miss Clara. You've been so kind." Jane kissed her daughter's forehead. "But your mama has to go to work. Why don't you see if Willow and Jay want to play dice?"

Ada groaned, her head dropping back. "Oh dear. I'm no good at that. Jay finds my failure rather amusing."

Jane chuckled low. "I'm aware. It's like the amusement Cole gets from the fact that all these years later I'm still no good at poker. These men and their games."

Cole plucked Clara from Jane's lap so she didn't try to lift the girl. He tossed Clara in the air, grinning as she giggled wildly. "You play. We'll be back soon."

Ada nodded. "We'll be in the restaurant around one for lunch. That is Alma's time, yes?"

"It certainly is." Jane smiled at the governess before heading to the door. Soon as the door closed, she spoke low. "Ada is working out quite well. The children all seem to like her."

"Except Willow." He frowned, glancing back at the room. Willow had come to flat out avoid Ada whenever she was in the apartment. "Have we figured out what that's about?"

"No idea." At the top of the stairs to the pit, she paused. The room was fairly crowded for a Thursday morning, but seeing as many people had gone to the funeral, it wasn't a total surprise. Jane squeezed his hand as her gaze wandered through the crowd. A bright, if fake, smile crossed her lips before she descended the steps.

Moments later, the smile became more genuine as she got to the bar. Cole had no doubt in his mind why.

"Mr. Hamm. You're looking much better today. A good dose of Cora's stew truly does heal all ailments." She kissed the man on the cheek.

Hammy nodded. "It sure does."

"I'm glad to see you." She remained at his side in a half hug.

Cole circled to get behind the bar. "Need a refresher, Hammy?"

At the mere suggestion, Hammy drained the remaining half of his beer. "Sure wouldn't mind."

"As if you had to ask," Jane scolded. At least for the moment she didn't look to be on the verge of misery, so he'd take the scolding.

"Lady Jane." Hammy set his beer drinking hand on hers. "Wanted to let ya know, I don't think Mike did nothing. He's a good man."

Tears sparkled in Jane's eyes, but her smile remained in place. "Thank you, Gilbert. I wish more thought like you."

Hammy blushed under her follow-up kiss to his cheek. "Just bein' honest."

"I know, and I appreciate it. Now drink your beer."

Cole eyed her as she came around his side of the bar. "You good?"

"Better, not good." She poured several drinks and handed them out before the guests could even ask. For an all-too-brief moment everything felt like it had returned to normal. Far too soon, all hint of joy or humor drained from her features. "Get out of my casino."

"Jane." David's voice emerged through the low murmur of conversation.

"I said get out." Jane backed away from the bar and made a beeline for the exit near Cole.

David raced her there, reaching the end of the bar right as Jane passed behind Cole. When she skidded to a stop, David's brow furrowed. "Please, Jane. I just want to talk."

"Is it about Jesse?"

"No."

"Then get out." She raced out onto the floor too quick for either of them to catch her.

Cole moved to stand in front of David when he got set to make chase. "What do you need her for?"

"I just wanted to see if she's all right."

"And?" He wasn't stupid enough to believe that was all David wanted.

"I had a couple of questions for her."

"Thought so." Cole rubbed his hand over his face. A quick glance told him Jane had been stopped by Graham. The pair carried on conversation animatedly. Jane's mood seemed improved by whatever the new mayor was saying. "I'll talk to her, but I've never seen her this mad at you. Even when you arrested her."

"I know." David sighed deeply. "Tell her…I don't even know."

"That you don't believe Mike did it? That's all she wants to hear, you know."

"I do. I don't want to believe it, if that helps." David rubbed the back of his neck. "Lewis is delayed and won't be here until after Christmas. I'm hoping Tom comes up with something other than Sally's deal with the cigarettes."

Cole only grunted acknowledgment. He thought Sally had a point, but the fact that those could have been there any time was a problem. After the distraction, he waved off David to approach Jane and Graham. He nodded to his friend. "Mayor."

"Shut the hell up." Graham chortled as he shook Cole's hand.

"What? You've been mayor for a couple of weeks now. Best get used to being called it." Cole grinned, then winked at Jane.

"Don't know that I will." Graham set a hand on Jane's shoulder. "Janey's setting me up at the roulette wheel since the Silver room isn't open for a couple of days."

"He was just telling me he doesn't think Mike could have done this, even if Michael did once break his nose." Jane's smile had returned.

"You broke my nose once, too." Graham touched the bridge of his nose. "Glad you haven't felt I've needed it in a while. Too bad Cole can't say the same."

Cole fought the urge to touch his own still healing nose. The bruising had faded, and it almost felt back to normal.

"Leastwise this time I had someone to set it straight instead of your fool attempts."

"I didn't care enough to set it straight." Graham held out his arm to Jane. "Don't see your woman complaining, none."

"Careful, Graham." Jane led him through the crowd toward the roulette table. Once again her mood had been lightened, but it could turn again at any time.

When she returned behind the bar, she held out a finger before he could say a word. "I don't want to hear it. He didn't have to arrest him."

"You weren't this mad at him when he arrested you."

"That was justified, or so I thought. This was not."

"You're gonna have no friends left, you keep this up."

"If they don't believe in his innocence, then maybe they weren't friends."

"Thought you were better at logic than that."

"Logic matters little in matters of the heart." She snatched a towel to start cleaning a glass.

"Who said that?"

"I did."

Some natural sorrow, loss, or pain
That has been, and may be again?
-William Wordsworth

Cole tucked the letter addressed to Jane in his pocket. He once again had to suppress jealousy over the sender. It would do him no good for Jane to figure out it still irked him. She made it a point to remind him that it had been several years since Al had proposed to her, and he'd moved on and been married. Even if his brain knew it, Cole couldn't get rid of the annoyance over their continued friendship.

He hadn't gotten halfway across the platform to leave when Kathy called out behind him. "Cole. Wait."

He really wanted to get back to the Inn to see how Jane's visit with Mike went. Still, he stopped. If nothing else he could divert her from approaching Jane until he was sure of her mood. When he turned, he could tell Kathy'd been crying. "Kathy."

"I—How's Jane?"

"Not good." He glanced down the street to where he could see the Inn peeking over the top of Kathy's home. "She went to visit Mike this morning. Once she knew David wasn't watching, she felt she could go. Took her near four days to make it there."

"Oh. Good. I mean that she could visit. I, oh…"

"She's not talking to Davie, neither. Won't talk to no one that doesn't think Mike's innocent. Pretty damn sure she woulda cut me off if I hadn't believed it."

Kat swiped some tears from her face. Her kerchief worried between her fingers. "I suppose I can't blame her. If it was her…"

"It was her."

She lifted her gaze in surprise. "What?"

"Five years ago, right at this same time, she was arrested. Remember?"

"How could I forget?"

"You all defended her even though she might've been guilty. Told her it wasn't her, it was Clara. Now that it's Mike, and you've known him longer than you knew her then, you can't bother to say the same."

"That isn't fair."

"Isn't it?" Cole took a few steps back. "Tom isn't giving Leanne a boo, either. The Young's? They stick together."

He hopped off the platform to head home. Along the way he exchanged greetings as Jane had taught him. When he spotted her on the porch, he stopped dead.

Her eyes were turned up toward the cloudless sky. Seemingly without awareness, her hands ran along the small swell that had formed there with her pregnancy. It seemed a peaceful moment, but it wasn't. There was a tremor in her hands, and her eyelids fluttered closed more than normal.

Something was even more wrong than it had been for the past week.

The closer he got, the more he noticed she seemed paler than usual. Her lean on the post somehow felt a necessity rather than casual. When her head moved slightly he could spot the glimmer of a tear.

Panic seized his heart until it pounded fierce as anything. He raced forward, willing away the sudden lump in his throat. "Jane? Is something wrong with Mike?"

She offered a subtle shake of her head. A wobble in her chin preceded her clearing her throat. When she finally turned her gaze on him, an eerie calm lie there despite the tears shimmering in her eyes. "I believe I need to go to the clinic."

"Jane." He raced up the steps to pull her close. "What is it?"

"It's happening again." Her lip trembled fiercely. Her nostrils flared, but not a single tear escaped her hold. "I'm losing our child. I'm sorry."

"I..." His throat stopped working at that point. Dread coursed through him until he felt almost numb. It had to be a mistake. "Are you sure?"

"I've been bleeding, and I'm having pains." She pulled herself free of his hold. Her hands trembled as she smoothed them over her hair. "Bonnie isn't back in town, so we'll have to see Andrew. Let's go see if I'm correct."

He couldn't move a muscle for nothing. This couldn't be happening again. Not now. Not with everything else. Jane was holding on by a thread as it was. "No."

"Saying no will change nothing." She skirted around him to descend the steps. When she spoke again, her voice trembled. "You don't have to come along. I wouldn't ask you to sit through it."

That stirred him back into motion. He quick-stepped to catch up to her. "What's that supposed to mean?"

"I know how difficult it is for you." The last words squeaked as if she'd choked on them.

"You too." He had to stop short when she turned to face him.

She stubbornly clung onto her tears so not one fell. Once again her lip trembled, and though she opened her mouth to speak, no words emerged.

"I told you long ago." He cupped her cheek gently. "I'm all in. Even for the moments we hate, I'm not going anywhere."

Her eyes closed, forcing a few tears free. She dropped her head to his chest. After a few seconds, she lifted her head again. "Not now. We don't…it may not…let's go see."

He held her in place long enough to kiss her forehead.

She entered the clinic with barely a knock. "Dr. Cross?"

Andrew rose with a smile. "Hello Jane, Cole."

Cole barely managed a nod.

Seeming to sense the mood, Andrew's smile faded as he looked between them. "Is there something I can help you with?"

Jane cleared her throat. "I'll need you to examine me. I believe I'm having a miscarriage."

Andrew stared at her in silence for a moment before moving forward. He clasped Jane's hand. "I'm so sorry. Please, come in the exam room and we'll see what's going on."

Cole followed Jane into the room. While she got settled, he stayed close. The moment she lay down he clasped her hand in his. He held her gaze as he ran his free hand over her hair. "It's going to be nothing."

"I wish I could believe that." Her hand clasped his back, tightening when the doctor began the exam. Rather than keep looking at him, she kept her gaze on the ceiling. The tears that had made her eyes shimmer a few minutes before appeared to have dried. Her lips thinned into a tight line, and she spoke not another word for the whole thing.

He did his best to control his own inner agony. Her current lack of emotion or reaction made it worse. The first time she'd been pregnant and lost their child he'd expected her to disappear, had almost hoped for it so he wouldn't have to feel. This time he swore she was disappearing before his eyes, and the thought of that killed him. He murmured low in her ear, "Stay with me, Jane. Please. Stay with me."

A splash of water startled Cole. Andrew cleared his throat. "I'm so sorry, Jane. Cole."

Jane jolted at the voice, but then went still again. She stared at the ceiling still, her voice now soft, weak. "Thank you, Doctor."

"I can give you some medicine to help."

"No. I've been through this before. Thank you."

Cole pulled her to sit when the door shut, settling himself between her knees. He cupped her face in his hands. "Jane? Don't you go giving up on me. You proved it wasn't too much."

"What if this time it is?" Her hands settled on his, the tears back full force, slipping down her cheeks. "I'm so sorry I failed you."

"What?" He stepped back in surprise of her apology. "What do you mean by that?"

"You know what I mean."

"You didn't do anything wrong." He moved even closer to press his forehead to hers. "Only way you could fail me is if you gave up this time. You're stronger than this. You know you are."

"How can you be so sure?"

"Because the woman I know, the woman I love is the strongest I've ever known."

"Even the strongest have their breaking point."

"Last time you didn't have anything and you fought."

Her eyes fluttered shut. "So?"

"You've got more to fight for this time." He brushed his thumb along her jaw as he embraced her neck with his hand. When her eyes opened again, he nodded. "You've got me. You've got our kids that love you and would be lost without you."

"I don't feel so strong right now."

Cole thought for sure his heart broke in two at the utter defeat in her tone. "Let's go home. We can grieve together this time. We'll take care of you. All of us will."

"Our child—our baby." A deep sob welled out of her. She collapsed against him.

"I know," he murmured. While she wept, he pulled her as close as he could, allowing her to release her grief into him.

Another child lost, to be buried far too soon. The curse he'd thought he lived with had seemed so far away once the twins were born. He'd been so happy and content. Wet racks of tears formed on his own cheeks. He let himself grieve with her, holding her close as they both shook.

He had no idea how much time had passed when a door closed nearby, startling them both from their hold on each other. He offered her his handkerchief to dry her tears until they could get home. Satisfied she was together enough, he offered his hand.

She took it, but didn't move. "Would you carry me?"

The request sent another pang of worry to his heart. Jane hated to appear weak to anyone. She walked on her own unless absolutely impossible. "What?"

"Please?"

"Whatever you need." He said it automatically, and meant it. Still, the burning concern made him almost unable to scoop her into his arms. It went against his better judgment, but they'd both longed for this child, and she would likely be bedbound until the miscarriage was complete.

He picked her up easily, holding her close to him. "You're gonna get through this. You've got to."

She didn't respond, only nestled in closer to him.

His nerves taut, he got her outside. As he headed toward the Inn, he spotted Kat walking their way. He shook his head at her before she could say whatever she opened her mouth to say. Kat stopped short, looking from him to Jane, concern puckering herbrow.

Cole carried Jane around the building so they could enter directly into their apartment without any questions from the patrons. He got her inside, and into their room. The moment he kicked the door shut behind him, her sobs rented the air again.

Always before he'd known they could fix it, even when they nearly lost the Inn in a fire. In Jane's current state, he worried that perhaps they wouldn't be able to.

*Friends show their love-in times of trouble,
not in happiness.
-Euripides*

The bell rang above the bed. Jane didn't want to know what it was, or who it was. She didn't want to move, or for Cole to leave. She curled tighter against him so he wouldn't move.

The past three days she hadn't left the room. Two days prior the baby had been expelled, and Cole had seen to burying their child in the back near the barn, with a stone to mark the spot. Eventually she would go out to see him, but for the moment she didn't want to move.

Cole kept telling her to be strong, repeated so often it had become his mantra. She knew she needed to be, so many needed her. Yet, she couldn't force herself to push through any of it.

The bell rang again. This time Cole moved. "If I don't answer, they'll keep ringing."

"Fine." She couldn't put in the effort to argue with him to stay. She wasn't much worth staying for any longer anyway. When he shifted away, she turned over, curling into a ball. His soft kiss to her shoulder reassured her that he hadn't fully given up on her yet. Not that she'd blame him at all if he did.

The playful cheers of the children and barking from the dogs that rang into the room in the brief time the door was open only served to make her pull the blanket over her head. All she wanted to do was burrow under the covers forever.

The worst feeling of all was her own bodies betrayal. She'd felt and witnessed the baby leaving her body, but her body couldn't seem to get the message the child was gone. Her stomach still swelled, her breasts ached. Her heart kept reaching for the child that wasn't there.

A deep sob erupted, the tears flowing before she could begin to try to stop them.

The noise from the other room interrupted her solitude again for several long moments before the door blessedly shut again.

A hand settled on her shoulder, another on her hip, and a third on her calf. Jane startled out of her sobs at the multitude of hands. With one hand she pushed back the edge of the blanket to find Kat looking down at her, tears in her friends eyes.

All of Jane's anger flew away at the sight of her friend. She sat faster than she'd moved in days to throw her arms around Kat's neck. She clung to her as another hug came from behind, and warm hands clasped hers. In that moment she knew all three of her friends were there with her.

"I—can't—do—this," Jane cried, hiccupping between each word.

"Of course you can," Leanne soothed. "You're one of the strongest women I've ever met. You'll get through this, and the next thing, and the one after that."

"And you won't do it alone, either." This from Cora, who kept a firm hold of Jane's hand when she pulled free of Kat's hug. "You've got Cole, and you've got us."

"No matter if you're still mad at us. It won't sway us one bit. You need us now." Kat wiped tears from Jane's cheeks. "We are still, and will always be, your friends."

"How'd you convince him to let you in?" Jane sniffled, managing to speak without sobbing through it this time.

"Didn't give him much of a choice." Cora pointed to a tray at the foot of the bed. "I told him you wouldn't get your food if he didn't let us in."

"I think he was happy to let us." Leanne rested her head on Jane's shoulder. "You've been in here for days now, as has Cole. Tom had to tell us what was going on."

Kat cleared her throat. "All right. We are going to get some food in you, then get you a good relaxing soak in the tub."

"No." Jane shook her head. "The food is fine. Cole will be upset if you're the one giving me a bath."

Kat laughed heartily. "There's our Jane. True enough. We'll get you dressed anyhow. Let's open the windows to get some sunshine in here. We'll get you through this, Jane. I promise."

"Thank you. I'm sorry I…"

"Hush." Cora carried the tray over to the small table under the window. "It's of no matter now. We don't deserve your apologies, you deserve ours."

Jane found herself on her feet, her clothes being changed before she could begin to form any sort of protest. The cheer and warm support of the women around her worked on the stupor of depression until she began to feel more coherent. Dressed in a simple chore dress, sitting at the table with a large bowl of stew before her, her shoulders relaxed for the first time in ages.

"Eat," Cora urged. "Based on what's been brought back to the kitchen, you've hardly eaten a thing in days."

"I haven't. My stomach is in knots." Jane pushed a few potatoes around with her spoon. After a pointed look from Cora, she scooped some meat on her spoon and took a bite. The warmth and rich flavor of the stew stimulated her hunger.

When she dove in with several more bites, Kat smiled. "That's more like it."

Leanne hopped to the edge of the bed. "You always said Cora's stew could cure a great many ails."

"There are many it can, but a few it can only temper." Jane's stomach turned again and she dropped her spoon.

"None of that. Keep eating." Kat took a brush to Jane's tangled mass of curls. "Cora was saying that Arthur will be home shortly after Thanksgiving for six weeks."

"Thanksgiving. I'd forgotten." Jane didn't mention that at the moment she didn't feel very thankful. That seemed selfish with the large family she had sitting just beyond the door.

"I'll be cooking, and if I remember correctly your mother is of the sort that will insist on helping." Cora's smile warmed. "She'll be here in a few days."

Jane had forgotten that, too. She seemed to have forgotten everything outside of the four walls she had hidden within. Rather than daring to broach the subject, she turned to other things. "How are the children? Your girls, Katherine. Isaac. Jesse."

"We all went ice skating out on the lake the other day. I worried it hadn't become cold enough to hold us all, but it did." Kat kept working on Jane's hair as she spoke. "I believe that is the one time I wish I had all the layers of petticoats to protect myself. I swear I bruised my tail with how often I fell."

Cora laughed with her. "I remember you being much better when you were younger."

"Unfortunately, I'm out of practice and fell more than I skated. I got marginally better after a time, but it wasn't fun for a while there."

Jane finished off her stew. Her scalp tingled under Kat's attempts to style her hair, the soothing sensation trailing down her spine. With a soft sigh, she picked up the tea to take a sip.

Under her friends ministrations and distractions, nearly an hour passed. They continued with gossip and stories from town until they slowly departed. Cora first, for she had to take care of cooking for the dinner rush. Then Leanne, so that the brothel might open for business on time. That left Jane with Kat alone, now sitting opposite her at the small table.

Kat grasped her hand tight. "I'm so sorry, Jane. I was so looking forward to us going through all of this together. I would understand if you don't wish to see me."

"I remain happy for you. I know how long you've waited for this joy." Jane's lip trembled despite her words. "That will not stop me being sad, but it won't change."

"Forgive me. For doubting Mike's innocence."

"I will." Jane lowered her gaze. "When you believe his innocence."

"I do. Your husband made a valid point to me the other day."

For that, Jane lifted her gaze. "He did?"

"Yes. He pointed out how much we'd all supported you, and now we've done the opposite with Mike." She pulled Jane's hand close to her heart. "I trust your belief in his innocence."

Jane collapsed into a strong hug with her friend. "Thank you."

"You are, first and foremost, my friend. I should have remembered that." Kat took a deep breath, releasing the hug. "I should let him back in here. Two of us have left already. You know the man is fretting something fierce out there."

"You're probably right. Thank you."

"No thanks needed."

"Would you tell him I'd like a bath?"

"Of course." Kat kissed her cheek, then darted from the room.

Jane set about cleaning up the tea she and Kat had shared. It was several minutes before the door opened again. Cole entered with Colton on his hip. Worry lined his brow as he studied her. "Someone was demanding to see you. Hope that's all right."

"Of course it is." Jane crossed the room to take the boy in her arms. Her wrist smarted during the transfer, but she didn't care. Holding one of the children right then seemed like the most important thing. She curled him close against her, kissing his dark curls as he snuggled into her chest. She lifted her gaze to Cole's. "Thank you."

He breathed out a gust of air. "Thought you'd be mad, but they wouldn't let me say no."

"I'm not mad. I'm hurting and infinitely sad, but I'm not angry. Not with you." She grabbed his hand. "Would you draw me a bath? I need to clean the d-e-a-t-h off me."

He kissed her forehead, lingering there for an extra few seconds. "You're coming back to me."

"I'm trying."

"Thought I'd lost ya."

"You almost did, I think." She lifted her lips to meet his kiss. "I'll be right there."

She sat on the edge of the bed with Colton still in her arms. The boy played with the buttons on her dress. She smoothed her hand along his back. "Have you been good for Miss Ada, Colton? I'm sorry I was in here so long."

"Mama." He hugged her tight. "Come play."

"I will. In a little while. I need to get cleaned up first." She cupped his small face in her hands, then kissed the tip of his nose. "I need to see all of my children, I think. We'll spend tonight all together. Do you think you can convince Sally to join us for tonight?"

Colton's bright eyes stared at her with wisdom well beyond his near-three years. He nodded solemnly. "She scared. Me scared."

"I'm so sorry I scared you all. I promise, tonight it's just us." She kissed his forehead and lifted him down to the floor. "Go on. I'll be out soon."

When he toddled on out of the room, she shut the door behind him. She turned to find Cole watching her from the doorway to the bath room. He held out his hand. "I've got your bath ready for you."

"I think I misspoke."

He frowned. "How's that?"

"I wanted you to draw a bath…for us."

A smile broke through his concern. "Think you can handle it?"

"I will make my best effort to do so."

"There's my Jane."

The one who cannot restrain their anger
will wish undone, what their temper
and irritation prompted them to do.
-Horace

Jane studied her features in the mirror. She'd added some rouge to her cheeks to add life, but still appeared tired and wan. Everything lately took enormous effort, except when she was around her family.

Part of her still wanted to curl up under the covers until spring. Her children deserved more, Cole deserved more. On top of that, the Young's were due in the next day to support Michael through his arrest.

Thanksgiving was too soon, and Christmas right around the corner. Due issues in other counties and the lack of a judge in town, Michael was expected to remain in the jail until after Christmas. She hadn't seen him since before she'd lost the child, and had asserted that she would go see him today, before their parents arrived.

All she had to do was gather the strength to get up and go. The door opened, but no loud ruckus filtered in.

"Kids went to eat," Cole said by way of greeting. His hands settled on her shoulders. "I told them you'd be along after you went to see Mike."

She reached up to grasp his arms. "He'll know something is wrong. I can't seem to make myself look presentable."

"Because you look beautiful. The sadness is in your eyes." He kissed the top of her head. "Don't stay long. You don't want him worrying."

"I know I don't." She released a sigh and moved to stand. When he folded her into a hug, she sank into him willingly. Together they'd spent time with family, and each other the past couple of nights. Each small moment helped patch her back together, but she felt a long way off from healed. Her corset pinched too tight, and she gasped. "Damn this thing."

"What? What's wrong?"

"It's been several days, but my corset still pinches." Her hand to her side, she took a few breaths until the pain passed.

"Should you go see the doc?"

"No. It'll pass. Perhaps I put it on too soon." She leaned up to kiss him. "I'd best go. The quicker I go, the more likely I'll be able to eat before the children leave the restaurant."

"Sure you don't want me to go with you?" He tucked a finger under her chin. "I can distract the sheriff so he doesn't bother you."

"I'm perfectly capable of telling my ex-husband to back off." She walked with him to the door where she grabbed the basket sitting beside it. "I'll be fine. I won't be long."

He kissed her forehead. "I'll be in the casino. Tom's at the saloon."

"I know. I'll stop and see you after I've eaten." When she turned, he set her cape on her shoulders. "Thank you."

She stepped out into the cold, crisp air for the first time in days. A light snow had fallen the night before. The thin layer crunched under her feet as she went around the chicken coop to reach the path behind the barn. A smooth stone on the ground drew her eye even as she tried to avoid it.

Jane crouched beside the barn despite her better judgement. The small smooth stone had some flakes on top of it, which she dusted off. "I should give you a name. A good, strong name."

She set her hand on the stone that by Cole's account was larger than the tiny form he'd buried beneath it. "I'll think on it."

Her throat closed, her eyes burning with tears she didn't want to shed. She closed her eyes to offer a small prayer over the small grave before she rose. A glance over her shoulder told her Cole hadn't moved from the door, his strong gaze watching her carefully. She smiled in what she hoped he'd see as reassurance before circling the barn to head to the next street.

While she might have wanted to curl in bed until spring and mourn until she could mourn no longer, life didn't afford such luxuries. She'd learned that lesson long ago, even if she wanted to forget it more often than not at the moment.

When Jane entered the jail, she didn't bother to spare a glance at David. She went right to the cell where Michael sat hunched on a cot. He looked so defeated, her heart broke all over again. She cleared her throat. "Michael? I brought you some vanity cakes from Cora, and a few apples."

Mike lifted his head slow. He'd cleaned up since she'd last seen him. Then he'd still been out of sorts from his drinking binge. Now he was clean shaven, and had fresh clothes on. He blinked a few times before rising. "Jane? I—I thought you'd given up on me."

"No, of course I haven't." She lowered her gaze as he approached so he couldn't see what Cole said lingered in her eyes. "I had something to attend to."

He rushed across the cell. One hand reached through the bar to settle on hers. "What is it? What's happened?"

"Never you mind." She did her best to deflect the question. The focus should be on him. "It's you we must worry about in the end. Have you spoken to Thomas and Sally?"

"Yes, a couple days ago. Jane, what happened?" A bit of desperation raised his tone. "Tell me. You know you can't lie and say you're fine. I'll know."

"Michael."

"Please. I can't focus one more minute on what's happened, what I don't remember, or the fact that Daisy is…gone."

She lowered her head until her forehead pressed to the bars. Her heart clenched to say it again, but she did. "I had a miscarriage. My baby is gone."

"What?"

"What?" The familiar voice of David interrupted their conversation. "Jane, are you all right?"

She glared daggers over her shoulder. "It's none of your concern, Sheriff. I wasn't speaking to you."

"Oh Clarabelle." Mike's soft tone drew her gaze back to him. "I'm so sorry."

"I know. We all are." She blinked rapid against rising tears. "Now, do you truly still not remember anything?"

"Jane, please." Mike groaned his way into the chair opposite her. "I told you, I can't discuss it any longer."

"I'm sorry. I haven't seen you for several days." She deposited the basket on the floor before taking the seat on her side of the bars. "I wanted to be certain there was no update."

"I'm beginning to see why it bothered you so much that we checked so often to see if you remembered anything from your past." His fingers clenched in his hair. "The last thing I remember is the second bottle of whiskey the night after you kicked me out of the saloon."

"You told me you were going home to sober up. When you left I thought you were much improved. Still hurting, still angry, but you were making steps in the right direction."

He released his hair to meet her gaze. "I had it in my mind to go home and dunk my head in the trough. You talked sense into me. I remember that."

"What changed?"

"I can't remember." He closed his eyes. Turmoil rippled across his features before he groaned in frustration. "I've been trying, but everything is fuzzy, disconnected. I don't remember what is real and present, or what is past, or even my imagination."

She clasped his hand in hers. "We'll figure it out. You've only just recently sobered. Trust Thomas and Sally to put the pieces together. We have to. Remember, Lewis is the sort that wants justice, and won't jump to conclusion like some people."

He looked over her shoulder where David sat. "He was doing his job."

"Lewis is a fair man. Hopefully the judge that comes is as well. We'll tell them the truth. Nicholas will put the truth before the judge. There is no way you did this. Tell me you believe that. If you don't believe it, all is lost."

His deep blue eyes sought hers. Tears welled until one spilled over. "I don't know anymore. I was so hurt and angry. Is it possible?"

"No. It isn't. You love her still. No matter how bad she hurt you, you love her." She brushed some tears from his cheeks. "Remember that. We all know you aren't capable of harming someone you love with such malicious intent as this murder."

"How can you?"

"The same way you knew that I murdered no one when I had no memory to speak of. I know your soul. You couldn't do this."

He released a slow, deep sigh. "I did believe."

"Even when I doubted, you believed for me. Now, it is my turn to believe for you."

"Thank you."

"Promise me you'll fight. For your memories back. Against this charge. Fight."

"I may have already messed that up by saying what I did when David came for me." He took a shaky breath. "But I will fight."

"Good. Ma and Pa will be here tomorrow. We'll all help you fight."

Mike nodded, but said nothing else. Jane encouraged him to take some food, then did the same for him that her friends had done for hers just a couple days before. She offered distraction in the form of gossip and stories. By the time she knew she had to leave, he was in slightly better spirits. Considering he remained in the cell, she couldn't blame him.

"I'll be back tomorrow. Do you have any requests?"

"Some books to occupy some time would be nice."

"Books I can do. I'm good at that." She clasped his hands once more, then left the basket on the chair beside the cell. She stormed right past the desk outside.

"Jane." David caught her arm. "Wait, please."

"I don't want to hear it, David."

"Please. Don't you think it pains me to have him in there? To know I put him there?"

"No, I don't. You put him in there without investigating a single other person. You didn't even try. Once he said he didn't remember, perhaps he could have in drunkenness, you brought him in here and locked him behind bars."

"I had no choice."

"You always have a choice." She pulled her arm free of his grasp. "You waited to arrest me even after seeing the poster. For months."

"He all but confessed, Jane."

She spun to face him, ready to let him have it, but the sorrow in his features made her pause. The man looked ten years older in his grief. "All *but* confessed, David. I'm sorry, I cannot forgive your haste in this matter."

"He is my friend, and I hate what's happened."

"You should." Jane backed away from him. "I must get back to my family."

David offered no other protest as she walked away. Jane straightened her shoulders against the renewed grief. She didn't care to be fighting with David, after all they shared a son together. They'd also always been close. At the moment things were too raw for forgiveness.

Jane made it through the quiet apartment to the casino. Cole stood behind the bar helping the customers. In moments he caught sight of her. His anxious gaze swept over her as she approached. "You doing all right?"

"Fine as can be expected." Rather than scold him, she wrapped her arms around his neck. "Your concern is appreciated."

"I got a right."

"I know. I don't need to be checked on constantly, though."

"Then pretend Kathy stopping by is a coincidence."

"You are impossible."

"Aw, you love me."

"With all my soul."

Suspicion is not less an enemy to virtue than happiness; he that is already corrupt is naturally suspicious, and he that becomes suspicious will quickly become corrupt.
-Samuel Johnson

Sally glanced at the clock for the tenth time. She still had almost half an hour before she had to be at Nick's office. A knock on the door interrupted her attempts to go through her notes again. "Damn it."

"Sally?" Jane's voice was quiet, with a note of concern.

"Yes. Come in, Ma." She glared down at the mess of her notes rather than raise her head to greet Jane. "Hey, Ma."

"You look fit to be tied, what's wrong?"

"I thought I'd organize my notes, but I tore them all out to do so and now I don't know how to put them back together."

"You made yourself a puzzle of your own thoughts."

"A puzzle?" Sally straightened, taking in the cluster of papers in front of her again. "Interesting. That might do something."

A low chuckle sounded from the door.

Sally lifted her gaze finally to see Jane smiling. It was a good sight to see, as she'd been so distraught for days. "What are you laughing at?"

"Once again, you've reminded me of…well, me. Or Clara. Maybe both of us." Jane leaned on the door frame, the laughter fading slightly. "Clara loved puzzles. I enjoy them to a point, although Clara's were a bit much."

"You said her letters were full of puzzles."

"Many, many. She was trying to help her brother while hiding the truth from a madman so many of her puzzles were frustratingly vague."

"You figured them out, though. I just need to do the same with this." Sally stood to look down at them. "I need to write them better, but first I have to get them organized."

"You will. I think you're trying too hard. You could ask for help, too. What about your friend, Molly?"

"She went out of town for Thanksgiving. Possibly on a job. She was pretty vague." Sally spread the pages out wider, moving a few around. "I'm sorry. I'm distracted. Did you need something?"

"I only wanted to make sure you were planning to meet the Young's at the train with the rest of us."

"Hm? Oh, yeah. I'm going over to Uncle Nick's in a little bit, and we're all going over together once we're done."

"Wonderful. We'll see you there, then." Jane wrapped an arm around Sally's shoulders. "You're trying too hard. Step back for a few minutes. The notes won't go anywhere."

"You're right. I should probably head over to Uncle Nick's anyway. The wind is pretty fierce right now. Hope it slows down before the train gets here or there's going to be a large group of grumpy people on the platform."

"You'll be on the platform. I'll wait in the office if it remains like this."

Sally laughed along with her. "I think you've got the right idea, Ma."

"I usually do."

When Jane left, Sally took one last glance over the notes before giving it up to grab her things. She really wished she hadn't torn apart her notebooks before this meeting, her memory wasn't near as good as Jane's.

Sally threw on her muffler and coat, scrambling down the stairs. She spotted the tail end of Jane's skirt disappearing into the bedroom. The low murmur of Cole drifted out in the moments before the door closed.

Sally flushed, knowing what the couple were likely doing. She wondered if she'd ever feel such stimulation as she'd once told Jane she wanted. While she'd been getting the hang of flirtation, not one soul had caught her fancy yet.

When she came around the edge of the barn into the open, the wind buffeted her a few steps. Though the walk to Nick's office wasn't far, she was going to be frozen to the bone before she arrived, she just knew it. She didn't understand why they couldn't have had this meeting in her room or Tommy's. If they'd done that, she never would have had to step into the biting winds to freeze only to get warm again.

At Nick's office, she gave a quick knock before stepping inside. "My goodness, it's freezing out there."

"Have some tea." Nick gestured to the nearby stove. He and Tom were huddled around it. "It'll help warm you up. Grab a chair on the way."

"Thank you." Sally dragged a chair over before setting about making her tea. Once seated, she glanced between them. "Well?"

"You first." Tom slurped his tea. He ignored her exasperation to flip through his notebook.

Guilt for the destroyed notebook sitting at home rather than secure in her hands gnawed her. She frowned. "No fair."

"You're the one learning." Tom grinned over at his brother. "You know she caught the cigarettes at Daisy's place all on her own? She's got a keen eye."

"So you've said. Let's give her a chance to show it, shall we?" Nick shook his head at Tom before turning his full attention on Sally. "What have you managed to get?"

"Well, we all know Artie is one of her callers. He seems to have been at Banner's saloon, though. Several men placed him there." Sally was relieved to have the information come to her head quick enough. "Several really drunk men. I'm not fully satisfied with that alibi."

"Unfortunately, around here there'll be a lot of drunken alibis." Tom slurped again. Sally could swear he was doing it to annoy and unbalance her.

"Right. Of course." Sally primped her fringe in a nervous habit that only led to Tom staring her down. "I've also got Carl Denner, Caleb jones, Edgar Coonts, and Mark Payne that were regulars of hers for certain. I have about five more that are possibilities."

"Add Seymour Davis, Bryan Kendrick, and Zeke Jones to the list." Tom tapped his pad. "They were for sure visiting Daisy on the sly."

"Zeke? Caleb's brother?" Nick leaned forward. "That could have caused some strife."

Sally spoke out of turn and off subject, sort of. "Could this all be related?"

Nicke straightened at the change. He eyed her quietly. "Sally?"

"My attack, Ma's, Lucy. The deaths of Emily, and Daisy, along with Agnes' disappearance. Then there's Bob's death, along with Ellis, McKerney, Tully, and Chauncey." Sally rose to pace. "That's a lot of deaths for less than six months of time around here. Even on our worst winter we don't have so many, plus most of the men were all accidents. The women more cut and dry, straight-forward attacks."

"I think that might be a stretch," Nick said in a conciliatory tone. "Bob and Ellis were clear accidents. Chauncey and Opal were having troubles the past couple of months. While I hate to admit it, Mac always had it in for your Ma. The situation at Tully's bar is unusual, but almost seems like mob mentality."

Tom remained silent through Nick's litany of excuses. "Why do you think differently, Sally? Out with it."

"Daisy, Agnes, Lucy, Emily, and I were all whores at some point, and Ma has always been likened to it. We have no idea what happened with Daisy or Emily, but Ma and I were attacked with slurs saying as such. Georgie said something about temptation for Lucy's attack." Sally took a deep breath to replace the air she'd expelled. "As for Bob,

Tom said it was a complex knot. Such things don't happen by accident."

"She's not lying."

"You're also suspicious of everything and everyone."

"Ma said that the well cover Ellis smashed through was next to brand new, the boards fresh and sturdy. I don't care how drunk you are, you don't do that on accident. If it was rotted, perhaps. He'd been in there so long, it was hard to tell if there were any other injuries."

Sally turned her back on them to pace the floor. "Chauncey was never sick a day in his life, and then he's poisoned and dies. His wife hasn't been seen since, and while she certainly might have done it, why would she? A couple months of trouble isn't worth murder, it isn't like he was abusing her. She seemed happy enough when I saw her in town."

Tom grinned broadly at her when she turned back around. Nick's expression remained stoic as ever so she couldn't tell what he was thinking. Tom leaned forward. "Go on."

"All the men were good, church-going folk no one would say a cross word about. Ma and I saw them every Sunday without fail until their deaths." Sally sank into the chair she'd abandoned. "Opal was a whore before, and after, she and Chauncey married. After they bought out her contract, she lived and home and tended her garden. Has there been any sign of her at all since Leanne thought she saw her?"

"No. We searched everywhere, including the wells around town. Even checked a few expired mines if the entrances were wide enough." Tom leaned back, hands behind his head. "I told you, Nick."

"Enough with your pride over your protégé. We are here to figure out how to get Michael out of prison, not solve the world's woes." Nick shook his head. "I'm sorry, but I believe it has been a very unfortunate year for the town, nothing more. Right now, all that matters to me is saving Michael from the fate Jane suffered. I fear he wouldn't be as lucky as her to come out the other side."

"But what if it *is* connected?" Sally set her hands on her knees for emphasis. "Uncle Nick, I want to save him as much as you, but I can't stop feeling like this is all one big story that we're missing because we're ignoring something."

"I understand that, but I have to focus on Michael. You both can run with your wild stories and theories elsewhere. We need to find who killed Daisy, and we need to find them fast."

"He's right." Tom interrupted Sally's next attempt at protest. "Even if it's connected, someone killed Daisy. We need to focus on finding her killer, and when we do, maybe we can find that connection we are missing."

After a minute, Sally nodded her acquiescence. "Fine. Daisy first, then."

For the next two hours they worked tirelessly, going over every detail two or three times a piece. Debating alibis and possible other frequenters of Daisy's goods.

By the time they finished, it seemed to Sally they'd done little but go in circles over the same points. The whole afternoon seemed a waste.

Tom helped her into her cape, then swung his own coat on. "You've got the mind for this."

"Right now my mind feels like it's in a fog. We've gone in circles."

"That happens. You need a break from thinking. That's usually when things start to make sense for most of us."

"I just can't shake the idea we're missing something."

"Me too."

"If that's supposed to make me feel better, it makes me feel worse."

Tom chuckled. "Why's that?"

"Because if you're missing it, too—how can we ever find it?"

Man...cannot learn to forget, but hangs on the past; however far or fast he runs, that chain runs with him.
—Friedrich Nietszche

Jane wished she could do more to help Sally. Tom would tell her Sally had to figure it out for herself, but she could see Sally getting more frustrated as time went on. Hopefully the gentle nudge Jane had given her would help.

Downstairs the apartment remained quiet, for the children were occupied elsewhere. With the biting wind outside, Jane imagined most of them were in the casino with Ada. Most, but likely not all.

A quick peek told her that Willow was, in fact, in her room weaving some more beads. Jane chose not to push the issue quite yet. But, she'd noticed a definite withdrawal of Willow since Ada had arrived. Something was bothering the girl about their new governess. Today was not the day to get to the bottom of it, though. Not with her parents arriving in five short hours.

She considered going to join the children, but noticed her bedroom door partially open. Certain she'd closed it earlier, she pushed it open to find Cole inside. He sat on the edge of the bed, staring out the window.

"Cole? What are you doing in here? I thought you were going to the saloon."

He made no response, his body eerily still.

"Cole?" She approached quietly, concerned at his state. After the past six months her mind tended to go to the worst-cased- scenario first. When she touched his shoulder, he startled. "Cole. What is it? What's wrong.?"

"I…" He shook his head, returning to his constant staring out the window.

She moved around him to turn up the lamp When she turned to face him, his features were a blank mask. Eyes hollow, with a dark emotion she couldn't place. "Cole. You're worrying me."

He finally turned his gaze on her. After he licked his lips, he shook his head. "He's dead."

"What? Who?"

"My pa."

She stilled at the declaration, not quite sure how to react. Cole had hated his pa with a burning passion, to be sure. Even so, learning of his death had to be quite the shock. "But…how do you know?"

He tugged a telegram free of his pocket.

She took the telegram in hand, reading it over several times. It said Paul Spencer was deceased and requested Cole return to Holle Creek to see to the estate. An attorney had signed the missive. Confusion over where the telegram came from. "I don't understand."

"He's dead."

"Yes. I understand that. How did they find you?" Jane studied him quietly. "Did you tell anyone where you were after you left?"

"Ella's pa knew after a time."

"Oh." Jane sank to the bed beside him. "Oh."

Cole didn't say a word. She could only imagine the confusing mass of emotions this news could have caused.

"Will you go?"

"What for? Pa didn't have nothing."

"He was your pa."

"He was a no good son of a bitch."

Jane set her hand on his, and was surprised with the force he used to clutch it the moment she'd touched him. "What do you want to do?"

"I don't know."

"We'll figure it out. Together."

"Jane."

"Yes?"

"I didn't ever want to go back there. Not ever."

"I know." Jane leaned against him, letting him squeeze her hand until it was numb. "We can go with you."

"No ya can't. We got too much going on, too many kids."

"But if you need us, we will go with you. The rest will work itself out."

"I don't know what to do."

"I know."

To Be

Continued...

In Book 9 of the
Dominion Falls Series

Blizzard
Lights

About the Author

Sarah Cass, author of over twenty novels in 4 series, is devoted to giving her readers well-crafted, emotional stories, with depth to even her secondary characters—to give readers a full world to explore. Stories that explore not only the labyrinths of the heart, but the nightmares of the soul. A RONE finalist, she is also owner and creator of Redefining Perfect. By day, she's a nurse, a mother, wife and cat-mom to 4 mischievous beasts. By night she crafts stories that take her across centuries. From the old west of Dominion Falls, to the small town of Lake Point for the holidays, and even into the paranormal land of Shifters and Magic in The Tribe. She loves hearing from her readers. Visit her at www.authorsarahcass.com

Other Books in
The Dominion Falls Series

Independent Brake
Changing Tracks
Derailed
Dark Territory
Green Eye
Runaway Train
Home Signal
Red Zone
Dust Raiser

Coming Soon in
The Dominion Falls Series

Blizzard Lights
Dead Man's Switch
Bird Cage
A Highball Arrangement
Douse the Glim
Blood
Grave Digger
Bad Order

Books by Sarah Cass

The Tribe Series
The Tribe
The Wolf
The Chief
The Raven
The Lake Point Series
Santa, Maybe
Deep-Fried Sweethearts
Stalled Independence
Witch Way
A Thorough Thanksgiving
Eve's New Year
Heartstrings & Hockey Pucks
Luck of the Cowgirl
Stars, Stripes & Motorbikes
Free Falling
Love for Hire
Haunted Hearts
Stand Alone Novels
Masked Hearts
Leap